Murder in
The Buff

MAGGIE TOUSSAINT

This is a work of fiction. Names, characters, places, and incidents are a product of the author's imagination, or are used fictitiously, and any resemblance to actual persons living or dead, business establishments, events, and locales is entirely coincidental.

Murder in the Buff

Cover art by *Nika Dixon*

Muddle House Publishing
1146 Tolomato Drive SE
Darien, GA 31305
Visit us at www.muddlehousepublishing.com

Publishing History
Digital format, Muse It Up Publishing, 2012
Second Edition, Muddle House Publishing, 2013
Print ISBN: 0983361460
Print ISBN-13: 978-0-9833614-6-6

Published in the United States of America

"Me and the girls are sitting on a gold mine in real estate." Mama Leon said. "The powers that be want us o-u-t out, but we're not taking our sorry hides anywhere."

"Go on."

"Some new muckety-muck's been coming around here, trying to take our land away. There's a deluxe shopping complex going in out by the highway, and our land backs up to that. They want to knock down these beautiful trees and pave over the whole countryside. These live oaks are over two hundred years old."

"No biggie. Don't sell."

"It's not that easy. This guy has an insider working the system. Our property taxes keep doubling. Now they tell us we have to pay to hook up to city water and sewer, and we're nowhere near the city."

"Sounds like a cash-flow problem. Everyone in the county faces these same issues. Sell them a few acres near the shopping complex."

"Not a chance. That's our most sacred acreage. That's where we're gonna scatter Barbara Jean's ashes."

Enough. "I don't get it. You're getting squeezed by the big money players, but that type of squeeze play isn't front page news. I don't see a blockbuster idea in your misfortune. The world isn't out to get you."

"You're wrong." He glanced around the screened-in pool area and lowered his voice. "Because not only have they got me in a vise, they've taken their tactics to the next level."

The next level?

This sounded like page one material, something that went above the fold. I wanted to cover it. A story like this would keep my reporter job secure for weeks to come. I hung suspended in breathless silence.

When he didn't continue, I leaned forward to prompt him. "And what level would that be?"

His chin quivered. "Murder. They murdered my Barbara Jean."

DEDICATION

Murder in the Buff is dedicated to writers everywhere
whose stories don't fit the norm.

ACKNOWLEDGMENTS

I could not have written this book without the
support of my family, friends, and peers. I'm
especially grateful to Meg Gore for her recollections
and to Wally Lind of CrimeSceneWriters who
answered my questions about tox screens and
bullet wounds. Dawn Dowdle helped with edits.
Any errors in the book are mine
and mine alone.

Chapter One

One more minute.

That's all I would wait.

One more minute.

I drummed my fingers on the steering wheel and glimpsed the white band of skin where my ring used to be. Tears welled. I blinked them back. Couldn't fall apart on the job. Plenty of time in the dark of night to cry over a cheating husband. Soon-to-be ex-husband.

Shadows covered the parking area as I steadied my breath. Deer flies circled my Suburban, daring me to venture outside the fortress of my air-conditioned car. I didn't plan to step anywhere. I planned to roll down my window, grab the expanded obituary from the nudist, and floor it out of Naturalist Woods.

Another minute ticked off my life clock. The "Beware of Dog" sign on the weathered gate worried me. I feared rabid dogs, naked women, and hordes of blood-sucking deer flies. Our newspaper readers didn't need to know personal details about Barbara Jean McAllister's life. The full-length obituary could surely wait until the next edition, until one of them could put clothes on and drive it into town.

1

It wasn't like the dead woman was one of coastal Georgia's leading citizens. The townspeople had been mortified when the naturalists arrived a few years back. My mother, a bastion of Southern refinement, had led the battle cry to oust them, citing the certain decay of our moral fiber.

But she'd been wrong about their degree of bad influence. The nudists had kept to themselves, and we had only ourselves to blame for our lack of moral fiber.

I'd never met the woman who'd died here two days ago. My editor heard that Barbara Jean had a heart attack, but rumors in Marshview, Georgia shaded the truth with kudzu-like efficiency.

We'd also heard the naturalists were retired call girls. No telling what went on back in these dark woods. Wife swapping. Orgies. Wild rituals. Anything was possible in such a remote location.

I checked the time again and sighed.

If I left right now, my mother would never know I'd been here. However, Ted would fire me in a country-fried minute if I returned without this family-placed obituary. Jobs were scarce in our county of ten thousand people, and with my changed personal circumstances, I couldn't afford to lose this one. Air huffed out of my lungs, up my warm face, giving flight to the wispy bangs on my forehead.

I dried my sweaty palms on my jeans and ramped up the air conditioning another notch. What was taking so long? I rubbed the back of my neck to ease the stiffness.

Behind the stockade fence, briars and weeds flourished. Spanish moss and ropy vines choked the tops of the oaks, pines, and cedars, adding to the sense that anything could and would happen deep in that jungle of green.

Jungle love gone wild.

I grimaced at that carnal image. My gaze fell to the thick ground cover outside my door. I couldn't see the sandy soil at all. I gulped. There were probably rattlesnakes galore out here.

Cottonmouths and copperheads, too.

And ticks.

I bet every tick known to mankind lurked within the dark green foliage, waiting for me to step out of my vehicle. I'd have to be diligent as I checked every inch of skin tonight for ticks.

Without warning, a narrow-faced woman with gray braided hair peered over the top of the fence and waved her bare arms. My heart sunk as her lips moved. Dang, she was talking to me. With my windows up, I couldn't hear a word she said.

Please, dear God, let her have clothes on behind that fence. My heart hammered in my ears as I powered down my electric window.

"You the reporter lady?" the woman asked.

Deer flies funneled into my SUV, swarming my head. "Yes, ma'am. Molly Darter from the *Marshview Gazette*. We received a call you had a family-placed obituary for the paper. I've come to pick it up."

"Well, come on then, Miz Molly. I'll take you up to see Mama Leon. I'm Alma Howell."

I hunkered down in my seat. "I'll wait here until it's ready."

"Mama Leon wants to meet you. I'm to bring you up to the house."

Mama Leon had a lot of nerve. I did not want to meet two nudists today. I was already one nudist over my lifetime quota. I needed a miracle or a hurricane to occur, only we didn't get hurricanes in May, and I wasn't on anyone's miracle list.

I chewed on my thumbnail. That scary warning sign preyed on my mind as much as Alma's potential nakedness. "What about the dog?"

She shot me a lopsided grin. "Ghost won't be a problem as long as you're with me."

Crap. I had run out of excuses.

"Give me a sec." I turned off the car, grabbed my heavy reporter bag, and locked my doors. My heartburn intensified as I hurried to the fence. Ted owed me a huge bonus for doing this.

A rational part of my brain knew my mother had been too strict in her worldview of the human form. But another part of me was leery of seeing another woman's private parts. I had an eight-year-old son to raise. I had to set a good example.

I had a dilemma, all right. Get the obituary and keep my job, or risk the certain decay of my moral fiber. What would Emily Post do in a situation like this? Would she keep her eyes averted? Would she demand a blindfold?

But if I demanded a blindfold, I might step on a snake. Okay. Blindfold out. Time to suck it up and do my job. Adopting a SWAT-like mentality would help. Get in and get out.

I could do this.

Deer flies dive-bombed my head. I took a deep breath, closed my eyes, and stepped through the open gate of Naturalist Woods.

I raised my chin, but that didn't work because I only saw the top of Alma's head. She was shorter than I was. I lowered my gaze and went too far. Her waist-long braids slithered down her long skinny breasts. I closed my eyes immediately, but I forgot to adjust my line of sight because when I opened my eyes her nether parts were front and center.

Yikes.

I averted my gaze to the sandy path, where her feet were shod in scuffed brown cowboy boots. Alma appeared to be fifty-ish and about a hundred pounds. Every inch of her bronzed skin glowed. Not one insect bite on her. My mostly slender physique paled in comparison. I sucked in my stomach and offered her a business card.

Alma took it and held out a small bottle. "Bug

repellent, Miz Molly?"

Deer flies whined in my ears. I considered my options. Which was worse, bug bites or naked people cooties? Repellent might take care of the cooties and zap the bugs. "Thanks. I'll take a double dose of whatever you've got."

I rubbed the liquid gunk on my arms, neck, and face. Jeans protected my legs, sneakers covered my feet. What I wouldn't give for some duct tape to seal my pants to my shoes and repel ticks. Coulda, shoulda, woulda.

Alma nodded toward a crude, vine-covered wooden stall. "If you like, take your clothes off and release your inner vixen."

"I don't do naked."

She shrugged. "Suit yourself."

I handed the bottle back to her and waited while she wedged it between warped fence boards. The trees rustled, and my heart skipped a beat. I turned, half-expecting a huge junkyard dog to leap out and bite my head off, but it was me, the trees, and naked Alma.

"You ready?" Alma took off without waiting on my reply.

Dark shadows edged the twisting path. I hurried after her, wishing I was independently wealthy and safe at home. No way was this in my job description.

Alma's brisk pace made me hustle to keep up. The only thing worse than snakes or naked people would be getting lost in these woods where both of them ran free.

Or I could turn around, get in my car, and be home in fifteen minutes, and no one would be the wiser. No one but my boss who would ream me out for not picking up Barbara Jean's expanded obituary. Then he'd fire me.

Ted was famous for his threats. Usually I laughed them off, but this week I couldn't. Single moms needed income. Plus Ted had recently heard from an old friend who wanted to come to work for him. One misstep from me, and I'd be yesterday's news.

"How'd you come to be a reporter?" Alma's gray braids swung with her every stride.

"I submitted a story to the paper about the new jail a couple of years back and Ted hired me. I'm writing for the paper temporarily until I sell my book."

"You're writing a book? I always wanted to do that. I've got a great idea for a story—"

I downplayed our possible connection. "Anyone can write a book. That's not the hard part. Selling is where folks get hung up."

Alma glanced back over her shoulder, a familiar gleam in her faded blue eyes. "My book would sell," she insisted. "It's about a rags-to-riches onion farmer who divorces his wife to marry the teenaged babysitter. He invests everything in a Florida hotel. Then a hurricane comes along and destroys everything. He kills himself, and his family lives happily ever after."

"Interesting." The editorial assistant who opened the publisher's query letters would bounce Alma's submission back on the same day it was received. Been there, gotten that letter.

"That's not all," Alma continued. "I have another book idea about a man who raises peacocks for a hobby. They drive his wife crazy. She kills their entire family, starting with his interfering mama and ending up with his trashy kid sister. Then she feeds her husband to the peacocks."

Alma's fixation with death and killing worried me. At least with her being naked, she couldn't conceal a weapon in her clothing, and I didn't see a gun handle poking up out of her boots. With my longer legs, I could outrun her, as long as I didn't get mauled by the unstable and unseen dog.

Branches crackled to my left. I stumbled over a root on the narrow path, righted myself, and scurried forward. "Do peacocks eat meat?"

Alma ducked under an overhanging branch. "They

eat dried cat food."

The poor woman. She had no idea how to write for publication. I let her down gently. "Your story premise is flawed."

"Only if I don't grind up my deadbeat husband and make cat food out of him."

Air whistled through my teeth. Alma was queen of the crazies. I'd better not upset her or I'd be cat food.

We rounded another bend, and there, plunked in the middle of the woods, was the back of a freshly painted, white two-story Victorian house accented with double-hung windows and paneled doors. A modern heat pump hummed with vigor.

I'd expected grass huts. Outhouses. RVs. Not a regular home straight from the suburbs of anywhere U.S.A., a home as nice as any Justice County had to offer.

We mounted the back steps, passed the empty cane-seated rocking chairs on the back porch, and entered the house. Cool air rich with an exotic spice slid over my heated skin. A white ceiling fan whirled above a cozy grouping of dark colored sofas and chairs. A cluster of coconut-scented candles flickered on an expansive dining room table bordered by a dozen upholstered chairs.

The sheer number of chairs stopped me. Twelve seats implied twelve naturalists. That was way too many naked bodies for a cradle-raised Episcopalian. My pulse ramped even higher.

"Wait here," Alma said.

I concentrated on steadying my breathing.

Hyperventilating would be a bad idea.

I thought about sitting down, but naked people sat on that furniture. Nope. Standing was good. I sat all day. Nothing wrong with my legs.

On the plus side, Alma's nakedness hadn't made me go blind or crazy. And I'd learned something. Viewing one naked person didn't kill me. Hope flickered.

And so did curiosity. I strolled about the room,

touching the velvet-like texture of the garnet-hued walls, making notes about the contemporary furnishings. You never knew when you might need decorating ideas for a book.

"Miz Molly, thank you for coming. I'm Kim Merritt."

The dulcet tones came from a naked female extending her hand to me. Her face was surrounded by a curly riot of dark hair, her full-figured body a golden brown. Her breasts swayed when she walked.

Envy washed over me. My demure plum-sized breasts didn't sway. But my no-account sister's did. Tears welled as a lightning bolt of emotion rent my heart anew. Rats. I wasn't going to think about her. I gritted my teeth together and banished my sister and her breasts from my mind.

I schooled my gaze on Kim's anxious face. Dark circles ringed her emerald green eyes. Her unadorned, full lips frowned. Was she distraught by McAllister's death? Or was she unhappy living here? My reporter's instinct revved up. I wanted to know more about her.

As before, heat suffused my face. But Kim was one person, my proven acceptable quota of nude people. Kim would take me to this head nudist woman, and she'd leave us alone to talk. I could survive this, one nudist at a time. I clung to that lifeline of hope.

I summoned a smile, shook her limp hand, and tried to speak without using the word naked. "Nice to meet you. This is quite some place you've got here."

Her doe-like eyes narrowed. "What did you think we lived in? A shack?"

My face tightened at her harsher tone. "I wasn't expecting it to be so modern."

"Embracing our natural state doesn't mean we don't appreciate nice things."

"Uh, sure."

"Mama Leon will see you now out at the pool. Follow me."

We traversed a narrow hall with mustard-colored

walls and the same plush red carpet. A series of botanical prints lined the walls. The air temperature warmed. The faint sound of music and splashing water reached my ears. As we neared the door, the noise level increased. Elvis was singing about his blue suede shoes.

Odd that a song about shoes would be playing in a place that shunned clothing. Odder still that rowdy music played in a mourning household.

Kim opened a screen door and gestured toward the water. Alma and three other naked women sunned facedown on cushioned loungers by the screened-in pool. My heart sunk. There was no sign of a written obituary anywhere. I had to start from scratch. Why couldn't they have gone through the normal channels of a funeral home to get the information to us?

The urge to flee took hold of my brain. A thin voice whispered how fast I could run, that I didn't need to subject myself to this level of intense anxiety.

Common sense countered with the facts. I didn't have the luxury of falling back on my soon-to-be ex-husband Hadley's income. Anger strengthened my courage. Hadley put me in this predicament. Hadley wouldn't beat me.

There were four unclad people around the pool. I took a few steadying breaths and looked elsewhere. Swimming laps in the pool was the darkest skinned person I'd ever seen. Her skin tone reminded me of the mud banks in our tidal creeks.

She had honed muscles reminiscent of a weight lifter. As the athlete churned through the water, I dug out another business card, my notebook, and a pen. When she stopped, I wanted to be ready.

Kim eased down and dangled one foot in the water. At the signal, Mama Leon stopped at the near wall and wiped the water from her angular face. Diamond earrings sparkled along the rims of both ears. "You're here," she said in a husky voice.

My grip tightened on my palm-sized notebook. I could do this. Artists looked at naked people all the time and they didn't go insane. I blinked rapidly at her closely shorn head. "Yes, ma'am. Ted Page from the *Marshview Gazette* sent me to pick up Barbara Jean's expanded obituary."

"About time you got here." Water sluiced off Mama Leon as she climbed up the pool ladder and faced me on the concrete deck.

Air whooshed out of my lungs. From afar, I heard my notebook clatter to the ground.

Mama Leon was a man.

Chapter Two

Seconds ticked by. My brain struggled to assimilate the gender inconsistency. I was standing beside a pool with a naked person.

A person whose private parts proclaimed his gender.

Four naked women lounged nearby. Anticipation swirled like a June thunderstorm through the steamy pool enclosure.

None of the rumors about Naturalist Woods had hinted at a man living out here. In spite of my shock, curiosity grabbed hold of me and wouldn't let go. What was his story?

Mama Leon bent to pick up my scattered belongings. "Kim, get me a cigarette."

Kim scrambled to fill his request. Was he their retired pimp? I shook his strong, very male, wet hand. My stomach clenched when he examined my hand front and back.

"Mmm, your hands are buttery soft," his baritone voice purred. "How'd you like for Mama to read your palm?"

He appeared to be older than me, forty-ish, by my guess. At five foot seven, I was two inches taller than he was. Uh-oh. Short men were always trouble. This one more than most because I had to look down to meet his gaze, and there was all kinds of manly real estate down there.

I extracted my hand, averting my eyes to the rippling pool water. "No, thanks."

"You can read my palm, Mama." Kim handed Mama a cigarette, but not before she squeezed in between us and planted a kiss on Mama's moist lips. I didn't miss the smug glance she shot me over her bare shoulder.

I read her unspoken message. Mama Leon was taken. Good thing. I sure as heck didn't want him.

Mama Leon chuckled and patted Kim's butt with obvious affection. "'Nuther time, sweet cheeks."

I rolled my eyes upward to the screened ceiling. I'd rather have open heart surgery than watch two naked people flirt. I cleared my throat. "Why don't we write that obituary?"

Mama took a long drag on his cigarette. His cool, assessing gaze swept my fully clothed length. "You're not comfortable with our natural appearance?"

I didn't want to meet his gaze, and I most certainly didn't want to look *down there*. I struggled to lock gazes with him. I wanted to wipe that self-satisfied smirk off his face, but I was on his turf and at his mercy.

Determined to hold my own, my eyes drilled into his. "I'm working on a deadline. If the obit isn't ready, bring it by next week for inclusion in a subsequent edition."

He gestured toward two vacant lounge chairs. "Have some compassion. One of my girls died, and I got other troubles too."

I winced inwardly. "I apologize for being so direct. I didn't mean to sound crass, but I am on a tight schedule. I'd appreciate it if we could get started."

He appeared to consider my words. One thinly plucked eyebrow arched. "You always this bossy?"

I trailed him over to the cushioned loungers. The

chlorine in the pool water and the sun's rays probably disinfected the furniture. I perched on the edge of my chair. "Yes. Being bossy is my second worst fault."

His dark brown eyes lit up with amusement. "What's your worst?"

The unexpected camaraderie loosened my tongue. "I have a tendency to talk too much. I get carried away during my interviews and don't ask enough questions." As I was doing now. I was supposed to be interviewing him, not the other way around.

He leaned forward. "Do you know why I asked Ted to send you out here?"

I leaned back in my chair. He requested me? Did he know me from somewhere? I was forever getting names and faces confused. No. That couldn't be it. With his muscular physique and the aura of power he wielded, Mama Leon wasn't someone easily overlooked.

I didn't know where this was headed, but it didn't feel like a short conversation. Mama Leon clearly had an agenda. "You should've requested Ted. He does the real news."

Mama Leon's nostrils flared wide. "Ted is a Johnny-come-lately. You're old school Justice County and that's what I need. Someone who knows the ins and outs of this place."

Mama had done his homework. Ted Page had moved here from Macon five years ago when the then-ailing *Gazette* came up for sale. We wouldn't have a paper if it wasn't for him, and I wouldn't have a job. Loyalty fueled my defense. "Ted knows his stuff. Plus he has a degree in journalism." My degree in general studies hadn't prepared me for much more than matrimony.

"Ted is a man. I wanted a woman. And I like the features you write."

Flattery was nice, but I needed to move this along. I tapped my pen on the slim notebook resting on my jeaned thighs. "In that case, let's get started."

With a twitch of her hips, Kim set down a tray containing two tall tumblers of amber colored liquid on the glass-topped table between us.

Mama gestured for me to take a glass.

My throat tightened. What was in that glass? Was he being hospitable or was I being set up for something bad? "No, thank you."

He waggled a finger at me. "Mama doesn't like it when you refuse his hospitality. It's safe. I'll show you." He drank from both glasses. Like that was supposed to reassure me. How did I know he hadn't spit in my glass? No way was I drinking after him.

I shifted in my seat. "I really need to get that obituary. Perhaps we could start on it now."

"We'll get to that. I'm offering you my hospitality. You refusing it?"

Dang.

My wants and needs kept getting trampled. I was tired of it. Like this Friday afternoon assignment. I didn't want to come here today, but Ted had made it a condition of my continued employment. The entire universe of men thought they could push me around. Why did they think I was such a pushover? Was there a sign on my forehead?

I took a few breaths to calm myself. I shouldn't lash out at Mama Leon because I was spitting mad at my soon-to-be ex-husband Hadley. Mama's offer of hospitality was a business gesture, a prerequisite to us developing a professional relationship.

I squirmed under his scrutiny. Then something inside me snapped. Living in fear wasn't the way to go. I sipped from the glass and sputtered immediately at the strong alcohol taste. "What is this?"

"It's writin' juice." He nodded his approval. "I want you to write down every word I say."

I smacked the tumbler down on the glass-top table. The liquid burned from my throat to my empty stomach. I shuddered convulsively. That had to be the most rotgut whiskey I'd ever tasted. "We charge by the inch for family-placed obituaries." As soon as the words left my mouth I blushed again. Inches. I was not thinking about inches of anything.

"It ain't the obituary we're gonna work on. It's something else. Folks in this county needs to know the truth. That's why you're here."

Alarm bells clanged in my head. "And what truth would that be?"

Mama Leon crushed out his cigarette in his empty glass. "What I'm about to tell you cannot be repeated."

This oversexed lunatic must be hyped up on a conspiracy plot left over from the Nixon era. I didn't care about his personal, religious, or political beliefs. "I'm leaving." I started to rise.

He grabbed my wrist and tugged. "Sit."

I glared at him. "Look, it's been a long week and I need to get home to my son. If you don't have information for the paper, you're wasting my valuable time."

Mama Leon released my arm. "What if I told you something so big, so gripping, that it could turn this county inside out? What if I told you it was a guaranteed best seller idea for a book?"

My heart sunk. Odds were, he was conning me. But what if he was telling the truth? I couldn't afford to pass up the story of a lifetime. "Talk."

"Me and the girls are sitting on a gold mine in real estate." Mama Leon stroked his angular chin. "The powers that be want us o-u-t out, but we're not taking our sorry hides anywhere."

"Go on."

"Some new muckety-muck's been coming around here, trying to take our land away. There's a deluxe shopping complex going in out by the highway, and our land backs up to that. They want to knock down these beautiful trees and pave over the whole countryside. These live oaks are over two hundred years old."

"No biggie. Don't sell."

"It's not that easy. This guy has an insider working the system. Our property taxes keep doubling. Now they tell us we have to pay to hook up to city water and sewer, and we're nowhere near the city."

"Sounds like a cash-flow problem. Everyone in the county faces these same issues. Sell them a few acres near the shopping complex."

"Not a chance. That's our most sacred acreage. That's where we're gonna scatter Barbara Jean's ashes."

Enough. "I don't get it. You're getting squeezed by the big money players, but that type of squeeze play isn't front page news. I don't see a blockbuster idea in your misfortune. The world isn't out to get you."

"You're wrong." He glanced around the screened-in pool area and lowered his voice. "Because not only have they got me in a vise, they've taken their tactics to the next level."

The next level?

This sounded like page one material, something that went above the fold. I wanted to cover it. A story like this would keep my reporter job secure for weeks to come. I hung suspended in breathless silence.

When he didn't continue, I leaned forward to prompt him. "And what level would that be?"

His chin quivered. "Murder. They murdered my Barbara Jean."

Chapter Three

Murder.

The word careened through my thoughts. There hadn't been any mention of foul play in Ted's terse account of Barbara Jean's death. No homicides had come through on the police incident reports because I'd typed up this week's "Police Investigations" for our police column this morning.

We'd had the usual assortment of drunks and broken hearts. Riveting copy in a tabloid kind of way. But nothing murderous had been recounted in those formulaic reports. I would've remembered that.

A murder story was every reporter's dream. But could I trust this man? He could be playing me, pushing my hot buttons to gauge my reaction. Time to do a little pushing of my own. "Murder? Are you smoking crack?"

He glared at me with enough venom to dissolve my pale pink toenail polish. "Don't sass me, gal. I'm neck-deep in sassy women and I don't need one mo' telling me what to do."

After being a cop's wife for nine years, I knew a thing or two about substantiation. "What evidence do you have?"

"I don't have jack. They made darned sure of that."

I had wasted enough of my afternoon. I needed to cut my losses and get the heck out of there. "I appreciate that you're grieving for Barbara Jean. But I can't help you."

"Hear me out. You're the right person, all right, and we've got to act fast. If we don't come up with the tax money by next week, the mayor will start condemnation proceedings on this alleged 'blight on society.' We've got to stop him."

A harsh laugh escaped my throat. "You're asking me for money? That's crazy."

He studied me for a long moment. "I heard about you kicking your no-account husband out of the house."

I flinched. "My personal life has nothing to do with the death of one of your, er—" I paused to search for a suitable word. "Residents."

Tears trickled down his angular cheeks. "Barbara Jean was more than a resident. She was family. She made everything better. It ain't right that she's dead."

His emotional response triggered a faint hope that he might have a basis for his claim. I located a fresh tissue in my reporter bag, and handed it to him. "Who found her?"

Mama Leon pointed his thick finger at the recumbent woman with straight, long black hair. "Tildy found her collapsed in the woods."

I glanced over and saw that all four women watched us. I turned back to Mama Leon. "If you believe she was murdered, go to the cops."

He slapped his palm against his thigh. The crisp smack of flesh on flesh echoed through the screened-in pool enclosure. "Cops are the problem, not the solution. We take care of each other out here. Cops don't have time for free spirits like us."

Bull. Cops couldn't let feelings or personalities hamper their investigations. "Why do you think she was murdered?"

"Because it wasn't her time to go."

Did Mama Leon decide who lived and died around here? It was one thing to be played for a fool, quite another to be suckered into a murder plot. I shot to my feet. "Look at the time. I've got to meet the school bus."

"Mama, quit scaring the girl. You spooked her something terrible." This from the other gray-headed woman I didn't know. Her long gray hair was clipped on top of her head in a lop-sided mass. She was thin through the face and shoulders, but the rest of her was curvy in all the right places. "Quit grandstanding and get to the point. Tell her about the records."

"Heck-fire, Norma, you shore know how to suck the fun out of everything." Mama Leon folded his arms across his chest and glanced at me. "Sit down, gal. I ain't told you all of it."

Curiosity made Swiss cheese of my resolve to leave. I eased back down in my chair. "What records?"

Mama Leon cleared his throat. "Barbara Jean was always scribbling."

The woman called Norma let out a humphf.

"All right, already." Mama's hands waved expansively. "She was our bookkeeper."

"She scribbled on your financial records?"

"We never should've put you in charge of this." Norma came over and sat beside me on the foot of my lounger. "Mama can take something simple and make it so complicated you can't figure it out. That sorry 'Y' chromosome. It clouds his brain."

Norma's sandalwood scent washed over me. She seemed nice and normal in a grandmotherly kind of way, if you overlooked her lack of clothing.

"Is there a point to this?" I glanced down at my watch. "I really need to meet my son's school bus."

"There is, and Mama is taking a long time getting to it. We believe in nature out here. We eat healthy foods. You may have noticed our roadside place, the Back to Nature Produce Stand."

I snapped my fingers with recognition. "I know that place. I stop there all the time. But I don't recognize any of you."

"Barbara Jean ran the stand. She didn't mind suiting up to sell our beautiful produce. The rest of us work the garden."

Barbara Jean? She was the nice heavyset woman perpetually garbed in a flowered muumuu at the produce stand? She gave my son strawberries so that he could tell her which ones were the sweetest. "She told me her name was Bea."

"It is. Bea is her nickname," Norma explained. "She must have liked you if she introduced herself as Bea."

Bea didn't have any reason to like or dislike me. Dismay filled me at the thought of never seeing her again. I'd liked her sunny warmth. "I never knew y'all grew those foods here. I thought they came from Florida or somewhere."

"Organic farming is a big deal. We have greenhouses and farmland on our property. To use the "organic" label, our cultivation and harvesting has to follow rigid standards. Even our seed stock is special order. We want to live peacefully, but trouble came looking for us with that new sheriff, Otis Blizzard. His relatives over in the next county have an organic farm. He keeps showing up out here, asking us questions about our operation. If he closes us down, they could expand east into our established customer base."

I loved organic produce, and I paid top dollar to get it. Which meant someone in the supply chain made money. Greed could have motivated a killer.

Norma had a point about the new sheriff. Justice County had been downright surprised when Otis won the sheriff job from my soon-to-be-ex, Hadley, the incumbent sheriff. "You're implying Otis had Barbara Jean killed?"

"Someone tried to steal our financial records. Barbara Jean happened to be in the wrong place at the wrong time, and they killed her."

"The cops aren't the bad guys." But what if they were? Was something nasty lurking along the mud banks of my precious hometown?

"Well they shore as heck ain't the good guys," Mama interrupted. "I've got the mayor and the sheriff poking their noses where they don't belong. I'm telling you, this farm is a cash cow, and the sheriff has a bug up his butt about moving this place. Mark my word, he's got a bead on us. He'll pick us off one by one and set his relatives up here."

"You want me to investigate the sheriff?"

Mama Leon leaned forward. "We figured your man would be wanting his sheriff job back. It would be a win-win situation all the way around if you was still together and he helped you with this. You thinking of taking him back?"

I didn't air dirty laundry in public. "My personal life isn't at issue here, but Hadley won't be helping me with anything in the future. Your worries about Otis are out of my hands."

I'd lived with a cop long enough to know that you needed proof to go up against the law, and these people had nothing but accusations. Worse, I still didn't have Barbara Jean's obituary.

I stood. "I have a school bus to meet."

Mama Leon shoved to his feet, his hands fisted at his side. "Doggone it, Norma, if I wanted to run her off I could've done that twenty minutes ago. Your 'X' chromosomes are as squirrelly as my 'Y' ones. Barbara Jean was murdered. They want our land and our business."

"Get the envelope, Kim," Norma said.

Envelope? I held my breath as Kim left the room. Was there actual proof of their claims?

Norma patted my bare forearm. "Once you get home, look through the information, think on what we said, and come back out here tomorrow."

I didn't want comfort from a naked woman, no matter how grandmotherly she appeared. I put three steps between us. "I'm not coming out here tomorrow. The weekends are my time with my son. If there's any breaking news in Marshview, it'll have to wait until Monday."

Kim returned with a small brown envelope. "Here's Barbara Jean's obituary, plus information about our organic farming procedures. We want you to write a feature on our farming operation, on how we're here to stay. We're not going to let the sheriff or the mayor run us out of town like they did up in Macon. This time around we're standing our ground. We're not doing anything illegal out here. Your article will prove we have nothing to hide."

With relief, I tucked the obit in my bag. "We're always looking for copy, but Ted won't go for a front-page gardening piece. He wants to know why y'all are naturalists, more of a personal interest story."

Kim stepped forward, her smoky eyes brimming with an inner fire. Her pin-up physique would stop traffic even if she were draped in a nun's habit. "I'll go first. Natural is beautiful and life-affirming."

Alma lifted her head from her lounger, flipping one of her long skinny braids over her back. "Natural frees us from the dictates of fashionistas."

Tildy joined us on the pool deck, her overripe figure past the flush of youth. Her pudgy hand glided down her rounded torso. "Natural makes me feel good."

Norma pinned me with a direct gaze. "Natural exposes your vulnerabilities and enhances your unlimited personal power."

I wrote faster. Heat steamed off my face when I noticed Mama Leon was sitting with his flag a-flying. He crooked his finger at Kim, and she laughingly straddled him.

Mama's broad grin filled his tear-streaked face. "Natural puts me in a sea of titties."

Chapter Four

It seemed I'd been transported to the set of a raunchy movie. Kim and Mama Leon were doing it right in front of me. My cheeks flamed like hot coals at their athletic gyrations. The musky tang of sex perfumed the air, mesmerizing me. My eyes recorded the action in slow motion, taking in every grunt, thrust, and throaty moan.

Shock shuddered through my frozen limbs, threatening to knock me off balance. Inside my head, my mother's cultured voice harped at me: decent women didn't watch other people having sex. Crackers did that. Low-class, white trash. Munros were better than that.

I'd put my morals aside to obtain Barbara Jean's obituary. I'd survived the shock of interviewing naked people. But this uninhibited display of carnal relations, it took the love out of love-making. And it was more than I could bear.

I bolted for the door. My heart pounded in my chest all the way through the darkly sinister woods. I swatted through branches and jumped over briars in the path, hoping I didn't come across the bad dog. I breathed a huge sigh of relief when I passed through the gate and saw my car sitting in an oasis of sunlight.

My normal car that I drove in a normal world where people wore clothes. I jumped in my Suburban and floored it. With trembling fingers, I punched in my editor's number on my cellphone. "I don't care how much money you pay me, it isn't enough."

"I assume you got the obituary," Ted rumbled in a deep voice. "What about that human interest story to accompany the piece?"

"Every one of those naturalist people is crazy."

"Why do they walk around with no clothes on? Where'd they come from? Did you take any pictures?"

Pictures? I didn't want pornography on my camera. "They're crazy, I tell you." I shivered with cold in my closed-up ninety-five degree car. "One woman is seriously psycho. She kept telling me about the books she plans to write. In every book she kills a man."

"We'll talk about it when you get back to the office."

Ted's solicitous voice irritated my frayed nerves. "I'm not coming back in. It's time for the school bus."

Ted groaned. "Can't Hadley help with the child care?"

"I wouldn't put Hadley Darter in charge of a flea circus, much less my precious son."

"Write up your obituary and email it to me this afternoon. Then start on the color piece."

"That's just it. I don't have enough for an article about the nudist colony. They want me to do an infomercial story about their fruit stand. Did you know they had an organic farming business hidden in their woods?"

"I assumed they made money somehow. Makes sense now that I think about it."

"But you didn't know before?"

"Nope."

His cluelessness offered slim comfort on this sunny afternoon. "At least I'm not the last one to know."

"Did you get anything else?"

"Some allegations about the new sheriff."

"Dirt? Do I hear dirt?"

I winced at the hopeful tone in his voice. "No dirt. Allegations. They think Otis will take over their business and the mayor will run them out of town."

"Hmm. Follow up on that. See what you can dig up."

"I'm not digging anything up right now. It's the weekend, remember?"

"Tough. I need copy, and you're all I got. Email me the obit and a page one feature by nine on Sunday, or you can find another job."

I ended the call, but my stormy emotions kept me off balance. I wanted to relax with my son this weekend. Feeding the copy monster was getting old. I needed to see about getting a grown-up job, one that didn't involve working so many hours, one that paid decent wages, one that didn't include interviewing naked people.

Fat chance of that happening here in Nowheresville.

Dodging the gnarled oak trees growing in the middle of the road and the hunk of Spanish moss which had fallen on the corded dirt road was standard fare for Justice County. I'd moved to Marshview Plantation with my husband Hadley Darter and our son Jimbo five years ago, thinking this would be the last time I ever moved.

If I lost my job, I'd lose my house.

I loved my house.

As I approached the familiar pink stucco house framed by sago palms, I realized I couldn't pay the mortgage on my meager salary. Despair clawed at my stomach. By this time next month I could be living in a mobile home and paying for my groceries with food stamps.

If only Hadley hadn't lost the sheriff's race.

If only he hadn't screwed around with my sister.

If only he hadn't broken my heart.

I stopped at the mail box to pick up today's mail. A familiar red pickup in the driveway gleamed in the dappled sunlight around the oak-shaded house. Hadley's truck. I thought of all the times the sight of his truck had brought me pleasure, of how we'd sneak away to snatch some together time.

Little did I know he'd been sneaking around other places as well. He wasn't worming his way back into my life. No way, no how. I'd rather starve and go to the poor house before I allowed him one ounce of sympathy.

A tide of anger came over me, washing away logic and common sense. I wanted to hurt him as much as he'd hurt me. He loved that freshly waxed truck more than life itself. I gunned my Suburban and rammed his truck. Glass broke. Metal crunched. I rocketed forward against my seatbelt restraint.

The air bag from the steering wheel engulfed me, coating me with a powdery substance. I punched my way through it, swiping at the tears on my cheeks with trembling hands.

To my immense satisfaction, the center panel of his tail gate bowed in, with an ugly gash the size of Africa. I'd left a mark on that which he held most dear.

My door opened, and Hadley drew me out in his arms. "Molls, you okay? What happened?"

For a split second his warmth and familiar scent comforted me. Then I remembered he was a traitor. I squirmed to get away. "Let go of me."

"Not yet." A slow smile played over his face. "I rather like having you right here."

I punched him square in the stomach. A stomach which he kept flat by working out for hours on the weight machine in our guest room. The room that was supposed to have been my office. But he'd taken it from me. As he'd taken my youth and my trust.

To his credit, he didn't wince from the blow though I'd socked him as hard as I could. His hands stroked soothingly down my back. It felt so good to be held that I savored the human contact. The gentle motion down my spine had me fighting back more tears and breathing in his masculine fragrance, the good stuff that he only wore when he was intent on getting laid.

Chemistry flared hot as July lightning between us. I didn't want to respond to his nearness. I hated that he had this power over me, but I was not letting him take advantage of me.

Not ever again.

Suddenly his hands stopped moving. His breath quickened. The silence around us darkened, a fierce thunderstorm brewing in my immediate vicinity. In the blink of an eye, Hadley had gone from the soother to the one needing to be soothed.

I knew how to soothe Hadley Darter's temper better than any person on the face of the earth, but I wasn't in the mood for his hysterics. I was in the mood for some of my own.

"Where have you been?" he snarled in my ear. "Why do you smell different? Why is your skin slick with oil? Is that liquor I smell on your breath?"

"Where I've been is no business of yours." I pushed against him, but I might as well have been trying to stop a tsunami from coming ashore.

"That's where you're wrong. You're still my wife."

"Only because I can't afford to go to a lawyer and divorce your sorry, two-timing self."

"No lawyer in this county or the next will take your case. I've made sure of that."

"There are other lawyers in the state of Georgia. You don't know them all."

"Who were you with, Molly?"

A distant rumble of the school bus reminded me that time was short. I struggled anew. "Let go of me."

He held me at arm's length, his brown eyes boring into mine. "You will tell me where you've been before either of us moves. I don't care if we have to stand here until dawn."

Heat rose up my neck, flushing my face. If Jimbo saw me in Hadley's arms, he'd be overjoyed. My eight-year-old son wanted us back together. That was never going to happen. "I don't owe you any explanations. If you don't let go of me right now, I'm calling Sheriff Blizzard to lock you up for harassment, assault, and anything else I can think of."

He glared at me.

I glared right back.

"Dad!" Jimbo yelled from the street.

I blinked back fresh tears as Jimbo ran toward us. We'd told him we were living apart for a little while, and he'd seemed to take the change in stride. I hadn't summoned the courage to tell him that I intended to divorce his father.

"Tell me," Hadley demanded.

He was stubborn enough to hold me here until dawn. I huffed out a breath of air. "I used an oil-based bug repellent for a deep woods interview today. Let me go."

Jimbo slammed into Hadley's leg, rocking us. "Dad! I knew you'd come home soon. I knew it."

Hadley reached down and picked up his son, tossing him in the air like he weighed ten pounds instead of eighty. "How's my Jimbo doing? I've missed you, sport."

Jimbo squealed with laughter and hugged his dad. My heart went out to the little guy. He hadn't laughed like that all week. From inside the house Goldie, our golden retriever, barked. She didn't like being left out either.

We'd once been a happy family. That tether had broken. Now we were drifting apart, forging our own identities, making separate lives for ourselves. Emptiness socked me hard in the gut.

Hadley had thrown our family away the moment he'd stepped into Clarice's open arms. My hands tightened into fists. I couldn't stand here and pretend everything was fine. We weren't a family any longer.

I circled around them, intending to go inside and be

mercifully alone. Hadley caught my arm. "Not so fast, Molls. You have some explaining to do."

With Jimbo watching, I was limited in what I could say. I nodded toward the house. "Your father and I need a moment alone. Would you go on in the kitchen and fix yourself a snack?"

Jimbo's hopeful expression fled. "Aw, Mom, do I have to?"

"Yes, you do."

Jimbo looked to his father, hoping for a reprieve. Hadley's lips thinned. "Do as your Mom says, squirt. I'll see you in a few minutes."

"You won't leave?"

"He won't leave without saying goodbye," I interjected.

Jimbo stared at our connected vehicles. "Did someone have an accident?"

I motioned toward the house. "Scoot. I'll be right in."

Once Jimbo went inside, I snatched my arm out of Hadley's grasp. "You are not welcome here. Get back in your truck and get off my land."

"It's your land, but it's my house." Hadley's voice hardened. "Why doesn't my key unlock my house?"

My chin came up. "I had the locks changed. You don't live here anymore."

He swore using several choice words. "You're not being reasonable. This whole separation thing was a bad idea. I never should've humored you."

"You never should've slept with my sister."

There. I'd said it. I'd let the big ugly monster out of the closet. It felt good to get those words off my chest.

He backed me into his truck. "I didn't sleep with Clarice. I would never sleep with Clarice. I'm married to you."

"I saw you embracing my sister. You'd been out all night together. You can't deny that."

"I can't talk about an ongoing investigation. Did you

29

talk to Clarice yet?"

"Why would I believe her? Both of you must have been lying to me for years."

"You have every right to be angry. I didn't tell you about spending time with her. I couldn't. But I didn't sleep with her. Call your sister."

"Forget it. I'm not talking to her for the next five hundred years. If we were stranded together on a desert island, I still wouldn't talk to her."

He swore again and then took off for the house.

I loped after him. "Where do you think you're going?"

"I'm saying goodbye to my son. Then I'm getting your air bag fixed."

I grabbed his arm to slow him. "My car isn't your responsibility. I'll replace the air bag as soon as I can afford it."

He kept moving. "I'm not risking your safety."

Jimbo looked up from his peanut butter and banana sandwich. The hopeful expression on his face nearly crushed me. "You staying, Dad?"

"Not yet, son, but I'll be home soon. Until then, you do as your mother says."

Hadley left, the screen door slamming behind him. When I realized he was in my car, I dashed outside. "Wait. I need my purse and my reporter bag."

He handed them out the window to me, and I promptly slung the long straps over my shoulder. Hadley tossed a set of keys at me. "I'll pick up my truck in the morning."

His keys were warm from being in his pocket. Glass fell and metal screeched as he pulled away. Both headlights were busted on the driver's side of my Suburban, but the nasty dent in his tailgate made it all worthwhile.

It wasn't until he'd driven away that I realized he'd made off with my keys. The ones that matched the new locks I'd had installed on the house two days ago. I ground my teeth together until my jaw ached. Hadley Darter didn't like being locked out of his house anymore than I liked finding him in my sister's arms.

I sagged against his truck, and then recoiled from the contact. Had he been with my sister in this truck? There'd been lots of nights he hadn't come home while he'd been the sheriff. "Work" had been his ready explanation. I'd always believed him.

Except for the time I'd caught him pawing my sister.

What a lousy day.

I had nothing for a feature story, I had nothing for a husband, and I had an impoverished future as a single mom. Maybe I'd have to move into the nudist colony and grow organic vegetables to provide food and shelter for me and my son, either that or rely on the adulterer to pay child support.

Poor Jimbo.

He deserved a real family. Eight was too young to understand about adult problems, too young to understand how it felt to have your heart yanked out through your nostrils.

Grandma Dee always said Munro women didn't shrink from trouble. They were known for stoutly defending their interests, all the way back to the original Scottish Highlanders who'd settled here. I wouldn't stomach adultery, in that I was a true Munro who believed in loyalty and honor, but how could I protect my son from heartbreak over his father's wrongdoing? I didn't have any answers.

With a sigh, I carried my bags inside, kicking my shoes off at the door.

"Mom," Jimbo spoke around a wad of sandwich. "What's adultery?"

31

Chapter Five

Adultery.

My son's question struck me mute.

I dropped my bags on the counter. Goldie trotted over, her claws clicking loudly on the ceramic tile floor. Her furry head shoved into my trembling hand. I needed to say something to my son. Anything.

"Where'd you hear that word?" I winced inwardly at the shrill tone of my voice.

Jimbo wiped his mouth with the back of his hand. "It's one of the 'thou shall nots.' We learned about it in Sunday school last week. I know people get committed to the crazy house. How do you 'commit' adultery? Is it like going crazy?"

Lord, help me. How could I answer this one without destroying whatever illusions he had left about his dad?

I unclenched my jaw. "It's a lot like going crazy. But kids don't have to worry about adultery. It's a grown-up thing."

Jimbo nodded sagely, light glinting off the lenses of his wire framed glasses. "Like when you and dad close your bedroom door and make grunting noises?"

My face heated, and my knees wobbled. I clutched

32

the kitchen counter for support. I'd told Hadley we shouldn't fool around when Jimbo was awake, but Hadley had been all about gratifying his own desires.

Which should have alerted me to his inherent lack of self-control.

But that was another matter entirely. Right now I had a little boy's questions to answer. A little boy who had asked very astute questions.

I cleared my throat delicately. "The physical intimacy a husband and wife share in the privacy of their bedroom is not adultery. Adultery is when a husband or a wife becomes intimate with someone other than their spouse."

"Intimacy." Jimbo slowly repeated the word, rolling the syllables around on his tongue as if he were memorizing the word for a spelling bee. His forehead furrowed. "What is that?"

His question hammered at me. I'd always thought Hadley would give Jimbo the birds and the bees talk. Of course he wasn't here to handle this. "Boys and girls have different body parts and when they grow up, they find pleasure in lying with each other, touching each other, even joining together."

Awareness dawned bright on my son's face. "You mean humping? Like when Goldie locks onto my leg?"

Between the sex-crazed nudists claiming their friend had been murdered and me ramming Hadley's truck, I was having one terrible day. I swallowed the hysterical laughter welling up in my throat. "That's a crude way of putting it, but it's the same idea."

Jimbo bit off a hunk of sandwich and chewed thoughtfully. Glad for having navigated safely through these treacherous waters, I contemplated pouring myself a glass of wine. A glance at the clock confirmed what I already knew. Four-fifteen was forty-five minutes before cocktail hour officially started. Too bad. I deserved a libation to settle my nerves. I opened the fridge and removed a bottle of white zinfandel. I was reaching for a wine glass when Jimbo spoke again.

"Did Dad hump someone else?" he asked. "Is that why you threw him out?"

The thin-stemmed glass slid from my hand and shattered on the ceramic tile floor. Cuss words filled my mouth, but I held my tongue. Shards of glass were everywhere, and my feet were bare. Jimbo's shoes were with mine over by the door, and Goldie the dog didn't wear shoes. This was a bad time to be barefoot.

And an even worse time to be talking about Hadley's adultery. I couldn't do it. Not with Jimbo.

"I can't talk about this right now." I bent over and collected the larger glass pieces in my palm. My hands shook so bad they hardly worked. Jimbo's chair scraped across the floor. Fresh alarm filled me at the thought of him walking on the floor. "Stay put. Wait until I sweep up the glass."

The kitchen quieted. A few seconds later, the dust pan and the whisk broom dangled down from the counter. "Here, Mom. Use this."

I looked up to see a serious little boy perched on my countertop. None of my problems were his fault. My son was an innocent. Hadley deserved my anger, not Jimbo. My shoulders sagged. "Thanks."

Worry creased his youthful face. "I'm sorry for upsetting you."

I deposited the glass pieces in the dust pan and swept up the rest. "You didn't upset me. I was startled by your remark. Big difference." I swept the floor an extra time and netted a few more shiny slivers of glass. "Why did you think your father was seeing someone else?"

He shrugged. "You guys get mad at each other and yell, but this is different. You never threw Dad out before. He must have done something bad to make you so angry."

Gingerly, I tiptoed across the cold floor and emptied the dust pan. I wet a paper towel and wiped the floor to pick up any remaining shards. "He made a bad decision.

Let's leave it at that, okay?"

"What did he do? Was it adultery?"

"I'd like to promise you it will all work out between us, but I'm not sure about anything. I don't trust your father now." My voice broke. "I don't want him to live here anymore."

Jimbo's eyes widened. He stepped back, shaking his head in denial. "You're divorcing him?"

The weight of Jimbo's disappointment was almost too much to bear. "Please, don't worry. Your father and I will come to an agreement about the future. No matter what happens, he'll always be your dad."

"He won't ever live with us again?"

I tossed out the wet paper towel and patted Jimbo's thin shoulder. I shook my head, a lump welling in my throat as large as the Titanic.

Tears glistened in Jimbo's eyes. "Can't you forgive Dad? He's sorry he messed up."

I didn't want to forgive Hadley. I wanted to hurt him in an Old Testament, an eye-for-an-eye kind of way. "It isn't that easy. Trust is a fragile thing. Once it's broken, the pieces don't fit back together the same way. Like that broken glass. Even if it was glued back together, it wouldn't be whole."

"Will you think about forgiveness?"

Forgiveness. It was a great concept for Sunday school, but it was impractical for the everyday world. If you forgave people who did you wrong, they'd take advantage of you again. Hadley Darter wouldn't get a second chance at breaking my heart. Once was enough for this lifetime.

I ruffled Jimbo's red hair. Motherly love welled up in me. I couldn't crush his hopes so cruelly. "I'll think about it."

He threw his arms around my neck and stole a hug. He glanced up shyly. "Will you also think about pizza for dinner?"

I managed a smile and reached for my heavy reporter bag. "Pizza it is. You choose the toppings and call for delivery. I've got a story to write for work."

Upstairs, I flopped down on my bed and powered up my laptop. I had to find a way to get through this pre-divorce period without losing my sanity or emotionally crippling my child. Everything was so jumbled up in my head, it was hard to set priorities. I needed a lawyer, and I needed a confidant. Someone who could help me reorganize my life. Someone who could explain to my mother that I would never be in the same room as Clarice again.

Thinking about my sleazy sister sent my pulse into overdrive. How could Clarice kiss my husband? That was so wrong. She'd screwed up her life, and now she was screwing up mine.

The blame wasn't all hers. Hadley had been a willing participant, no matter what excuse he used to justify his actions. I'd caught them together, and it had really opened my eyes.

My empty stomach lurched. God, what a fool I'd been. They'd probably been sneaking around for years and had finally gotten complacent enough to get careless.

I definitely needed a lawyer. Hadley was right about my slim chances of getting a local one. Every lawyer in a thirty-mile radius owed him. None of them would go up against the former sheriff. I needed someone from upstate. And for that I'd have to ask my mother because she knew everyone.

But calling Mama would invoke a barrage of questions I didn't want to answer about my marriage and my former sister. Right now, I had two pieces to write for my editor.

I should polish off the obituary first, and then tackle the longer organic gardening feature. For Barbara Jean's life history, I needed the information the naturalists had provided.

I dumped out the large manila envelope. Mixed amongst the typed pages and glossy tri-fold pamphlets on organic gardening were black and white eight by ten inch photographs. They rained out onto my turquoise spread, snapshots of intimate acts.

I gasped in morbid fascination. The photos were of the allegedly murdered nudist, only Barbara Jean appeared very much alive here. And very much enjoying sexual relations with Marshview's leading men.

One candid shot caught and held my gaze.

I'd never seen that particular expression on my father's face.

Chapter Six

My father had slept with Barbara Jean. He'd committed adultery against my mother. My brain reeled. The stark photos and my colorful bedspread whirled into a kaleidoscope of abstract, pornographic art. I grabbed a wad of spread and held on.

The door. I needed to close the door so Jimbo didn't see these graphic pictures. I stumbled over and locked the door. Then I climbed back in bed, tucking my legs underneath me, wrapping my arms tightly around my belly.

Adultery.

In Marshview, it wasn't limited to my cheating husband. It was also an activity of the middle-aged, the retired, and the "they'd-be-better-off-dead-and-gone" crowd. Tears filled my eyes, and the pictures blurred. My stomach sank down to my toes.

Mama would have a cow when she found out. Not that I would tell her about Daddy's transgression. Heck, no. I didn't want her coming after me with a shotgun.

I'd always thought of my father as old, but time had altered my perspective. Two women I went to school with had married men my father's age. Daddy was in remarkable shape for a man in his late fifties. His trim physique easily took twenty years off his calendar age.

Barbara Jean was in pretty good shape herself. Those shapeless floral dresses had hidden breasts the size of ripe cantaloupes, a narrow Barbie doll waist, and broad hips that would have borne a dozen babies effortlessly. I would never again view cantaloupes without remembering Barbara Jean screwing my father's brains out.

Heat rose to my face. It was beyond weird to be viewing my father's sex life. I didn't spontaneously spring forth from their union, but my parents were asexual in my presence. I'd never seen them kissing or touching while I was growing up. Intimacy at five-oh-eight Waters Street had been conducted behind closed doors.

Fascinated by the ecstatic pair, I studied the photo again. I couldn't believe Daddy had allowed himself to be photographed like this. A thought niggled at my brain. Maybe he hadn't allowed it at all. Had the picture been taken without his permission?

My reporter brain kicked into gear. I knew who was in the pictures, but where were the pictures taken? Bits of brown showed in the edges of the photo. With effort, I focused on the setting. The walls seemed to be roughly planked, like an old shed. Definitely not the plush velvet walls out at Naked Woods. Definitely not the pastel-hued drywall of the house I grew up in.

A thought struck me out of the blue. Not a shed. It was the storage room of the Back to Nature Produce Stand. That made sense, especially since Barbara Jean spent most of her time there. From the muted natural light in the photo, these liaisons had occurred during daylight hours.

I picked up the other photos and studied them one by one. The sweaty mayor with his Coke-bottle glasses askew, frozen in mid-thrust. The fast-talking preacher of that new holy-roller church out by the highway—his face aglow with something more than the glory of the Lord as Barbara Jean licked his Popsicle. Well-rounded police deputy Noah

Marvel snorkeling in Barbara Jean's cleavage. Skin-and-bones Judge Humphrey who glowed with male virility as if he'd impregnated a prize brood mare.

My father was in some pretty exalted company, but his appointment as the city attorney had him rubbing elbows with Marshview community leaders quite frequently. I laid the pictures out on my turquoise bedspread like playing cards. One thing struck me right away. From her blissful expression, Barbara Jean either enjoyed her work, or she was a superb actress.

How had these photos been developed? I turned Daddy's photo over. No identifying marks. Which probably meant these were digital images printed on a personal computer.

Anyone could have printed these shots.

Why?

I couldn't get away from that basic question.

Mama Leon and his naked lady friends insisted Barbara Jean had been murdered. I'd believed their claims were preposterous because she'd seemed like such a nice lady, but these incriminating pictures gave credence to another side of the woman. I doubted Barbara Jean kept a scrapbook of her conquests.

Which left one awful possibility: were these blackmail photos?

Blackmail.

Cool air skittered over the base of my neck, raised the hair on my forearms.

Blackmail was a good motive for murder.

I'd considered using it in the book I was writing, but I'd chosen greed as the motivation for my on-paper killer. In any event, it wasn't a stretch to believe someone in real life would have killed to get rid of a blackmailer.

According to these photos, these four men had motive and opportunity to kill Barbara Jean. Were there more photos elsewhere? Were other men involved?

I hugged a pillow to my chest. Even if Barbara Jean

had been murdered, how could I prove it? Should I open that can of worms if my father was involved?

My temples throbbed. I cradled my head in my hands and tried to sort out my jumbled thoughts. How could my life this week be so out of control? Last week I'd had a loving, committed husband and a father that doted on me. This week I had neither.

God. My father.

He'd given me life and so much more. He'd held my hand in the hospital birthing room because Hadley had passed out at the first sign of blood. Daddy couldn't possibly be mixed up in anything wrong.

I wouldn't have believed it possible that he'd be mixed up with a woman like Barbara Jean if I hadn't seen this photo. Was it evidence of a crime? Was I an accessory to the crime if I sat on the pictures?

What was I going to do?

Should I ask Daddy about the picture? No. Both of us would die of embarrassment.

Should I give these photos to my editor? Ted would have a field day with them. Newspapers would fly off the shelf. But the community infrastructure would be ripped asunder.

Should I turn the photos over to the new sheriff? He'd like nothing better than to humiliate the old guard of Marshview and fill those positions with his friends.

The magnitude of what lay before me slammed home. These photos would change the face of how Marshview did business for the next twenty years. Was that what I wanted to do?

Heck no.

I couldn't ruin so many people's lives.

Barbara Jean was dead. She couldn't blackmail folks any longer. The people in these pictures needed to leave the past buried in the past.

With that thought, I stuffed the photos back in the brown envelope and took several deep breaths before

41

scanning the other information. Besides Barbara Jean's brief obituary, an assortment of text and brochures on organic farming completed the information packet.

I tapped one brightly colored pamphlet against my nearly colorless palm. Could I really write a fluff piece about organic gardening, knowing that the roadside stand had been used to lure men into a sticky web of blackmail?

Chapter Seven

I hit the delete key and the sophomoric words vanished from my laptop screen. Nothing I wrote for the organic gardening story worked. Every descriptor seemed full of innuendoes. All mentions of fruit and vegetables reminded me of sex. Sex, sex, sex. I couldn't get away from it.

"Can we go to the store now, Mom?" Jimbo asked from the doorway of my bedroom.

Thirty minutes ago, I'd told him we could go out for breakfast as soon as I'd finished my first draft. Trouble was I couldn't get past the first line. If I could get the lead right, the rest of the story would fall into place. "A few more minutes, hon."

He drifted closer, a hopeful expression on his face. "What do you have so far?"

"I've got nothing." I sighed. "This is the hardest story I've ever tried to write."

Jimbo's face lit up as he studied the glossy brochures on organic gardening. "You're writing about the fruit stand? Awesome. Let's go there. Bea has the best strawberries."

His suggestion reminded me that Jimbo didn't know

43

Bea was dead. Poor baby. He expected to see Barbara Jean at the fruit stand. Better prepare him for her absence. "Bea isn't there anymore."

Light glinted off his glasses as he cocked his head. "Where did she go?"

How would an eight-year-old handle this very adult topic? I patted the space beside me on the bed and Jimbo sat. "There's no easy way to say this. She died a few days ago."

"Died? Like the bunny in our second grade class?"

At least he had a reference point for death. "Yeah."

"Is she in heaven?"

Naked, promiscuous Barbara Jean. From the photos, I assumed she'd been a blackmailer, which made her heavenly ascension improbable. I swallowed around the lump in my throat. "I don't know."

Jimbo thought for a few minutes. During the silence, the dog's leg thumped loudly on the wooden floor as she scratched an itch. "She was a nice person," Jimbo said. "I'm sure she went to heaven."

The innocence of youth. I'd like to have a faith as solid as my son's, but I'd seen too much, been too hurt by the powerful in this life. I patted his shoulder.

Jimbo tugged on my arm. "Why don't we go there and you can take pictures for your story?"

I hadn't planned on going to the produce stand, but once he suggested it, that was exactly what I needed to do. Fresh photos would jar me out of my writer's block. "Because they are in mourning, her family might not open the stand today."

"So? We could still go out to eat or buy the cereal I want, couldn't we?"

Guilt slammed into me. What kind of mother made her kid wait for breakfast? The way this story was going, I could still be sitting here with nothing by lunchtime. Jimbo was more important than any story or my phobia of driving Hadley's truck. "You convinced me. Let's go."

"Can Goldie come too?"

Goldie was shedding her winter coat. I smiled. "Absolutely."

"Cool."

We rolled the windows down and Goldie hung her head out the passenger window, lapping up sunshine with her lolling tongue. Tufts of dog hair blew around the cab of the pickup like dandelion seeds. Jimbo laughed as he tried to catch them, and then he petted Goldie and released more wads of hair.

There were no cars at the Back to Nature Produce Stand, but a blue bike rested against the rear of the shed-like structure as I approached. A white helmet dangled from the shiny chrome handlebars.

The roll top front door of the wooden stand had been raised. Bright red, green, and yellow fruit and vegetables crowned the sales counter. They were open for business.

I signaled a left and pulled into the empty lot. Goldie whined with expectation. Without a leash she'd be out on the highway in ten seconds flat or upturning the mounded displays of produce with her wagging tail. "No," I told her. I caught Jimbo's eye to make sure he knew I meant business. "If Goldie gets out, we're turning around and heading straight home."

"Yes ma'am," he said in a resigned tone.

Miracle of miracles, the dog behaved and we emerged from the truck without incident. "Hello? Is anybody here?" I called out.

Norma scurried out of the back room in a cloud of sandalwood scent. Like yesterday, her long gray hair was clipped on top of her head at an odd angle. She was loosely clothed in one of the flowered shifts Barbara Jean used to wear. On her feet were Alma's scuffed cowboy boots.

They must not have a lot of call for clothes at the nudist colony. Did they pool their clothing according to who was going out in the world that day? When I looked at that familiar dress, it seemed like it should be Barbara Jean standing before me, and that irritated me.

"What can I get for you today?" Norma beamed a fake smile at me. Then she held out her palm to Jimbo, an aging Eve bearing fruit. "How'd you like to try a fresh strawberry? I'm not sure this new batch is as sweet as the last one."

She didn't offer me a strawberry. I'd never noticed before that I hadn't been offered free fruit. I'd thought the strawberry gesture was a bribe to placate kids so that the parents would shop longer. But now I wondered if the offer had to do with the fact that Jimbo was a male.

Perhaps they were accustoming the local males to receiving "treats" at their stand. If the naturalists got the Justice County kids hooked on sampling their wares, hormones would do the rest as they matured. How diabolical.

Jimbo wolfed down the strawberry. "I couldn't tell it if was sweeter than the last batch. I need to test another one."

His angelic, considering expression didn't fool me for a second, but Norma apparently bought it. She handed him three more berries. "This should do it."

Jimbo started to swallow them whole but I nudged his shoulder. "What do you say?"

He hung his head and mumbled, "Thank you."

"Enjoy." Norma beamed a smile at him and then turned to me. "What can I get for you?"

At a sound from the store room, Norma backed up to cover the open doorway. My internal radar pinged on. Did she have a male customer back there right now? If so, how'd he get here? I'd assumed the bike was hers, but maybe not. Maybe it belonged to someone who liked to bike on Saturday mornings.

I hesitated. That blue bike had looked familiar. Very familiar, now that I thought about it. And I knew from recent photos of someone who frequented this stand and liked to bike. "Daddy? Is that you back there?"

My father's mop of graying curls appeared behind Norma. He glanced at me, but he didn't quite meet my eye. "Hey."

"Grandpa!" Jimbo shouted around his mouthful of strawberries. He ran and jumped into Daddy's arms. "What are you doing here?"

"Same thing as you, sport." My father whirled Jimbo around in a tight circle and then put him down. I noted he still wouldn't look me in the eye.

At Jimbo's squeal of delight, Goldie barked from the truck. I prayed the dog would stay put. Goldie in the fruit stand would put Jesus in the temple to shame. And I'd be stuck with the bill. Organic fruit wasn't cheap.

Jimbo licked the last of the berry juice from his hand. "Did you test the strawberries, too?"

Daddy turned strawberry red. "Yes, and I believe I'll buy a quart of them today."

Jimbo tugged on my shorts. "Mom, can we buy two quarts?"

"We'll see. We came here to take photos for the newspaper article, remember?"

My father blinked in apparent confusion. "Photos?"

My thoughts went to those other, incriminating photos in my bag. Did Daddy know about them? Because if he did and she was murdered, he'd be a prime suspect. What was I thinking? This was my father, a man I trusted implicitly. Until I'd seen those photos.

What he was really doing here today?

Was he doing Norma, too?

"I'm writing a feature on organic gardening," I said. "Maybe I could get a photo of you buying your strawberries."

Daddy tugged at his shirt collar. "Uh, I don't think that's a good idea."

I dug my camera out of my purse. "It's a great idea. It

will generate more interest in the story if there are local people in the picture. Don't be shy."

Jimbo clasped Daddy's hand. "Yeah, Grandpa, don't be shy. I'll be in the picture with you."

Silently, I cheered my son. We'd boxed Daddy in quite nicely. Refusing to be in the picture would hurt Jimbo's feelings. Daddy thought the sun rose and set on his grandson.

He shifted uncomfortably and then nodded. "Okay."

I snapped off five photos of the two of them pointing at various plastic containers of bright red fruit. "What about you, Norma? Can I take a photo of you?"

She shook her head so fast I worried that clip would fly right out of her gray hair. "No. I don't photograph well."

I understood her negative reaction. I hadn't given her any warning, and it did look like she'd slept in her current hairdo. Plus, she was wearing someone else's dress and shoes.

Norma shot a quick glance at my father and Jimbo, and then leaned in close to me. The scent of sandalwood grew stronger. "Did you have a chance to review the material we provided about our operation?"

Those pictures of "Barbara Jean-does-Marshview" flashed into my head. I shivered in spite of the warm temperature. No way was I mentioning the photos with Jimbo nearby. I chose my words with care. "The material. Well. Yes. I looked it over, but——" My voice trailed off. How was I going to phrase this? "The information raised more questions, and I'm having trouble getting an angle for the article. Would it be possible to come over later and get some clarifications?"

Annoyance stormed across her dark brown eyes. "Why wait? I can answer your questions right now."

My throat closed suddenly. I wasn't looking forward to being around naked people again, especially now that I knew Mama Leon was a man. But I couldn't write the article as is. It didn't have any heart. And I sure couldn't ask Norma about the lurid photographs with my eight-year-old son eavesdropping on every word I uttered. I made a show of glancing at my watch. "I don't have time now. We've got errands to run."

"Suit yourself. I'll be here all day if you want to come back. Mama and the others are spending a day in quiet reflection."

Rats. I'd have to find something to do with Jimbo and I hated shuffling him around more than anything. He wasn't a burden, he was my greatest joy in life. And I wanted to spend my entire weekend with him, not a bunch of whacked-out naturalists. "I'll make child care arrangements and swing back by later today. How much do I owe you for two quarts of strawberries?"

Daddy whipped out his wallet. "I'll get them." He handed Norma a twenty, and then hustled us into the truck.

Jimbo scanned the empty lot. "Did you walk here, Grandpa?"

"I rode my bike." He tousled Jimbo's red hair. "Take these strawberries for me, will ya, Molly? I'll pick them up later today."

"They'll be on the back porch if I'm not home."

He frowned for a moment as if he'd counted heads and came up one short. "Where's Hadley?"

Jimbo clicked his seat belt. "Mom and Dad had a fight and she kicked him out."

"What's this?" Daddy asked, his lawyer-sharp eyes focusing on me for the first time today. "He didn't mention anything about this at the office." When Hadley lost his bid for re-election to become the sheriff of Justice County a few months back, he'd gone back to work as my father's law partner. During his slack times, he freelanced for the Georgia Bureau of Investigation.

"Because he doesn't believe I mean it. I do." I gripped the steering wheel. Now that the moment of truth was here, I could barely get the words out. Both Jimbo and Daddy needed to hear my decision. Tears welled in my eyes. "I won't take him back. Hadley and I have separated for good."

Daddy paled. "It can't be as bad as all that."

"He committed adultery." A solemn expression filled Jimbo's face. "He incubated with someone that wasn't Mom."

He incubated, all right. Only there better not be any long-term consequences. My sister was so self-absorbed, she'd be a disaster as a parent. Hadley and I had given up birth control after Jimbo's birth because we wanted another child. Hadley didn't carry condoms in his wallet. Or he hadn't the last time I'd looked in there to get money for the pizza delivery guy a month ago.

Consequences.

Dear God. What if Clarice was pregnant with my husband's baby?

Chapter Eight

As I drove down the sunny highway, I couldn't get the image of Clarice swelling with Hadley's child out of my head. Jimbo should have at least three siblings by now, but all he had was me.

How entangled would our family tree be if Jimbo's brother was also his first cousin? Clarice's baby should have been mine.

I grabbed a handful of my hair and held on, the pain grounding me. What was I doing? I didn't know if Clarice was pregnant. All I knew for certain was she'd been fooling around with my husband, making a fool out of me.

Now I was stuck driving Hadley's pimpmobile and wishing I was pulling my sister's hair out. *Focus, Molly. You have a story to write.* With Jimbo entertained by swimming in his friend Eric's pool, I was free to consort with nudists, prostitutes, and murderers until dinner.

I slowed to turn off the highway at the Back to Nature Produce Stand, noting the other dark-colored vehicle in the lot. My teeth ground together at the sight of that particular SUV. That car used to be Hadley's. Now the sheriff's vehicle belonged to Otis Blizzard, a man who'd challenged the sheriff's election after he lost and demanded a ballot recount. A recount which netted him Hadley's job.

Otis Blizzard was not my friend. He might even be the murderer. I'd better be very careful.

He stood under the awning in the shade, Mr. Perfectly Groomed, with one hip cocked against Norma's sales counter. He tipped his hat as I approached. "Miz Molly."

I unclenched my teeth. "Sheriff."

An awkward silence followed. I fumbled through my reporter bag for one of the organic gardening brochures. Otis made no move to buy anything. I could hardly quiz Norma on the naughty photos with him around. "You here on business?"

"You might say that," Otis drawled. "I was asking Miz Norma about her yields."

Yields. I blinked, trying to fit the word "yield" into my mindset of naturalists and a dead woman. Mama Leon had said the cops were a problem, so I wasn't going to bring up Barbara Jean's death. Not when Otis had a gun strapped to his waist and another one strapped on his ankle.

I must have looked clueless.

"Crop yields," Otis went on. "I'm especially interested in their onion production."

Norma's lips thinned. "That information is confidential."

"My cousins over in Waycross said the market for their organic potatoes dried up. Have you noticed a similar drop in sales?"

"Our potatoes are selling fine."

"What about losses to insects?"

"We plant enough for the bugs too."

The sheriff hounded Norma with a few more farming questions, and then cleared his throat several times. I thought for sure I would be stuck here all afternoon waiting for him to leave. Thankfully, his phone buzzed. He excused himself and stalked off. He brushed past me on the way to his car, his cologne nauseatingly sweet in the heat of the day.

After he drove away, Norma whipped out a cigarette and lit up. "He's going to shut us down and take over our business."

I maneuvered away from the smoke plume, not wanting to alienate Norma, but not wanting to leave without asking my questions.

Gardening was a lot of hard work. My Grandma Dee was a gardener. She put in several hours each day in her yard. With his job as sheriff, no way would Otis have time to work the farm, much less run the produce stand. "Maybe he's interested in farming."

"Did you hear him? He wants this place. I'm quite a good judge of character and that man wants this place bad."

I shared her distrust of Otis. He tried to come across as a nice guy, but there was something about him that put me on alert. Best to get the conversation back on track. "Did he mention anything about Barbara Jean's death?"

"Her case isn't important to him. He wants to persecute us."

Norma's name should've been Relentless. "It didn't sound like persecution to me."

She took another drag off her cigarette, blew the smoke at me. "He's got it in for us."

My patience frayed enough to loosen my tongue. "I can't believe you're smoking. For someone who believes in being pure and natural, you are polluting your body with smoke."

Her hand fluttered in the air. "I've tried to stop a million times. Then jokers like the sheriff come along and punch my hot buttons, and I gotta have a cig."

Mental note to myself: don't try to reason with the naturalists. For that matter, I had to get back on task. I had a reason for coming back here. The blackmail photos. I scrounged around my bag for them, found them, and dumped them on the worn counter. "Can you explain these?"

Norma paled. "Where'd you get these?"

"They were in the envelope with the infomercial stuff on organic farming. You gave them to me yesterday."

"I most certainly did not." Her hand trembled as she studied each one in turn. "But I can't let you keep these. People would get the wrong idea about us."

Alarm flashed through my veins. I wasn't giving up custody of the photos. I couldn't. Daddy's photo had to be handled discreetly. I pried the photos out of her hands and zipped them in my bag. "No kidding. Did you know Barbara Jean was seeing these men?"

Norma gazed pointedly at my bag. My pulse kicked up a notch. Would she try to take them back? We watched each other. She took a drag on her cigarette. "Barbara Jean was a free spirit. If she had an itch, she'd scratch it. She had quite a few itches where men were concerned."

I thought of my father's embarrassment at being found here earlier today. "Is more of that itching going on now that she's no longer around?"

Norma froze. "Are you accusing me of something?"

I studied her for a long minute. As much as it distressed me to ask, I had to know how I happened to receive those photos. "Why were those pictures in my packet?"

She seemed agitated, which was appropriate given the revealing nature of the photos. But she didn't seem enraged or murderous. Just irritated. Curious. What were these naturalists up to?

"I can't say."

"I believe you can. Why did you give them to me?"

Norma retreated toward the storage room, her hand covering her mouth. Her gaze dropped to the wooden planked floor. "Why are you so hung up on that? I didn't give them to you. I swear on Elvis's grave."

I wasn't born yesterday. She was hiding something. What was it? And how did my father's visit play into this mess? "I assume these men are the suspects you and your family thought might have murdered Barbara Jean, the ones you want me to investigate."

She leaned forward. "You believe us now? Because of those pictures?"

Was she going to steal them from me? I tightened my grip on my bag. "If these photos are related to her death, we need to get them to the police. I'm not a cop. I'm a reporter."

Norma's expression tightened. She pointed to my bag. "You've got a cop and a judge in those pictures. The cops won't take our word over theirs, particularly when the top cop wants to close us down. Getting the cops involved won't help, not unless you have proof."

I chewed on my bottom lip for a minute. Justice for Barbara Jean seemed out of my domain. Seeking it could be detrimental to my father. "Police detectives are trained to investigate. I'm not. Besides, my father is in one of these pictures. How objective would I be?"

She shrugged quickly, too quick for me. "Mama Leon said you were the one to call, so we called you. The ball's in your court."

"If you knew how bad I was at tennis, you wouldn't use that metaphor." Why were they bothering with an amateur like me for the investigation? Questions about Barbara Jean's death circulated in my head, as if this were a plot for a murder mystery. Except I was no real-life amateur sleuth.

"What about the coroner?" I asked. "If foul play occurred, he should find forensic evidence during the autopsy."

"Betcha anything he lists Barbara Jean's cause of death as a heart attack. But she recently had a check-up, and her doctor said her heart was fine."

Our county coroner, Bubba Brown, had been sweet

on my grandmother for the last decade. He moved at the speed of molasses. "Is the autopsy complete?"

Norma shuddered. "Well that's plain ole gross. Don't be talking about autopsies while I'm smoking a cigarette."

Talking about an autopsy wasn't gross. Gross was when you got dispatched to an auto accident and you were expected to take photos of everything. "Murder is gross. If you're right about Barbara Jean being murdered, it will get a lot more inconvenient and messy."

"I hate messy."

Messy seemed to be my middle name. If I had a chance of helping them, I needed to know more about the dead woman. "What can you tell me about Barbara Jean?"

"She was like the rest of us. She lived and died and paid her taxes."

No help there. What would motivate a person to kill a semi-retired prostitute? "Who were her heirs?"

Norma took a drag on her cigarette and blew out a long stream of smoke. "She was the last of her line. All she had was us."

"And her sexual conquests."

"Those guys wouldn't hurt Barbara Jean. She was their safe harbor in a cold, cruel world."

"You knew about the photos?"

"The photos didn't come from me." She picked fuzz off her dress. "I should have suspected something was up though."

"Why is that?"

Norma rearranged a basket of tomatoes, adjusting each one so that the darkest red side showed. "After we moved here, Mama Leon forbade us from engaging in our former line of work because of the trouble we'd had upstate. He said he'd keep us all satisfied that way. Barbara Jean complained loudly, bitterly, and often. She slid into a deep depression. Because she was so miserable, Mama allowed her to staff the produce stand, hoping daily contact with people would bring her out of her funk. She became much happier, much more content."

"Because she slept with her customers?"

Norma's face clouded up like a sudden July thunderstorm. "Those men are having the time of their lives. Barbara Jean was an expert at her craft. There was none better. A few years back, she'd have men waiting for two hours to have a date with her. They'd wait for her, even though the rest of us were available."

My brows shot up. "Professional jealousy is a strong motive. Maybe one of y'all got rid of the competition."

"We did not kill her." Norma stabbed out the cigarette on the back of the wooden counter. "Barbara Jean was the sweetest, dearest woman. No one wanted her dead."

"Someone wanted her dead. Someone killed her."

"You're going to catch them so they'll rot in prison."

"What makes you think I can unmask her killer?"

"Because Mama Leon believes in you."

I had no patience for brainless minions. "Don't you think for yourself? Does he have all of you women brainwashed?"

I didn't mean to vocalize either of those thoughts. My lungs stilled as the cords on her neck stood out.

"My brain works." Norma huffed out a blast of air. "I'm thinking I should tell Mama Leon he made the wrong call about getting you involved."

"Why? So you can set up another blackmail operation here at the stand? Do y'all split the money or does he take everything?"

"Barbara Jean didn't have sex with those men for money. She did it for love."

"Come on. She couldn't romantically love all those men."

"She loved sex. Someone took advantage of her weakness and snapped these photos without her knowledge."

"How convenient. Someone would've had to know

what was going on, hidden a camera, and kept the operation a secret."

"It wasn't Barbara Jean."

"How can you be sure?"

"Barbara Jean didn't need money. For her, sex was about satisfying her inner needs and pleasing the man she was with."

"Besides the people in the photos, who knew she was having sex here?"

"I certainly didn't. And I don't believe the others did either. Someone from the community must have found out. That's why Mama Leon believes you can help us. Because of your long-standing ties to the community."

"Why would someone from Marshview spy on Barbara Jean?"

"Blackmail. It's the oldest game in the book." At my pointed glare she amended her statement. "Well, the second oldest game."

"I'm confused. The killer was blackmailing Barbara Jean?"

"They wouldn't have to. She'd have given them all her money if they asked. But I looked through her bank records. There are no unexplained withdrawals or deposits. Whoever took those pictures targeted the men involved. It wasn't us."

"All I have to do is find a local who is unexplainably flush with cash? Wouldn't it make more sense to ask these men if they'd been blackmailed?"

She shrugged.

"Is the camera still here?"

"Nah. See for yourself."

The back room consisted of a narrow cot and stacked empty bushel baskets. No cameras were in sight. I remembered the orientation of the photos and backtracked to where the camera should've been. All I found was a few empty screw holes. Something had been mounted here. But it wasn't here now.

Who would be most affected by these men having sex with Barbara Jean? An answer came to me in a blinding flash. Their wives and girlfriends.

Chills ran down my spine. My mother routinely threatened to shoot my father if he strayed. She had the intestinal fortitude to confront a rival. But did I have the guts to ask her about it?

Nope.

I needed help.

And I knew the person to give it.

Chapter Nine

Grandma Dee was up to her elbows in raspberry impatiens when I parked the Hadley's truck in her driveway. Her lush landscaping was the envy of the county. She'd taught me the names of her rainbow-hued flowers, and she'd shown me how to care for the cuttings she'd given me. However, my impatiens never looked as nice as hers. Neither did my petunias, zinnias, black-eyed Susans, or roses.

She coaxed the best out of everything and everyone, and her down-to-earth practicality nearly drove my status-conscious mother nuts. Not that my mother needed a reason to go nuts; she was headed there on her own.

With the envelope of photos tucked under my arm, I joined Grandma Dee under the moss-draped oak tree. The shade chilled my sweaty skin. "Hey, Grandma Dee."

"Well, if it isn't my first grandchild." Grandma Dee waved me down on my hands and knees. "Help me finish weeding. These weeds have no business in my flower bed."

In our near-tropical climate, especially after the wet spring we'd had, Grandma Dee constantly battled weeds. I'd lost the war in my yard, which would sadden her the next time she visited. I dropped to my knees, set the incriminating envelope aside, and obligingly pulled the one-inch weeds from underneath the delicate, heart shaped petals.

Now that I was here, guilt riddled me. I should sort out my own troubles. Grandma Dee was no spring chicken. She didn't need the additional burden of my problems. I shot her a quick glance. "You doing okay?"

"I'm fine. The Garden Club is due in here next week, and I won't have that pack of snooping, backstabbing old biddies gossiping about the weeds in my yard." She gazed skyward and muttered something under her breath. "You know how those old women talk."

Though my grandmother didn't think she was old at eighty, her hair was snowy white, and smile lines wreathed her thin face. She moved with a stiffer gait these days, but she never mentioned her aches and pains. Old people did that.

She nodded toward the driveway. "I see you're in Hadley's truck. Is something wrong with your car?"

"Yeah." I choked back a harsh laugh as emotion got the best of me. "I rammed the back of Hadley's truck with my Suburban, busted my headlight, and activated the air bag."

Grandma Dee's busy hands stilled. "That's not like you, dear. What's going on?"

Tears blurred my vision. "I feel like a dog for coming over here and talking about my troubles, but you always know what to do."

Grandma Dee stood and extended her frail hand to me. "Up you go. Let's talk on the porch. These weeds will keep."

In moments, she had installed me in a wicker rocker, the envelope of photos in my lap. The faded rose-sprigged cushions comforted me, as did the tumbler of lemonade Grandma Dee placed in my hand. Her compassion brought my personal troubles to a head. I'd come here intending to ask about Daddy and the dead nudist. Now that I was here, I wanted to tell her about Hadley and Clarice.

"What's wrong, dear?" Grandma Dee asked.

"Hadley." A big lump filled my throat. I'd been hoping I'd wake up from this bad dream of seeing my husband kissing my sister. That wasn't going to happen. I hated them both.

"What did he do?"

I stroked my thumb across the condensate on my glass. "I caught him kissing Clarice."

Grandma Dee's lips pursed. "In ten years, there's never been a hint of trouble between you. Are you sure you didn't misinterpret the situation?"

I couldn't look at her. Reliving the moment was gut-wrenching, but maybe confiding in her would stop the scene from replaying endlessly in my head. "I was headed to work when I remembered I'd promised to take Clarice's bags of old clothes to the Thrift Shop. I didn't call first. I showed up. Hadley's truck was parked in her back yard, big as you please."

I gulped in a breath of air. "They were standing on the back steps. Their arms were cinched tightly around each other without a hint of daylight in between their hips. They were so wrapped up in each other they didn't hear me approach. Seeing his hand on her breast made me nauseous. It cut me through to the heart, Grandma Dee. I screamed at them, and then picked up everything I could find and threw it at them. Potted plants, rakes, a tennis ball, a bag of garbage."

Grandma's face paled. "How awful."

I scrubbed my face with my hands. "I lost it. I've never been so out of control in my life. I was furious with Hadley. I couldn't believe he'd betray me. With my sister. God. Hadley keep saying he could explain everything and Clarice stood there with that sickening smirk on her face."

Grandma Dee froze, her hands fisted in her lap. I let

out a deep sigh because she understood. And because she knew I needed to tell it.

"I kicked him out. I changed the locks. I refused to take his calls. When his truck was in my driveway on Friday afternoon, all I could think about was hurting him the way he hurt me."

"How did you explain this to Jimbo?"

"Jimbo figured it out for himself, even the adultery part."

"Always knew my great-grandson was a sharp cookie."

"There's more." I rubbed my face again. "I came here because of another problem."

"What?" Grandma Dee stopped rocking. "Is it your mother? Did Lila shoot Clarice?"

"No. But I can't say I haven't thought about shooting her myself. The new problem is Daddy." I flipped through the photos in the envelope and handed her the picture of Daddy and Barbara Jean.

The lines around Grandma Dee's face tightened as she studied the picture. She handed it back to me without a word.

Her brooding silence made no sense. Unless this wasn't news to her. "Did you know already?"

"Joe's always been interested in the pursuits of the flesh."

Her voice sounded bitter. "He's done this before?"

"It's not my place to revisit the past."

"Does Mama know?"

Grandma Dee leveled an icy gaze at me. "Lila chooses not to look. She talks a big game, but that's all she does is talk. That's how she tolerates his shenanigans."

I couldn't believe my mother wouldn't notice such a major transgression. But who was I to judge her? I hadn't caught on to Hadley and Clarice's affair until this week. We hadn't had any hint of marital woes and our sexual relationship had been fine. Nope. It had been fine for me.

Obviously not for Hadley.

"It's hard for me not to condemn her attitude, but being in the same boat myself, I can't see how she tolerates adultery."

"She loves him."

Love. I thought Hadley loved me, but I'd been wrong. He loved himself and his stupid truck. I'd been one of his women for a bit. Now I wanted no part of him. Especially not the parts he shared with other women.

"Grandma Dee, people believe this woman in the picture was murdered. If so, Daddy's involvement with her will come under investigation."

She grimaced. "He can handle it."

"What if he killed her? What if this is a blackmailing picture?"

Grandma Dee resumed rocking. "Shaky ground, that universe of 'what-ifs.' Don't go borrowing trouble. It'll find you all on its own."

"Should I give this photo to the sheriff?"

"That's up to you. Too bad Hadley lost his bid for re-election last November. It would have been easier if we could keep this in the family."

I wasn't sure I understood her advice. "Should I take these pictures to the sheriff?"

"Talk to your father. Don't air our dirty laundry in public."

"That's the thing. I can't broach this subject with him. Not now. Maybe not ever."

"Come now. Where's our intrepid reporter? You're stronger than that. I raised you to be strong. This thing with Hadley and Clarice will blow over, but your dad, well, it's time he was held accountable for his actions."

Hadley and Clarice wouldn't blow over if she was pregnant with his child. My chin jutted out. "How can you trivialize Hadley's adultery?"

"Clarice has had her eye on Hadley for a long time."

That brought me up short. "She has?"

"Yep. She took advantage of him. He strayed. But he didn't sleep with her."

My jaw dropped. "How could you possibly know that?"

"Because he loves you, gal. It's as plain as the nose on his face."

"Mama loves Daddy, and look where that got her."

"Ah, but your father didn't put Lila first in his affections. Hadley would go to the ends of the earth for you or Jimbo."

My fists clenched. "What was he doing with his tongue down Clarice's throat?"

"Men are opportunists. Do you think for a minute that a happily married man wouldn't look at a photo of a naked woman?"

"Entire magazines are built on the premise of men looking at naked women. Hadley did more than look."

"And he got burned."

"Wait a minute. Has he been here talking to you?"

Grandma Dee stopped rocking. A muscle twitched in her sun-kissed cheek. "He's staying here, dear. He wants you back."

"He's here?" I glanced nervously in the window. "That's not fair, Grandma Dee. You're my family, not his. You're supposed to take my side. Why didn't you say something? You let me go on and on, when all the time you knew about my humiliation."

"Hadley's grandmother was my best friend for fifty years. I won't turn her grandson away. He loves you. He made a mistake. He's sworn on Elizabeth's grave that he'll never stray again."

"He's a liar."

"He made a mistake."

"I can't believe this. You're my grandmother."

"I'm an adult. I make my own choices. Hadley screwed up. He admits that. It's not too much to extend that Christian charity that you profess in church to your husband."

"So, Hadley deserves another chance, but Daddy is pond scum?"

"I didn't say it quite like that, but, yes, that is the bottom line."

"This is nuts."

"Prove me wrong. Use those reporter skills to find out the depth of your father's involvement. Meanwhile, I'll keep Hadley safe here."

"You can have him. He hurt me."

"He's sorry. Sorry enough to sleep on my couch every night this week."

"Where is he now?"

"I believe he's at the auto parts store replacing your headlight."

"Crap."

"Don't swear, dear. It isn't becoming to a young lady."

"You've got it wrong. My father couldn't possibly be the pond scum you claim he is, whereas Hadley cheated on me with my sister. I know that for a fact."

"Prove it."

Chapter Ten

There was no time like the present to go head to head with Daddy.

I caught up with him down at the floating dock near the house. A glance at the exposed mud banks in the creek told me it was dead low water. Low tide meant no breeze and favorable conditions for insects. This situation called for bug spray. I rooted around in Hadley's truck until I found a can of bug spray and doused myself with insecticide.

Marsh hens called across the endless fields of slender cord grass. Gulls winged down the trickle of water in the oyster-lined creek. The afternoon sun glinted off the water, creating the illusion of flames on the surface. I shoved my sunglasses on. They weren't body armor, but they were the best defense I had against my father's scrutiny.

The pungent smell of gasoline permeated the stagnant air. Pieces of boat motor were scattered around my father in the small aluminum john boat. From his harried expression, the motor reassembly wasn't going well.

Metal clanged on metal. "You sonuvagun." Daddy's curly hair pulsed with each stroke of his hammer. A cloud of mosquitoes haloed his head.

How many times as a child had I watch him take apart this very motor? How many times had I stood here and been warmed by his inventive cursing until he noticed my presence? He'd always made time for me. His welcoming smiles were a powerful antidote to the woes of the world.

Now that he was in trouble, could I help him? I doubted a smile from me would cure his problems. With a child to raise, could I even involve myself in his mess? I hated adultery. Blackmail, too. I definitely couldn't help him if he'd been in on the murder. But this was my father, the man who'd sung me to sleep each night.

The envelope in my hand weighed a ton. I cleared my throat. "Hey, Daddy."

He startled at my voice, and then his face crinkled with warmth. He waved a grease-darkened hand at me. "Hey, sunshine. What brings you to mosquito central?"

I nodded toward the jumble of mechanical parts. "How many times can you revive that old dinosaur?"

"This is a fine motor. No reason to retire it."

Were we talking about the motor or him? My mother had been nagging him to take an early retirement so they could travel before senility hit. Had she stepped up her campaign now that Hadley was sharing the workload at Campbell and Associates?

As Daddy gave me another all-seeing glance, I was glad my sunglasses hid my eyes. He had an uncanny ability to read people and know if they were telling the truth.

Daddy sprayed WD-40 on a lever. "What brings you down here?"

"I realize you're right in the middle of something, but I needed to talk to you when Mama wasn't around."

One furry eyebrow kicked up. "You're keeping secrets from Lila? She won't like that."

"It isn't my secret. It's yours." I jerked the photo of him and Barbara Jean from the envelope and held it up.

Daddy bolted out of the boat like a thunderclap. His

instantaneous reaction stunned me. I lurched backward to keep the photo out of his range.

"Where did you get that?"

After arm-wrestling Norma for the picture, I wasn't about to let Daddy toss it overboard. I tucked it behind my back. "The 'where' doesn't matter. I want an explanation."

The muscles in his face tightened. "I don't have to explain my private business."

"It isn't so private if someone took your picture." My throat tightened with emotion. "How could you do this?"

His lips thinned. "Stay out of it."

"I can't." I cursed my hand as it shook. "This is a compromising picture of you with a woman who recently died. There are allegations she was murdered."

Daddy turned away from me. A marsh hen called in the distance, its tone mocking and derisive. The hot humid air pressed down on me, a giant weight pinning me in place. The longer Daddy held his tongue, the more my dread grew that he was involved in Barbara Jean's murder. I silently implored him to defend his actions.

"I can't believe she's gone." His voice cracked as he spoke. "Barbara Jean meant the world to me. I had nothing to do with her death."

Daddy sounded sincere, but I'd seen him work a courtroom to tears before. Now that he was under a cloud of suspicion, I had to be wary of his wiles. Fortunately, I'd learned a thing or two from him about interrogation. "I can't believe you were screwing her."

He flinched. "What we had together was beautiful."

"She was a prostitute, Daddy. She's slept with hundreds of men. She had sex for money."

"That was all in the past. I never paid her for sex. We loved each other. I was planning to leave your mother to marry her."

"Marry her?" My face must have shown my horror. Daddy stepped toward me, and I retreated into the dock ramp. I thought I knew him, but I only knew the side he'd shown me. And all my adult interactions with him had been viewed through the rose-hued glasses of an adoring daughter. Joe Campbell the man was a stranger to me.

I whipped out the photos of her with the other men and waved them under his nose. "She played you, Daddy. You were one of her many men."

The color drained from his face. He ran a greasy hand through his tangled curls.

I'd also learned from Daddy to look for tells, little signs a person gives off when they are nervous. He was normally quite fastidious. The fact that he'd coated his hair in grease was significant.

I forged ahead. "You are a married man. You promised to forsake all others for Mama. Have you forgotten those sacred vows?"

His chin jutted out. "That's between Lila and me."

He couldn't rationalize his way out of this. "Not hardly. Not when you're out screwing around. It affects me. Believe me, it affects me. But I'm not the only one tarnished by your immoral behavior. I don't want you anywhere near my son."

Splotches of red stained his rounded cheeks. "We're going fishing with Hadley tomorrow. That's why I'm overhauling the motor."

"Forget it. Jimbo's not going anywhere with you."

He grabbed me, his thick fingers manacling my wrist. I struggled to break loose, but he held fast. His eyes had a tortured look I'd never seen before. If it had been anyone else, I would have thought I'd gone too far. But because my father made a living out of manipulating people, I couldn't silence my questioning thoughts. Was his distress real? Could Daddy fake this degree of upset?

His nostrils flared. "You can't keep my grandson from me."

"I have every right to say who my son sees. If I'm not letting him see his adulterous father, you can bet the fleet I won't let him see you. You're an adulterer, maybe even a murderer."

My accusation colored the air between us. Daddy's pale face darkened with rage. I could have been more delicate about Jimbo's welfare, but I meant every word. My son's moral safety was my top priority.

"Let go of me," I gritted.

He shook my arm. "Not until you see reason."

My knees trembled. "If you don't release me immediately, I'm going to call Sheriff Blizzard out here and press assault charges against you. I'll make sure every sordid detail gets in the newspaper, too."

He let me go, but he stepped between me and the ramp, blocking my egress from the dock. "You'd ruin my reputation and my marriage over a photograph?"

Daddy had never snarled at me before. I massaged the greasy handprint on my wrist and wrestled with my thoughts. Adrenaline sluiced wide open through my veins. "You'd ruin our family's reputation and good name by whoring around Marshview?"

Daddy kicked an old Styrofoam float off the dock. "This is Hadley's fault. If he hadn't gone sniffing around your sister, you wouldn't be reading me the riot act."

My spine stiffened. "Don't you bring Hadley into this. He messed up, but so did you. According to Grandma Dee, you've been messing up for quite a while."

His hands fisted on the wooden rail bordering the ramp. "Dee's hated me ever since I married into this family. I was never good enough for her precious Lila."

"Listen to yourself. Every other word out of your mouth blames someone else. You can't blame anyone but yourself for this."

"You'll regret declaring war on me."

"Is that what you think I'm doing? So be it." Tears welled up behind my dark glasses. I blinked furiously in the waning light. "Your behavior has opened my eyes. You've been playing at the role of my father. Life isn't a game. Your actions have consequences. It's high time you faced them."

With that, I pushed around him and ran back to my car, my flip flops smacking against the rough wooden planking. As I drove home, I realized we'd passed the point of no return. I'd never be Daddy's sweet little girl again. He'd never be the superhero who was the rock of my world.

He was a sleazy, self-indulgent man with violent tendencies. A married man who worshipped another woman. A man who put his lust above the honor of his family. Grandma Dee was right. Daddy wasn't the man I thought he was.

But was he a murderer?

Chapter Eleven

Before I wrote Daddy off as a cold-blooded killer, I needed to find out if Barbara Jean had been murdered. For that, I had to talk to the county coroner. A glance at my watch showed I had time for a quick stop before I picked up Jimbo from his friend's house.

I turned off the highway onto the grassy lane to Bubba Brown's riverside cottage. Bubba had been the coroner for close to forty years, and when he stopped being the coroner, we wouldn't have one. This being a small town, he was also the Fire Chief and a deacon at the First Baptist Church of Marshview.

Though it was late afternoon, the temperature hovered in the mid-eighties. I hoped this springtime hot spell wasn't a portent of a long, hot summer. I had enough heat in my life without battling the climate.

Wooden steps creaked as I mounted them. I peered through the sagging screen door. "Bubba? You home?"

He ambled toward the door, a large-framed man with a thin salt-and-pepper comb-over. The inviting aroma of smooth bourbon wafted from his highball glass. "Who's asking?"

"Molly Darter. You up for a little company?"

"Always got time for a pretty gal. You want to come in, or does the porch suit you?"

I considered my options. It had to be hot as Hades inside his fan-cooled house. Here on the front porch, we had a chance of catching a breeze. "Out here is fine."

He raised his glass up to shoulder height. "It's cocktail hour. What can I get for you?"

Bourbon was the last thing I should put in my jumpy stomach. "A glass of water will be fine."

"Have a seat. I'll be right out."

Two faded green plastic chairs sat askew on his front porch. I settled on the one farthest from the door so that Bubba wouldn't have to walk around me. From the looks of the rotted porch railing and the peeling paint, the coroner didn't get paid enough to maintain his house. How in the heck were we ever going to get someone else to be the coroner after Bubba was gone if we only paid peanuts?

Thunder rumbled across the marsh, infusing me with urgency. Two weeks ago a storm dropped eighteen inches of rain on Marshview. Unless I wanted to drive in a deluge, I needed to keep this short. I hoped Bubba would tell me about Barbara Jean's cause of death.

Bubba shuffled through the screen door, his slipper-clad feet dragging on the bare decking. The collar around his polo shirt was threadbare, the cuffs on his shiny polyester trousers frayed. In his hands was a tarnished silver tray containing a whiskey bottle and two empty glasses.

He set the tray down on the plastic table between the chairs, and then poured me a glass and shoved it at me. "Here. Water is for sissies. A big-time reporter like you ought to knock back a glass of whiskey like a pro."

With reservation, I accepted the glass. I hadn't felt comfortable drinking with Mama Leon yesterday, but Bubba was a dear family friend. And after the go-around with Daddy, I needed something medicinal to steady my nerves.

But bourbon was trouble.

The last time I'd done straight shots of bourbon, Hadley had slung me over his shoulder and hauled me around like a cave man. We'd had wild sex on the stairs, in the bedroom, and in the shower. We would have had sex on the kitchen table the next morning if Jimbo hadn't started crying in the nursery.

I shook off that memory. Those days of uninhibited sex were behind me. I was a responsible adult now, a single parent, and I couldn't afford wild excesses of passion. But the idea niggled at me just the same as I took a polite sip. Probably because of all the bare skin I'd seen lately.

The booze burned all the way down. My eyes watered, and I coughed.

Bubba leaned back in his chair. "What can I do you for?"

"I'm here about Barbara Jean."

He nodded slowly. "The McAllister woman from the nudie place."

"Yeah. Her housemates believe she was murdered."

Bubba's knee jerked. "Why would they think that? She wore a Medic Alert bracelet because of her bad heart."

"Apparently she just received a clean bill of health from her heart doctor. Did you find anything out of the ordinary during your autopsy?"

"I haven't made my report to the sheriff yet. That information is confidential."

"I'm not asking as a reporter. I'm asking because I'm looking into the circumstances of her death, for personal reasons."

His piercing eyes lingered a bit too long on my slight frame. "Never figured you for one of those nudie girls."

I took another sip of the whiskey. It hummed all the way down. "Get real. You've known me all my life. I don't hang out with the naturalists."

He eyed me again. "Good. I'd hate to think you'd been holding out on my nephew all these years."

Bubba was also Hadley's great uncle and Hadley's only living relative. Did he know about our week-long separation and our pending divorce? Booze had lowered my guard, but it would take the entire bottle to make me air my dirty laundry in public. My private life wasn't open for debate. "I'm not here to discuss my sex life. I'm asking you, as a concerned Marshview citizen, if you believe Barbara Jean died of natural causes."

His hands shook as he drained his glass. The thin hair on his head stirred in the gathering breeze. "I could lose my job if the sheriff found out you knew this before he did, but what the hay, nobody else wants my job. Since the cause of death wasn't apparent, I collected blood and tissue samples and sent them off."

"When will you get the results? Monday?"

He snorted. "Not hardly. I didn't put a priority on the results because the most obvious cause of death is from natural causes. Heart trouble doesn't go away on its own."

"It could take days to get results?"

"More like a few weeks."

I savored a mouthful of whiskey as I considered the lengthy time frame. I wasn't familiar with forensic science, but I'd seen plenty of television programs where they did this kind of testing. "That's not how it happens on TV."

"Got news for you. Real life isn't scripted like those crime shows on TV. I'll be lucky to have the results in a few weeks."

"You'll keep her body in the morgue all that time?"

"The body has already been cremated."

My head bobbed. Was I too late? "Did you check under her fingernails for skin she may have raked off her killer?"

"Don't you worry your pretty little head about forensics. I know how to do my job. Here." He shoved the Lord Calvert bottle at me. "Refill time. I haven't had me a decent drinking buddy in days."

I glanced down in shocked surprise. My glass was empty. How had that happened? More to the point, why had I done that? I still had to pick Jimbo up from his friend's house. I needed high octane coffee, not more booze. I couldn't be drinking and driving my son around, even in Marshview. Especially now that my husband, correction, my ex-husband, was no longer the sheriff.

"No thanks. I really should be going."

"No fair. Things was getting interesting."

I studied him for a moment. Other than his shaking hands, he didn't seem the least bit tight. On the other hand, I wasn't so sure about my mental sharpness. "What are you talking about?"

"I wanna know about you and my nephew. Why'd you throw him out?"

I stilled, my mouth going dry. "How do you know about that?"

"His truck's been docked at Dee's house this week. A man notices when a younger man moves in on his woman."

Bubba had been courting my grandma for the last ten years. I should've known he'd notice anything that concerned her. Bourbon loosened my tongue. "Grandma Dee's taken pity on Hadley, but it's no use. I caught him kissing my sister."

"Can't blame a man for falling into a siren's trap. No offense, but your sister has the morals of an alley cat."

His comment infuriated me. Hadley shared an equal amount of blame for the affair. "Clarice is a tramp, but that's no reason for Hadley to sample her wares."

Bubba's trembling hand covered mine. "The boy meant no harm. He'd been up all night working on a project for the state. She came onto him while his defenses were down. Stuff happens. You can't hold that against him."

I didn't need this. I rose to go. The world wobbled. I

held still until it righted again. "That's where you're wrong. I can and will hold it against him. He's a lying rotten weasel, and he broke my heart."

"Don't be so quick to call the kettle black. Does Hadley know you went out to the nudie place yesterday?"

Fire brimmed in my nostrils. "How do you know about that?"

"Gal, I may be old as dirt, but I don't miss much. You said you'd talked to them, and I know good and well those folks run around in their birthday suits. If Hadley knew you'd been around a naked man, wouldn't he question your fitness as a parent?"

Words hurtled out of my mouth at supersonic speed. "His hand was on Clarice's breast. Mama Leon didn't touch my private parts, and I was fully clothed. It isn't the same thing. I had to go there for my job."

"My point exactly."

I'd had enough of gossipy old men so I lit out of there, a rooster tail of dirt spraying in my truck's wake. I didn't care if Bubba told Hadley about my trip to the nudist place. Hadley was ancient history. But he was also Jimbo's dad, and I couldn't pick Jimbo up after drinking so freely. Hadley would have to be the responsible parent.

Accelerating onto the highway, I punched in his cell number on speed dial. He answered on the first ring. Liquor made me direct and economical with Hadley. "Drop whatever you're doing," I told him. "Pick up Jimbo from Eric's house and keep him for the evening."

"Have you been drinking?"

I heard the censure in his voice, and his disapproval rankled. "Most definitely."

"I'll take care of Jimbo, and then you and I are going to have a long talk, Molls."

"I'm not talking to anyone tonight." I hung up on him and concentrated on staying between the white lines on the road.

Lightning crackled and gusty winds buffeted my SUV

as the storm blew in. A husky alto crooned on the radio about young lovers reuniting. Dang. I didn't need to think about sex tonight. Because of Hadley's faithlessness, I'd be sexless for a long time.

But when I pulled into my driveway, Hadley stood there, larger than life and sexy as all get out. Fire brimmed in my belly. The temptation to mow him down was stronger than ever, but I refrained and parked behind my green Suburban.

Never let it be said that Molly Darter was stuck in a rut. I could be flexible.

I could mow him down with my words just as easily, and my actions wouldn't hurt my car or my strained budget one bit. Being a writer, words were my weapon of choice.

Chapter Twelve

The gusting wind flattened my T-shirt against my chest as I exited the truck. I slammed the truck door hard, intending to march over to Hadley and lash him with my tongue. He didn't give me a chance to march anywhere. He was already in my face.

Confusion had me sucking wind for a second. If Hadley was here, where was Jimbo? As much as I wanted to blast him, my concern for our son trumped my anger. "Where's Jimbo?"

"I took care of it." Hadley backed me up against his truck, his palms pressed against the truck window on each side of my shoulders. Heat and dangerous energy swirled between us.

I shoved at his chest. "'It'? You think our son's an 'it'?"

"Quit putting words in my mouth. Jimbo is sleeping over at Eric's house tonight. What are you doing sloshed in broad daylight?" He sniffed my breath. "Have you been with a man?"

Darn it. He was too close. He'd boxed me in with his hands brushing my shoulders, his hips mere inches away from mine. His scent, the scent that used to drive me wild, filled my lungs, tormenting me with sensual memories from the past. Lightning flashed across my heart. Thunder boomed across the marsh.

I didn't love him anymore. He'd hurt me the worst way. With defiance bolstered by bourbon, I stared right into his narrowed brown eyes. "Yes. I've been with a man. And I had a good time, too."

A muscle in his cheek twitched. "Uncle Bubba called me."

"Why would he do that?"

"He wants me out of Dee's house. I'm cutting into his love life. And I want my wife back."

I pushed at him again. "You should have thought of that before you started shoving your tongue down my sister's throat. Go straight to hell."

His hand stroked through my hair, his lips whispered along my neck. "You do care, or you wouldn't be so all-fired up mad at me."

The lightning wasn't just shooting across the sky. It was arcing between us, raw and elemental. I shivered at his touch and hated myself for responding. "Don't," I whispered back. "You don't have any right to touch me. I don't want you anymore."

He stepped closer, until his hips and powerful thighs pinned me to the truck. His hard length pressed against all the right places. "I've given you time to cool down so we could talk about this, but that seems to have been the wrong strategy. You love me, Molls. You always have. You always will. We're a team, you and I."

His heat blanketed me until I felt I was going to suffocate. I planted my hands on his chest and shoved. He captured my wrists and held me still. I squirmed under the tight restraints. "You can't come in here and manhandle me. I'll call the sheriff."

"You won't call the sheriff. He wants you in the worst way, and you aren't available to him."

The unexpected information threw me. "Sheriff

Blizzard wants me? How do you know that?"

His eyes narrowed on mine. "A man knows these things. He watches you too closely. He stands too close to you."

"That's ridiculous. I'd know if he was interested in me." I voiced my protest aloud, but I was already thinking, what if he was right? I'd missed Hadley's affair with Clarice. Maybe all my relationship instincts were shot. "But, on the off chance you're right, now that I'm going to divorce your sorry ass, maybe I'll check out the competition."

A deep growl rose in Hadley's throat. His fingers tightened around mine. "You will not. You're my wife. If Otis Blizzard lays a finger on you, I'll shoot it off."

"Cut the melodrama. Let go of me. You don't have any right to threaten me or to tell me what to do."

"Call your sister. She'll explain."

"I no longer have a sister."

The pad of his thumb caressed my palm. "Now who's being melodramatic?"

His attempt at tenderness grated on my inflamed nerves. "I'm being honest, something you apparently know nothing about."

"It was a mistake to kiss your sister. I apologize and humbly beg your forgiveness. I was tired, and she smelled like you."

He was pond scum. I'd kill him except then Jimbo would be an orphan when I went to prison. I summoned the strength to shove him away, and then skittered around my SUV. "That's the lamest apology I ever heard. You'd been out all night and I came upon you glued to my sister on her back steps." I gave a grunt of disgust. "In a week, you couldn't come up with a better story than that?"

"I'm working on a case, Molls. I can't tell you about it."

My temper spiked again. "But you can tell Clarice?"

"Clarice is part of the investigation. She'll tell you her

part if you call her."

I banged my fist on the Suburban's warm hood. "I'm never speaking to her again."

"It's killing me to live apart from you."

"Don't you put this on me. You did this to us. You cheated on me."

He moved to close the distance between us, and I bolted for the house. I was fumbling through my tears, trying to stick the car key in the door lock when he took the keys from me and unlocked the door. But before I could enter, he enfolded me in his arms. "I love you, Molls."

My body didn't melt into his welcoming heat. "Don't."

His lips nuzzled my neck again. "I can't help it. I made a mistake. I admit to being a fool. I'm groveling at your feet. Please give me another chance."

The dog nosed the door open the rest of the way and dashed out, running in circles on the driveway, barking her head off. "Hush." I said it to Goldie, but I meant it for Hadley as well.

"I'll give you more time if you like," he continued as if I hadn't shushed him.

I turned around to give him a piece of my mind, but he had other plans. As soon as I faced him, he kissed me. I blamed the booze, but he'd always been a good kisser. I didn't participate, which drove him to try harder. So I waited for him to be done, all the while telling myself I wasn't buying his song and dance. He was probably out of clean underwear and wanted my laundry services.

When he stopped, there was an odd look in his eyes. A sad look. A defeated look I'd never seen on his face before. It tore at my ravaged heart.

I turned to go, but he caught my arm. I stared mutely at his restraining hand.

"Molls, Uncle Bubba told me you'd asked about the McAllister woman. Stay as far away from that as possible. I don't want you mixed up with those people."

Hot retorts sprung up in my throat, but no matter how hard I tried, nothing came out of my mouth. Finally, I managed two words. "Go away."

Mercifully, he let me pass. I ran to my bedroom and coiled up in my bed. Drawing the turquoise spread tightly around me, I hugged my knees to my chest and wept. Hadley had been my friend. My lover. My rock I counted on.

He'd betrayed me.

With my slutty sister.

Chapter Thirteen

Hot air bathed my face. I drifted in and out of sleep. It was so tranquil on my tropical island. Gentle waves lapped the pristine white sand. The sun warmed my bronzed skin as a muscular cabana boy walked toward me carrying a tray of umbrella-topped drinks. He was much too young for me, but he seemed riveted by my svelte body, his dark brown eyes boring into me with animal-like fascination.

I flushed under his rapt attention. He caressed my cheeks with long languid stokes, and my heart rejoiced. His breath came faster and faster, and it thrilled me that he was so attentive to my every desire.

There was something familiar about his scent. I inhaled deeply, freeing all the pent-up tension in my lungs, straining toward his heat. My eyelids drifted shut with pleasure at his repeated caress.

Something hard, cold, and wet touched my face. I startled awake, surfacing from my cocoon of sleep. I shoved the object away, blinking against the blinding sunlight filling my bedroom. As my brain booted up from dream mode, I was filled with a sense of profound loss.

I wanted to be back on that tropical island with my

handsome cabana boy.

"Five more minutes," I murmured, scrunching my eyes closed and burrowing into my fluffy comforter. The heavy object rolled up to my nose with a thud.

My eyelids popped open at the unexpected impact. Goldie's slobbery rock lay on my pillow. I groaned and then shoved the rock away, blinking against the bright sunshine. I squinted over at the clock. Seven.

Seven was the time my clock normally went off on a weekday. What day was it? Was Jimbo late for school? Jimbo. I frowned. There was something about Jimbo I needed to remember. Then it came to me. It was the weekend, and he was sleeping over at Eric's house. Relieved, I sagged back into my pillow.

My mouth seemed full of cotton, my eyes Sahara desert-dry, my stomach hollow and empty. I became aware of my pants snug around my waist, my bra tight against my chest. Glancing down, I realized I'd fallen asleep fully clothed.

Last night came tumbling back with dizzying disorientation. Drinking with Bubba Brown. Arguing with Hadley. Crying myself to sleep during the thunderstorm.

Goldie deposited the rock on the bed, her tail thumping against the wall. When I didn't respond, she nosed the rock onto my pillow and licked my nose, bathing me in dog breath. Ah, the scent of my favorite cabana boy.

My head pounded. I scrubbed my face with my hands, remembering the ugly confrontation with Hadley. Afterward, I'd come straight to bed. My stomach growled. No supper for me or Goldie last night. She must be starving. I certainly was.

"Okay. I'm getting up."

I swung my feet over the edge of the bed. Goldie licked my hand. She needed me. She wouldn't run off and betray me. It was me she loved. Well, I was a close second for her affections when Jimbo wasn't around.

The house seemed too quiet. Ignoring the emptiness, I fixed us both some breakfast and then sat on the front porch with my coffee and toast. I listened to the birds sing their dawn chorus. The chirps and trills grounded me, reassured me that life went on. Birds routinely lived through severe storms. They hunkered down during bad weather. When the sun broke through the storm clouds, they rejoiced in its rays of hope.

I'd never weathered a personal storm like this before, and I didn't feel much like rejoicing in the aftermath.

Hadley's half-assed apology wasn't credible. For him to actually kiss my sister, he must have wanted her for some time. I didn't believe his claim that the embrace had been a mistake. How did you mistakenly kiss someone? I couldn't imagine kissing my boss, the new sheriff, or Mama Leon accidentally.

And if I'd done something so heinous, Hadley wouldn't consider it a mistake. Accidents were things like running over a squirrel, or spilling coffee all over your grandmother's rug. Kissing wasn't an accidental pursuit. Either you kissed someone or you didn't.

That hurt look in Hadley's eyes last night—that had been the worst. I hadn't physically responded to his kiss, I couldn't because any response would mean I was nothing but a weak, hormonal creature. My heart had recognized the caress of my lover, but my head and my heart couldn't reconcile.

In my high school class, I'd been voted most likely to succeed because of my studious nature and my ability to obtain my goals. I'd believed my classmate's predictions were right. I'd gotten the man I wanted, the writing career I wanted, even the child I wanted. Now I was getting divorced.

A divorce I didn't want.

I'd failed. Failed at being a wife. Failed to read the signs that Hadley had a wandering eye. What else had I failed at? Was I screwing up at being a good mom to my son? Was I kidding myself about my journalist career?

I could end up dead and alone like Barbara Jean McAllister.

And naked.

Which did I fear most? Dead? Alone? Or naked?

The phone rang, but I didn't move. Goldie nudged my feet. I didn't want to talk to anyone. But it might be Jimbo calling.

I sprinted for the kitchen phone. "Hello?"

"Whatcha got for me, gal? Deadline's coming fast and furious." Ted's gravelly voice filled me with dismay.

With all the family hysterics yesterday, I'd gotten sidetracked. So far, I hadn't written a single sentence of copy. "I'm still fleshing the organic gardening story out. It isn't ready yet."

"Gotta have it."

I padded back out on the porch, Goldie at my heels. "It's not that straightforward."

"How hard can it be? They plant the fruit and vegetables, grow them, and harvest them. You can write a little fluff piece like that in your sleep."

"Those people are naked. It's very distracting to go out there."

"So? Finish the interview on the phone."

"I need more information. I didn't get what I needed on Friday."

Silence echoed through the line. "You said a mouthful there. I didn't get any on Friday either."

My temper flared at Ted's lame innuendo. "Don't reduce this to sex."

"Molly, everything is related to sex. Haven't you figured that out yet?"

"Are you referring to my sex life? Are you saying I can't do my job because I haven't been laid in a week?"

"Don't get so huffy. I was generalizing. People are programmed for sex. When they don't get it, they get out of sorts. It's a proven fact."

I rolled my eyes. "What's your source for that assertion?"

"Don't need a source. My own eyes have never failed me. When my best reporter can't write a word, I know what's wrong."

"I'm your only reporter."

"You're also in the midst of writer's block."

Was I? "You don't know that."

"Tell me your lead for your gardening story."

The seconds ticked by, and my brain wouldn't work. It couldn't. There was no lead, and Ted knew it. I lashed out at him. "Those people think Barbara Jean was murdered. Murdered. That's the real story, and I can't write it because there's not a shred of proof."

"Big deal. Get the proof you need."

I shuddered at the thought of returning to the nudist colony. Mama Leon's family jewels weren't my idea of eye candy. "You didn't tell me that the head nudist was a man. Everything was hanging out, and it wasn't a pretty sight."

"Did he tell you about the six men he allegedly killed?"

"He did not. He was too busy trying to make me believe Barbara Jean McAllister had been murdered."

Ted coughed. "Do you believe him?"

"I was so uncomfortable, I couldn't wait to get out of there. I don't have any idea if he was feeding me a line."

"What are you going to do about it?"

I took a deep breath, knowing what I had to do. "I'm going back out there today."

"To take pictures of the nudists?"

"To take pictures of their garden. To find out more about Barbara Jean."

"If you do uncover foul play, the story could get picked up by the Associated Press. It would prove the *Marshview Gazette* was a force to be reckoned with. Get the story and have it on my desk first thing in the morning."

The story. Ted's big dream was that folks in the big

leagues would take notice of us. But without pouring money into topnotch journalists, his chances of being on the journalistic map weren't great. I wanted to live in Marshview because I grew up here, but there wasn't much to hold an outsider like Ted. Unless he liked getting eaten by bugs and living with the sulfur-laden salt marsh smell.

How did he end up here five years ago? I couldn't fit him into a neat little box. Ted was a mystery, one I hadn't thought to solve. Not that I had time to do that, either.

That next-day deadline loomed in my head like a ten-foot-high brick wall. "Ted, I'll have the obit, but you can't count on the gardening feature."

"I've got a hole on page one. Write the story."

Desperation clawed at my gut. At this rate, I was going to be divorced and jobless. Lonely and broke. Without a means of support, I might lose my son. My worst nightmare was coming true. "I need this job. You need me."

"I'm the boss. I can fire you if I want."

My world was crumbling around me, and I couldn't fix it. Shaken, I hung my head. "Why don't you save us both the agony and fire me now?"

"Don't be an idiot. Get the story."

Chapter Fourteen

Snapping pictures of Back to Nature strawberry plants loaded down with lush red berries wasn't how I envisioned spending my Sunday afternoon. I'd planned to devote the weekend to my son, but so far I'd seen little of him. Just as well, because my boss demanded I finish the organic gardening story. I photographed the fancy-dancy irrigation system and the mixed rows of vegetables as I traipsed behind Kim, my naked escort for the day.

She'd met me at the gate wearing hiking socks, combat boots, and nothing else. Her curly hair draped around her shoulders and flirted with her pert breasts. There wasn't an ounce of cellulite on her butt. Her bodily perfection irritated the daylights out of me. As did this crazy hodgepodge of a garden.

"Watch your step," Kim said as she stepped over a mound of fresh dirt. "Tildy's been transplanting marigolds and she's left holes everywhere."

"Why are the plants all mixed up?" I asked as I framed out another photo. "I thought gardens were planted in straight rows."

"That's not how organic gardens work. Monoculture agriculture encourages losses by insects. By mixing the plant types, you bring in plants that are natural insect repellents, like marigolds. Tildy planted four flats of marigolds that she raised from seeds."

I paused to scribble that down. Though Kim had been nothing but helpful today, I hadn't warmed to her. Maybe I would hate all sexy, younger women because they were everything I wasn't—curvy, alluring, attractive, brimming with the blossom of youth. Nothing I could compete against.

And yet, I would be competing against the likes of her for a man, once I divorced my cheating husband. If I ever wanted another man. Only I couldn't picture me kissing another man.

The image of Hadley lip-locked with my sister flashed into my head again, merciless as a bald-faced hornet. Time to think of something else. "I was wondering what you thought about Barbara Jean's death."

Kim glanced over her shoulder at me. The move was meant to be coy and affected, but annoyance flickered in her eyes. Interesting. From what I'd seen of the family dynamic on Friday, Kim enjoyed her role as the reigning sexpot. Judging by the pictures of Barbara Jean with multiple sex partners, it was possible Barbara Jean had once held that role. Had Kim murdered Barbara Jean to remove the competition?

"Mama Leon thinks she was murdered," Kim said.

Clever of her to spout off the party line. But I wasn't dissuaded. "What do you think? Surely you have an opinion."

Kim shrugged. "Opinions aren't worth much around here."

Her comment aroused my curiosity. Was Mama Leon running this operation like a cult? Were the women terrorized by his iron-fisted rule? "I'd like to know your opinion."

Kim bent over and weeded around a few plants, displaying two tanned globes of buttocks. I ignored the moon staring me in the face and focused on her hands. I couldn't tell how she knew which plants to pull and which ones to leave, but the clumps of uprooted plants showed me Kim had the power of life and death over the garden seedlings.

Did she exercise that power anywhere else? Or was Mama Leon the group mastermind?

As silence settled on us, I realized she wasn't going to voice an opinion. I tried another tack. "What can you tell me about Barbara Jean? Where was she from?"

Kim straightened slowly, brushing the dirt from her hands. "I thought you knew."

My reporter instinct pinged. Was this the key to the woman's murder? I tried to appear calm. "I don't know anything. That's why I'm asking questions."

"She came from here. It was in the obituary information we gave you."

I hadn't started sorting through the obituary information yet. "Marshview?" I couldn't seem to wrap my brain around the new information. "She was born here?"

Kim nodded.

I searched my memory banks for a tie to her family and drew a blank. There was no outside industry to draw people here, so we didn't get transient families. "I don't remember any McAllisters living around here."

"Barbara Jean was homesick. That's why we all moved down here."

Her evasive comment further confused me. I'd left Marshview for college, but I hadn't pined away for sunrise over the marsh. I'd thought about finding a job elsewhere, someplace where no one knew me, my parents, my grandparents, and all my aunts and uncles. "I can see why she might've left a small town like this, but why would she come back?"

"The land. She inherited our place a few years back."

I tried to pinpoint when the naturalists moved in. The exact year escaped me. I remembered folks laughing about the nudies out in the woods, and I remembered Mama mentioning it to Hadley one evening when we'd been over to dinner.

"Can't you run them out of town?" Mama had asked. Hadley had been sheriff at the time.

"They aren't breaking any rules," Hadley had replied. "They're allowed to do what they want on their property."

"Can't we enact an ordinance to ban lewd behavior? I swear, it's like having a nasty worm growing right in the middle of the apple of our community."

"Ordinances work well, but Natural Woods would be exempt as it is already in operation."

Mama and Hadley had continued their skirmish, but I hadn't given another thought to the nudist colony after that. It was here and the people didn't bother anyone. Sure there were rumors about Mama Leon, but the wild rumors kept folks away. If he'd really killed six men, as Ted had implied, no one wanted to be number seven.

Unless Barbara Jean had been victim number seven.

She'd owned this land, but her death meant ownership would transfer to someone else. This land was valuable real estate. Ownership of such a lucrative resource might have put a target on Barbara Jean's back. I'd been sure those photos were related to her murder, but now I wasn't so sure. Greed was one of the oldest murder motives in the book.

This mid-county chunk of real estate was in a prime location. It would fetch a high price on the real estate market. "Who owns the land now?"

Kim's chin jutted out. "Us. We're her family."

Her family. Had Barbara Jean been killed by someone she lived with? Someone who knew about her heart condition might have set out in cold blood to take Barbara Jean's life and gain her estate.

How did the photos fit into this puzzle? Were they part of the murder scheme? Or were they intended to divert attention from the real killer? I didn't understand how these puzzle pieces fit together. Two things seemed certain. Barbara Jean had been murdered. And her heirs were sitting on a gold mine of real estate.

Kim seemed willing to talk, but I had to ask the right questions. "How'd you get mixed up with these people?"

"These people are my family."

"Sorry. I wasn't passing judgment on you or your associates. You're so pretty, so young, you could do anything with your life. Is this your life's ambition? To grow organic vegetables on a clothing-optional farm in the low country?"

Kim scowled. Deep lines marred her perfect face, lines that made her look fifteen years older than my thirty-three years. "What do you know about life? It's hard to make a living out there. I don't see you running off to work for the *Atlanta Journal* or the *New York Times*."

"We're not talking about me," I shot back, refusing to let this become personal. "We're talking about why someone with as much—" I paused to search for the right word. Sleazy, tawdry, flirty. None of those seemed quite right. Then the word came to me. "Someone with as much *presence* as you have, why would you waste your life here? Doesn't it feel like you're marking time?"

Kim puffed up like a rattlesnake in attack mode. "You don't know anything about me or my life, so stay away from me." She whirled and ran. "Find your own way out of here."

"Wait. Don't leave me here."

But she was gone even as I uttered the words. The birds quit singing. The sun slid behind a cloud. The woods sighed and creaked, giving me the creeps. Why was I standing here?

Because I didn't know which way was out.

Chapter Fifteen

Kim fled across the garden and turned left at the pole beans. Before I could remove the foot I'd lodged in my mouth, she'd vanished. I hurried after her but quickly stumbled to a halt. Near the pole beans were three paths leading into the woods. Which one had she taken? With the thick overhead canopy of vegetation casting long shadows, they all looked dark and forbidding.

I glanced around the disorderly garden. Which path brought me here? Did I come in by the leafy lettuce? Or was it closer to the strawberries? I paced the garden's perimeter, wishing I'd paid more attention when Kim led me out here ten minutes ago. I looked around, growing frantic. Even if I somehow chose the right path, it wasn't a direct route out of here. On the way in, we'd gone right at some forks, left at others.

My chances of getting out of here on my own were dismal.

And there was the additional worry of the bad dog somewhere on the premises. I'd been lucky enough to avoid him on my visit on Friday. But I wasn't feeling so lucky today.

My cellphone was in my reporter bag, but who would

I call? I'd need a helicopter to spot me in this maze of woods. If I had twine or lipstick, I could mark my passage through the woods, but I had neither. My clear lip balm was useless as a trail marker. The other items in my bag included seven ink pens, half a bottle of water, car keys, a mileage log, and an address book.

I thumbed through the address book. Who would I call? The mayor? No. The judge? No. The sheriff? No. My father? No. My husband? Absolutely no.

The sun slid behind a dark cloud, and the dense woods closed in on this tangled-up garden. A crow cawed in the distance, reminding me of my precarious position. I was alone, with no idea of how to get out of this maze. I shivered. Why hadn't I kept my mouth shut?

Kim projected the image of an agreeable sex kitten, but she wasn't agreeable at all. When I asked a pointed question, she'd turned tail and ran. I had to face it. She wasn't coming back.

Having grown up in this area, I knew something of the lay of the land. A highway bordered the property on the east and west sides. I'd parked at the picket fence, which was to the east of the garden.

Since it was late afternoon, the sun was closer to the western horizon. Therefore, if I kept the sun behind me, I should find my car sooner or later. It was the later that worried me. No matter how brave I wanted to be, I wasn't inclined to strike out on my own through these woods.

At least I wouldn't go hungry. I pocketed my camera and helped myself to a few delicious strawberries. It was easy to picture Kim as the murderer. She wasn't a balanced individual. She could have gotten mad at Barbara Jean and lost her temper. But there was a big difference between getting mad at someone and actually killing them.

I should know. My sister had betrayed me, and I had disowned her. The moment I'd caught her glued to my husband's hips hadn't put me in mind of murder, though I'd definitely wanted to hurt her. But killing someone went against everything I'd been taught about the sanctity of life.

But not everyone was raised right. Kim wasn't from around here, and I didn't know any of her people. Who knew what her morals were. She had a temper, and she got riled easy enough. Without moral bounds, passion could turn dangerous. The question I couldn't answer was why. Why would Kim murder Barbara Jean? Was it jealousy? Greed? Revenge? What would cause a breach between two supposedly kindred spirits?

A branch crackled off to the left. I grabbed my car keys. If that killer dog came at me, I'd jab him in the eyes with the keys. Sour notes of a popular country and western tune rang through the woods. Probably not the rabid dog singing about cheating hearts. But who? Was it the killer?

I hastily shoved the rest of the strawberries in my mouth and chewed fast. If this was my last supper, Bubba Brown would find the strawberries during autopsy. Maybe their presence would help him identify my killer.

The woman with elongated breasts strode into view on the westernmost path, singing for all she was worth. What was her name? Alma something. With her gray braids pinned to her head, she looked like an aging Swedish matron. Well, a naked one.

"There you are." Alma's pinched tone implied I'd wandered off and caused my current predicament.

Careful to avoid her nakedness, I trained my eyes on her face, lifting my hands in surrender. "Here I am."

"When the Princess stormed back into the house, I figured she'd had another hissy fit."

My eyebrows shot up. "You call Kim the Princess?"

"Yeah. Figured you must have reminded her she wasn't royalty."

Ah. Here was an opening I could use to my advantage. "We talked about the garden and Barbara Jean. Then Kim stormed off. Was she close to Barbara Jean?"

Alma sighed. "We all were. Barbara Jean was always

doing nice things for everyone."

"If that's so, why would anyone want to kill her?"

"Because some people wouldn't know a good thing if it bit them on the ass."

I flashed back to when I had to share a bathroom with my sister. After she started wearing makeup, Clarice spent hours gazing at her reflection in the bathroom mirror, hours that prevented my use of the facilities. With so many women living under one roof at Natural Woods, there had to be friction in their household. "So Kim didn't get along with Barbara Jean?"

"Kim doesn't get along with anyone but Mama Leon."

Interesting. Miss Sweetness and Light hated everyone. Kim vaulted to the top of my suspect list. "Did anyone else in the household have trouble with Barbara Jean?"

Sparks flew from Alma's faded blue eyes. "What are you getting at? None of us would've hurt Barbara Jean. She was good people. She was one of us."

"She's also dead. And y'all think it wasn't from natural causes."

"No way we would have lifted a finger against Barbara Jean, not even Princess K. Especially not her. She wouldn't want to jinx her karma."

Karma wasn't a word one ran across very often in Marshview. "Is Kim into the new age movement?"

"We're not Bible-thumping Baptists in here. We embrace alternative ideas. Fellowship and communion come in many forms."

Her comment jogged my sluggish memory. "Yesterday at the produce stand Norma mentioned the rest of you were spending the day meditating."

"Meditation centers us. It helps us to focus on the important things in life."

"Kim too?"

Alma nodded tersely. "Especially Kim. Though it appears that one day of meditation wasn't enough for her.

She probably needs a solid week of steady chanting to unblock her chi."

Hmm. I whipped my camera out and snapped a picture of the path Alma had arrived on, the one by the sunflowers. People that meditated didn't seem the type to commit murder, but I was pretty sure Kim could've killed Barbara Jean. For that matter, all of the naturalists had the opportunity to kill her.

As did the men in the compromising photos. I couldn't forget them. "What about the other people in Barbara Jean's life?"

"What other people?"

Since I didn't know who'd given me the photos of Barbara Jean screwing those men, I had to phrase this delicately. The last thing I wanted was to incite Alma to go haring off and leave me out here. Time to start using my head. Self-preservation was my top priority. "Never mind. I have enough pictures now for the gardening article. If you'd orient me in the right direction to leave, I'd appreciate it."

Alma pointed toward the path by the water spigot. It wasn't the same path she'd used. "Your car is that way. What other people?"

"Local people. She worked at the produce stand. She must have gotten to know various community members from clerking there."

"I wouldn't know about that. Barbara Jean was a woman of action. She wasn't big on talking about her acquaintances. If she made friends outside our boundaries, that's news to me."

Not the right answer. Was her ignorance of Barbara Jean's activities an act? I dug a little deeper. "What about men friends?"

"She didn't have men friends."

"The rumor around town is that men were your livelihood before you moved here."

Alma whipped around. Up ahead the trail forked and

I could just imagine her abandoning me here to wander the rest of my days in the woods. The canopy was too thick for me to tell where the sun was. Why couldn't I keep my big mouth shut?

"So what? You think a former client killed her?"

Yikes. I'd pushed her buttons. So much for keeping my mouth shut and using my head. I might as well go for broke. "I don't know who killed her. You asked me to help. Tell me about those pictures."

"What pictures?"

"The pictures of Barbara Jean having sex with men in the back of the produce stand."

Alma's chin jutted out. Her eyes blazed. "I don't believe you."

The pictures were still in my bag because I didn't want Jimbo finding them in the house. I pulled out the envelope and thrust the photos at her.

Awe spread across Alma's face as she studied them. Her hand trembled. "God, she was the best of the best. Look at these expressions."

I pointed at the curly-haired man in the photo. "That man is my father. He's still married to my mother."

Alma whistled in admiration. "She can thank Barbara Jean for that, too. Once men found Barbara Jean, they didn't look any further. She was a real pro."

I snatched the pictures out of her hand and stuffed them back in my reporter bag. "Her sexual proficiency doesn't impress me. These men might have had reason to kill her if these were blackmail photos."

"I see. You're afraid to investigate her murder because your father might be involved."

"I don't know who's involved, that's the problem. But someone from your household knew about her sexual partners."

"How do you know that?"

"Because that's where the photos came from. Your house."

"Damn Sam. Don't tell Mama Leon about the photos, whatever you do. He'll be furious. I swear I didn't know Barbara Jean was sexually active again. All I knew was that she was much happier once she started working at the produce stand."

I bet, but that didn't change the fact that Barbara Jean was dead. "Y'all moved down here because she was homesick. How could she be homesick and miserable at the same time?"

"That's the downside of being euphorically happy most of the time. Most days she'd be fine. But Barbara Jean would have days when she was so depressed she couldn't get out of bed. We learned to deal with her lows because she wouldn't seek medical attention. We had to drag her kicking and screaming to the heart doctor."

"Why's that?"

"She hated doctors. One butchered her female parts a long time ago, and she didn't have any use for the entire medical profession after that. Back when we were in the business, if we got a doctor in, even if he asked for her, she wouldn't do him."

With that, Alma scurried down the narrow path, and I hurried to keep her lithe body in sight. As much as I wanted to speculate on Barbara Jean's abhorrence of doctors, I wouldn't risk being stranded in the woods again. Whereever Alma was going, I was going, too. At long last I saw the familiar picket fence and my green Suburban. I breathed a huge sigh of relief.

Then I saw the uniformed sheriff leaning against my vehicle.

Otis.

What did he want?

Chapter Sixteen

Lordy, I didn't want to deal with Sheriff Otis Blizzard now. Not when I had the incriminating photo of Daddy and Barbara Jean in my reporter bag. Not when I'd gone behind the sheriff's back to talk to the county coroner.

But I wasn't related to Grandma Dee for nothing. I squared my shoulders and forged through the open gate into a bright pool of sunlight. "Afternoon, Sheriff."

My southern drawl sounded cool and refined, a testament to years of having my manners drilled into me. Or maybe it was that infinitesimal speck of blue blood coursing through my veins that wouldn't allow me to cower in the face of my enemy. Even if my insides were quivering like a hound's nose on a scent.

Otis tipped his hat toward me. "Miz Molly." He repeated the gesture to my naked companion. "Miz Alma. How's everyone doing?"

Well, well, well. He knew Alma's name, and he'd addressed her with respectful familiarity, same as he'd addressed me. I edged toward my vehicle. "Doing fine. And you?" Never let it be said that a southern lady couldn't converse under duress.

Relief filled me as soon as I touched the hood of my

dark green Suburban. A few more steps and I'd be home free. I drew in a deep breath under the pasted-on smile I sported.

"Fine and dandy," he replied.

Alma had remained behind the weathered picket fence. Even so, her upper torso had to be clearly visible to the sheriff. I glanced at him to see if he was fixated on her nakedness, but found his gaze riveted on me. Heat rose to my cheeks. God, was Hadley right about Otis being infatuated with me? Was that what his gawking was all about? Or was his interest more unhealthy?

The other day Mama Leon said Otis had it in for the naturalists. I'd thought the tie-in was because of the rival organic gardening farm his relatives owned, but what if it was something more? What if Otis was the killer? I shivered. No matter which way I looked at it, hanging out with Otis was dangerous.

Up until the election, Otis Blizzard had always reminded me of one of those fashion dolls - the ones with smooth sculpted plastic hair and a "G"-rated anatomy underneath their clothing. Or in this case, his freshly pressed uniform. When Hadley lost the election to Otis, Hadley had made the comment that Otis wore the uniform to remind folks he was the new sheriff. Hadley had never worn a uniform when he'd held that position. Never had to. He exuded authority.

I edged a step closer to my car door. Otis was an ambulance-chasing lawyer who'd relocated here about four years ago, right after he started working in Justice County part-time. No one had taken his bid for sheriff seriously because Hadley was a shoo-in. The vote recount told a different story. At the time, I'd assumed his win was because of grass roots support, but now I wondered if he'd manipulated the recount.

Why was he out here? My reporter curiosity trumped my need to escape. "Were you looking for me?"

He stepped in my path. "When I saw your car parked

here, I stopped to see if there was a problem."

"No problem at all. Alma and I were talking about her garden." He had an annoying dimple in one cheek when he smiled. His classic blond good looks rubbed me the wrong way too.

"What garden?"

I wasn't buying his dumb routine for one second. He couldn't be as stupid as he sounded. Stupid people did not pass the Bar. Hadley had studied for weeks for that exam, barely scraping through, and he was brilliant.

Well, not so brilliant. He'd screwed my sister.

My head pounded. I scrunched my eyes shut for a moment to divert my thoughts. This wasn't about Hadley. This was about me giving Otis the brush-off. I'd better start chit-chatting like a normal person instead of crying over my disaster of a marriage.

I clutched my reporter bag close to my side. "I'm doing a feature on organic gardening for the paper."

He nodded slowly, his tawny brown eyes creeping me out as they roved over me, as if memorizing every nuance of my expression. Yikes. I dug in my bag for my keys.

Otis moved forward again, blocking my exit. "Did you get what you needed?" he asked.

His question wasn't about sex, but he'd invaded my personal space. My mind began to panic. At his nearness, his musky fragrance filled my head. My sudden flurry of sneezes took both of us by surprise. I clamped my hand over my nose and mouth, but not until I'd already sneezed on both of us. "Sorry. I must be hypersensitive to your cologne."

His eyes rounded with surprise. "I'll make a note of it."

Gross. I really didn't like him, and I didn't want him making any notes about me. I made a show of checking my watch, and then hit the unlock button on my keypad. "Look at the time. I'm late to pick up my son."

"You be careful on the road now, you hear?" Otis

cautioned as he opened my door. It didn't escape my notice that his gaze lingered overlong on my sandal-clad feet. Once inside, I revved the engine and backed around his black SUV. Before I popped it into drive, I noticed Otis had moved toward the open gate where Alma stood waiting.

Interesting.

I pulled away slowly, watching my rear view mirror as I accelerated onto the highway. The sheriff didn't pull out behind me. Hmm. I made a U-turn and cruised past the driveway again. His empty vehicle sat there, but he and Alma were long gone. What was up with that?

What business did Otis have with the naturalists? Were they part of his grass roots support team? Or was he a voyeur and enjoying the "natural" scenery in the woods? Or were he and Alma up to something more nefarious?

If he had a reason for being there, then he'd made up that stuff about stopping to see if I needed help. Which made him a liar. I didn't care for liars.

I didn't care for Otis Blizzard, either. Daddy had called him a carpet-bagging shyster when he opened a law practice in Marshview. I thought the remark was prompted because Otis cut into Daddy's business. But maybe Otis was truly woven of a lesser cloth.

Was he out here on official sheriff business? Did he finally believe the nudists' claim that Barbara Jean's death was murder?

If that was so, I wouldn't need to investigate any further. But those pictures. My gaze fell to my reporter bag on the adjacent seat. What about those pictures? Did I have an obligation to show them to the sheriff? Daddy didn't deserve my protection, but he was family. Family always stuck together.

What the sheriff didn't know, wouldn't hurt him.

* * * *

Jimbo chattered about his sleepover at Eric's all evening. I was happy to see my son, even happier that he didn't question his good fortune. Usually I went overboard grilling him on the sleepover agenda. Both Jimbo and Hadley thought I was being neurotic with my questioning.

Boys will be boys, Hadley had said.

I hated that catch-all, Teflon phrase. I hated even more that there was some truth to it. In many ways this was still a man's world, one where men made up the rules.

Was that how Hadley and Daddy justified their adultery?

They couldn't help themselves? The fact that they could justify the ultimate betrayal made me nauseous.

The phone rang while we were watching television, and Jimbo jumped on it. "Hey, Dad!" Jimbo's face lit up. "Guess what I did last night."

His overt happiness tore at my shattered heart. I muted the television and carried the empty popcorn bowl to the kitchen. After I finished with the dishes, I stepped into the hall to give Jimbo more privacy.

I sat on the stairs, wishing I could keep my son's heart whole, wishing I could fast forward him past the next ten years of disappointment and anger against his father.

Goldie padded over and rested her large triangular head in my lap, her solid warmth a balm to my aching heart. I stroked her soft fur. The house fell silent as Jimbo listened to what Hadley was saying.

Tears threatened, and I blinked them away. I prayed Hadley wouldn't ask Jimbo to put me on the phone. I didn't want to speak to him. I didn't want Jimbo to see us fight, or to hear us yell at each other either. No matter how much I hurt on the inside, no one else needed to know. As far as the world was concerned, Molly Darter was doing fine without the adulterer.

"I love you too, Dad," Jimbo whispered.

A sob escaped my throat. I quickly crammed my fist in my mouth to keep from crying out.

"When you gonna come home?"

The answer was clear to me. Hadley was never

coming home. We were both much better off without him.

But I knew better than to count Hadley Darter out. He was tenacious. A tad ornery, too. If he wanted us back, he'd move heaven and earth to get us. He wasn't above using trickery to manipulate me, only I wouldn't let him get close enough to try anything.

Chapter Seventeen

Jimbo held the phone out to me. "Dad wants to talk to you."

I stared up at the white ceiling. I could refuse to speak to the adulterer, or I could accept the phone from my son. If only there was a thunderstorm right now. Hadley knew I wouldn't talk on the phone if there was thunder or lightning. But the only thunderstorm in the area was the one raging inside of me.

I made the mistake of looking into my son's eyes. His glasses magnified his earnest expression. He looked so hopeful, so keen on me talking to his dad, that I had no choice. I silently cursed Hadley.

With great trepidation, I put the phone to my ear. "Yes?"

"You've been ducking my calls, Molls."

Conscious of Jimbo's rapt attention, I swallowed my not-so-nice retort. "I'm fine, thanks for asking."

Silence pulsed ominously through the line. "Don't freeze me out. I want us to get back together. You want that, too. I know you do."

His husky voice was doing things it shouldn't to my pulse. I was so over him. "Principled people understand the difference between thoughts and actions."

He groaned. "You're killing me. I want my family back."

"It's a little late in the day for that thought."

"I'm going to make this right, love. Meanwhile, stay safe." He ended the call.

I tossed the phone on top of the bills on the kitchen counter. If not for the eight-year-old boy at my side, I'd be ranting about Hadley's arrogance. I'd be slamming things around the kitchen, ripping the traitor's smiling face out of every family photo, and shredding his clothes with scissors. I tried a deep breath to calm down, but it still felt like the top of my head was smoking.

"When is Daddy coming home?" Jimbo asked with innocent expectation. "He said it was up to you."

Hadley would. I unclenched my back teeth. "I don't have an answer for you."

"Are you thinking about forgiving him?"

I exhaled tiredly, hating being cast as the bad guy in this scenario which was so clearly Hadley's fault. "Jimbo, some things are easy to forgive, others are much harder. I'm not feeling very generous toward your father right now. We're working out a solution. That's the best I can tell you."

"You haven't ruled out forgiveness?"

This seemed so important to my son. I couldn't let him down. I summoned a weak smile. "I haven't ruled out anything."

After I tucked Jimbo in, I put Hadley and the dead naturalist out of my thoughts and wrote the organic gardening piece. Words boiled out of my fingertips as the story came to life. Who said I couldn't compartmentalize my thoughts? Every word sang.

My editor would love this story. With the garden being so secluded, I used the headline "A secret garden." It had been done before, but never by me and never in our paper. I emailed him the piece and went to bed feeling better than I had in days.

Even if my marriage was over, I was still a darned good reporter.

*   *   *   *

Monday morning, I put Jimbo on the school bus, and then I dashed back in the house for my peanut butter and jelly sandwich. No more costly seven dollar lunches at the diner for me. I had to economize if I was going to support us on my reporter salary.

Hadley's red pickup pulled in behind my Suburban as I exited the house. When I saw my sister with him, anger boiled out of me like a swarm of bees. His betrayal and disgust buzzed through my head. I banged my fisted hand on the warm hood of his truck. "Get out of my driveway. Get off my property."

Hadley marched around his truck and dragged my sister out. I noticed that she held onto the door and her seatbelt until he pried her fingers loose. He shot me one of his patented dark looks. The one that said he meant business. "You two need to talk."

Clarice rubbed her arm where he'd grabbed her. "If I get a bruise from this, I'm suing you for everything you've got," she hollered as Hadley drove away.

I glared at my sister. "I don't have time for this. Get off my land."

Clarice smirked at me with her hot pink lips. She was perfectly made up and in a low-cut, lacy pink blouse that showed off her tanned, plumped up breasts. Way too sexy for first thing Monday morning. My blood pressure spiked. Had she spent the night with Hadley?

"Or what? You'll call the new sheriff? You don't scare me, big sister."

I had on a white T-shirt and jeans. My hair was in its usual air-dry mode which meant it was not curled or alluring like her hair. My only concession to being a girl today was that I'd worn sandals instead of my customary sneakers. With my slender frame, I looked like a boring stick while Clarice's voluptuous curves fairly shouted her womanly status.

"I don't have to scare you," I said. "I have the law on my side and you're trespassing."

"You're quoting law to me, that's rich." Her brittle laughter echoed across the marsh.

Clarice had started law school, but she'd studied a succession of men instead of law and flunked out. She'd boasted as soon as a rich man came along, she was running off with him. When Mr. Right hadn't materialized, she'd taken my husband.

Waves of hatred crested through my gut. "Get out."

With a satisfied smirk, she crossed her arms. "I can't go anywhere unless you give me a ride into town."

"I'm not giving you anything. Slut."

"Tight ass."

I dropped my reporter bag and lunged for her. We slammed against the concrete driveway, rolling, punching, clawing. I yanked on her hair. She sliced open my face with her nails. Furious, I grabbed her hands and pinned them to the ground. I landed hard on her torso.

She bucked, trying unsuccessfully to unseat me. "Get off. You're squishing me."

"Too bad."

She glared up at me. Defiant. Smug. "Hurts, doesn't it?"

I rubbed my throbbing cheek on my shoulder and winced at the pain.

Her eyes flashed pure malice. "I'm not talking about your stupid face. I'm talking about your precious Hadley."

My back teeth clenched. "What about him?"

"It hurts not having a man in your life."

I lifted up and purposefully sat down hard on her torso. Gouging her eyes out would be too good for her. I wanted to rip her toenails off one by one and then drip caustic fluid all over her precious curves. Maybe tear all that strawberry blonde hair out by the dark roots, too. I opened my mouth to curse at her, but only a gurgle of anger came out.

Speechless.

I was so mad I couldn't even talk.

"Now you know how I—" Clarice's lower lip trembled as her eyes misted with tears. Her lip stiffened. "How I feel all the time."

She was lonely? She'd seduced Hadley because she was lonely? I wasn't buying it for one minute. My body tightened with fury. She wasn't about to win an ounce of my sympathy after what she'd done to me. Those tears in her eyes were probably crocodile tears anyway. "I don't give a hoot how you feel. I hate you for what you did. I don't have a sister anymore."

Her chin quivered. "You can't mean that."

I still wasn't buying her poor-me routine. "I never say stuff I don't mean."

Disgusted, I rolled off her and stood. I was shaking all over. All this drama and it was barely nine o'clock. I still had to go to work. I touched my cheek where she'd scratched me. I needed to clean that wound. No telling where those skanky pink nails of hers had been.

I scooped up my reporter bag and headed for my front door. "Get off my land and never speak to me again. If you're still here when I come out, I swear to God I'll run you over."

"I kissed Hadley. He didn't kiss me."

I ignored the hysterical note in her voice. Clarice had always been good at manipulating people. But I was onto her tricks. I slid my key in the door lock without looking back.

"We'd been working all night on a case for the Georgia Bureau of Investigation," Clarice continued as if I cared what she said. "He walked me to my door and was going to kiss me on the cheek like he always does. I blindsided him and kissed him full on the lips."

I stilled in the threshold. I couldn't look at her, but I

couldn't close the door either.

"I wanted him," Clarice cried. "I know it's selfish. But I've always wanted Hadley. And," her voice broke again. She paused for a moment. "He's only ever had eyes for you. So what if I took advantage of him? He doesn't love me. He doesn't even like me anymore. He won't speak to me."

Even if Hadley hadn't initiated that kiss, he'd still participated. His hand had been on her breast. I would never forgive him for that. As a law enforcement officer, Hadley had received training on repelling assaults. He didn't put up the slightest fuss. I'd seen the embrace with my own eyes, and my eyes didn't lie.

I slammed the door and spent the next ten minutes trying to get my pinging nerves under control. It wasn't happening.

If I called in sick, my boss would probably kill me. On Mondays, we assembled the pages of the paper and proofed everything. Ted's rule was that every page had to be proofed twice. Since it was only the two of us, my participation was mandatory. Ted wouldn't care if I was shaking. As long as I was breathing and able to proofread, he would be happy.

When I went outside, Clarice was no longer prostrate in my driveway. I sped past her walking on the road into town. It was a good five mile hike and the high-heeled strappy sandals she wore were better suited for a cocktail gown. And deer flies were in season.

She probably had a cocktail of gel, mousse, and hairspray in her hair. Natural insect attractants, every one of them. She had to walk past ditches full of standing water, so she'd be mosquito bait, too. Nice big red welts on her face would look perfect with her bright clothes. Maybe she'd contract West Nile virus from a mosquito bite.

That thought stopped me. Crap, what was I thinking? I didn't want her to die. I dialed my mother on my cell.

"Can't talk," I hurriedly stated, once she answered. "Your daughter is stranded on the highway between my house and town. You need to go pick her up."

"Why are you calling me? Why don't you get her yourself?"

"I no longer have a sister." I turned my phone off. Mama would demand an accounting, but I wasn't in the mood for more family drama right now.

"Holy cow. Did you run into a buzz saw?" Ted asked when I hit the office.

I glanced down and for the first time noticed that my shirt was torn and dirty. Self-consciously, I skimmed my fingers over the scratches on my face. "Something like that. I don't want to talk about it."

"Good girl. Suppress all those emotions and you'll end up a bitter, lonely man like me."

"I'm not answering the phones here today. If anyone from my family calls, I'm busy. Except for Jimbo. I'll speak to him. Everyone else is *persona non grata.*"

"Aye aye, boss."

I shot him a dirty look. "What have we got?"

He slid two sheets over for me to proof. "I used the obituary, the organic gardening story, and photos you emailed me. Good going on that gardening article. It was page one all the way. That photo of Jimbo and your dad at the produce stand was good human interest stuff."

What would Ted think if he knew my father had been screwing his brains out in the storage room of that same produce stand a few weeks ago? Would he print that? I clamped my mouth shut.

"What about the dead nudist?" Ted prompted. "Was she murdered?"

"Seems very possible to me. Did you know Barbara Jean McAllister was from here?"

He didn't answer. His chair creaked as he leaned back in it. His thinking position.

Sensing a story, I tossed my red pen down on my

desk. "You knew? You knew her?"

He shrugged. "I knew about her."

"Who was she?"

"She's an Olden."

"Duh. That was in the obituary. She left town before I grew up, so how did you know her?"

"Didn't say I knew her. Said I knew of her."

"I don't get her story. Where was she all the years old man Olden was bedridden? Why would he leave her a penny when she didn't give him the time of day?"

"Now you're asking the right questions."

"Don't keep me in the dark. Spill."

Ted steepled his fingers under his chin. "What I know is old news. Her Mama died soon after childbirth, and Barbara Jean's Daddy let her run wild. When she ran off in her late teens, he did the only thing he could do to make her come home. He cut off her money. Then he lost track of her. When he found out she'd turned to whoring, he went on a two-week drunk, wrecked his Cadillac, and spent the rest of his life fighting bedsores."

"Dang. Why didn't you give me that background before I went out there?"

"I wanted to see what you thought about the place."

"The property was well maintained. The people were weird." I studied Ted for a minute. He seemed to be waiting for me to say something else about Barbara Jean. So I said the first thing that came to mind. "You think she was killed?"

"Definitely."

My breath stilled in my throat. "Who did it?"

"I don't know, but my gut tells me to follow the money."

"One of the women out there told me they inherit the property. You think they all were in on it?"

"We need to find her lawyer and read her will."

"I'll check it out later today." I had a sinking feeling I knew who Barbara Jean's lawyer was: Daddy.

Chapter Eighteen

An hour later, Mama stormed into the office. She'd dressed in full battle gear, from her shiny lavender pumps and matching patent leather handbag to her severely tailored violet suit. Her hair had been flattened into a compact helmet with glossy hairspray. Electrical energy sparked from her body like heat lightning across a summer sky.

I gulped. This would be ugly.

Mama leveled a manicured finger at me. "You. Come with me."

Ted could save me by insisting I was invaluable to his editing process. It was Monday after all. I shot him my best *help!* look. In response, Ted lifted the proof page higher and slunk down in his chair. Coward.

I sighed heavily. "I'm working. We've got a paper to put out."

Mama didn't look impressed. "I'm gonna give you three seconds to get out of that chair, then I'm gonna snatch you up and drag you out of this dungeon."

I shifted uneasily in my squeaky chair. "This is our busiest day of the week. I'll call you when I get off work tonight."

"Margaret Catherine Campbell Darter, you know how I feel about airing dirty laundry in public, but unless you come with me right now, I'll do it."

She'd used all my names. I was in big trouble. Amidst a wave of humiliation, I swallowed my further protests. I was thirty-three years old, and I couldn't stand up to my mother. What did that make me? A wimp of the first degree? "Yes, ma'am."

No point estimating a time when I'd be back. Ted, the big coward, would have to make do without me.

I shoved on my sunglasses as the blinding sunlight hit me. Maybe it was a little dark in the office, but we liked it that way.

"Get in the car." Mama pointed to her mammoth luxury sedan. There wasn't a scratch, ding, or even a speck of dirt on her white car, but then in her world, cleanliness was next to Godliness. I scanned the car anxiously for Clarice, and then heaved a sigh of relief she wasn't there.

If I got in that car, I'd be on my mother's turf. No telling where she might take me. She'd pried me out of the office, which was as far as I was going today. "Let's take a walk in the park, Mama."

"Dirty laundry," she warned, her lavender clad feet not budging.

"There are no secrets in Marshview. If you want to talk to me, this is how we're gonna do it. Come on." I struck out for the park at a brisk stride.

I wasn't being disobedient. I was a grown woman after all.

Her pumps slapped against the pavement at a fast clip behind me. She wouldn't like following my lead. I was betting she was praying a mile a minute back there. I kept up my rapid pace until I came to the Marshview Oak. The town landmark had endured for two-hundred and fifty years. A little Campbell dirty laundry wouldn't bring it down.

I turned and faced her, hands on my hips. "What did

you want to talk to me about?"

Mama skidded to a stop. "Your shameful treatment of your sister. That's what."

Clarice had always been able to wrap mama around her little finger. Why should I have assumed mama would actually take my side for once? I momentarily lifted my glasses to show her my scratches. "Your *daughter* sliced my face open."

She crossed her arms. "After you attacked her. You were raised better than that. I'm so mad I could spit."

I'd had it with Clarice getting dibs on mama's sympathy. "Clarice is no angel. She's a tramp, and if you don't wake up, you'll be the last person in town to know that."

"Don't you slander your sister's good name."

"Mama, she's slept with every man in town."

"She has not. Take it back or I'll wash your mouth out with soap."

Heaviness settled in my heart. "I caught her kissing Hadley."

Mama's hand fluttered and went to her chest. That's just what I needed, to be responsible for sending mama to the Emergency Room with a heart attack. I stepped forward, supported her elbow, and guided her over to a shady park bench. "I'm sorry to disillusion you," I said, softening my voice. "Truly, I am, but I'm hurting here, too. She wrecked my marriage."

"I don't believe your preposterous accusation. She said you'd make up something spiteful."

Irritation flared. She was my mother, too, and she could darn well hear my side of the story. "That was Clarice trying to put her spin on recent events. I hate her, Mama, and she's not welcome in my life."

Mama gasped. "What about Thanksgiving dinner?"

"What about it?"

"Everyone always comes to the house for dinner."

"You can forget about a full family gathering. I won't

be under the same roof with her."

Mama's hand covered her mouth. "You'd ruin Thanksgiving?"

I huffed out a blast of air. "I'm ruining nothing. Clarice ruined everything."

Mama was quiet for a moment. "You'll feel differently once you work this out with Hadley."

I held her gaze. "He cheated on me, Mama. I don't trust him."

Mama's face tightened until the fine lines around her mouth deepened into well worn furrows. Funny, I'd never noticed them before. Her voice came out whisper-soft. "That's how it is with husbands. You have to overlook that sort of behavior."

From her comment, I inferred she knew about Daddy and Barbara Jean. But this conversation wasn't about her marriage limitations. It was about me, and I wasn't veering off topic. "I don't have to overlook anything. I'm not the one in denial here."

The color drained from Mama's face. "I don't know what's got into you today. First you attack your sister. Now you're attacking me."

"Does that make it easier for you, Mama? To blame me? Well, I'm tired of shouldering all the blame. I'm tired of Clarice always getting her way. I'm dead tired of you always believing her over me."

"Clarice is delicate."

I snorted. "You're wrong. She's tough, manipulative, and spiteful. If she wasn't your daughter, you wouldn't give her the time of day. Clarice has been getting by on her looks for years, waiting for the perfect Sugar Daddy to keep her in the lifestyle she thinks she deserves. When she got tired of waiting, she took my husband. Now she's ruined my life. Yet you're defending her."

"Because she can't defend herself against you. You attacked her."

"Did you see a mark on her?" I lifted my dark glasses

again. "Take a good look at which daughter is hurt. I can guarantee that my heart is broken. I've loved Hadley all my life. Do you know how humiliating it is that she crooked her little finger at him and he went to her? Do you have any idea of the shame I've felt this past week? Do you?"

The fight went out of Mama. She deflated in front of my eyes. "Yes, I believe I do."

As much as I wanted to comfort her, doing so would lose me every inch of ground I'd gained. "Then don't defend her to me."

"But you're so strong. She's always needed protection."

"From who? I never understood why you always took her side. Tell me the truth. Do you think I bullied her around all these years?"

"No, I never thought that. You were always sure of what you wanted and of where you were going. You never needed me."

"Never needed you—how can you say that? I was strong because of you and Daddy. I needed you plenty, but you never had time for me. You were always off running bake sales for the poor kids in town that didn't have shoes. Or organizing community blood drives. Or polishing brass for the church. After what Daddy's done behind your back, you, of all people, ought to know that you can't buy your way into heaven through good works."

Mama's lips thinned to the vanishing point. "How dare you attack my acts of service? It's not enough that you roughed up your sister? No wonder your husband left you."

"He didn't leave me. I kicked him out."

Mama stood, tall and regal. "No, dearie. He left you first. You couldn't give him what he needed. So he went out and got it from another woman."

With that, she swept out of the park in a blur of lavender and violet.

Her caustic words echoed in my ears as I stared at the

squirrels running up the rough bark of the Marshview Oak. The May sun beat down on me, but I'd grown cold, inside and out. Was it true? I'd never understood why Hadley kissed Clarice, and I certainly didn't believe it had been as simple as she claimed. I'd seen them embracing, and I knew what I saw.

Had he grown tired of me? Was that why he'd touched Clarice's rounded breast in broad daylight? The tears came fast and furious, and I was glad of my dark glasses.

He'd known what he was getting with me from the start. If he'd wanted a wife with voluptuous breasts, he should have chosen someone else.

I kicked the dirt. This was getting me nowhere. I wasn't about to get breast implants to win my husband back. I hated my sister. I hated my mother for taking Clarice's side, when Clarice had clearly wronged me. I didn't drive Hadley into Clarice's arms. No way. But now that she'd mentioned it, that ugly thought wouldn't go away.

The only family member I hadn't had a run-in with today was Daddy. I gave a dismayed sigh. I needed to talk to him about Barbara Jean's will, to find out if he was connected to the money trail that led to her murder.

I started toward the parking lot. I might as well shoot the moon and ruin my relationship with my father, too.

Chapter Nineteen

The U.S. flag and the Georgia state flag flanked the deserted receptionist counter inside Campbell and Associates. Despite my heated emotional turmoil, I shivered at the cooler temperature in here. This was one place where Daddy controlled the thermostat, and he kept it polar-bear cool.

Clarice wasn't at the front desk. But then I hadn't expected her to come to work today, not after our run-in this morning. Knowing my ex-sister, she'd take the entire week off, gorging herself on talk shows and butter pecan ice cream, and whining to Mama about how I'd bullied her.

The click of a keyboard sounded from Daddy's rear office. I followed the noise, marching past Daddy's military medals above the credenza. Framed copies of the Declaration of Independence and the Constitution hung between the mahogany paneling and the heavy gold drapes.

Joe Campbell's patriotism went bone deep. Which was why his involvement with Barbara Jean McAllister, and lying about it to mama, caught me so off guard. I thought I knew my father.

I knew the father who'd raised me, the parent who'd encouraged my every decision, the adult who'd told me he loved me throughout my life. But after seeing the picture of him and Barbara Jean, I realized the truth. Joe Campbell the man was a stranger to me.

I dreaded our upcoming conversation. He would, of course, expect that I'd changed my mind about him being pond scum. I hadn't. Adultery wasn't something I would overlook, in a husband or a father.

Even so, my heart lurched at the sight of him. His curly hair was smashed flat in the back, his posture was stooped, and grim lines bracketed his mouth. His rolled up shirt sleeves gave him the air of a harried man.

His deeply ingrained manners wouldn't allow him to remain seated when a woman walked into the room. But I didn't take his courteous gesture of standing to greet me as conciliatory. I'm sure he didn't want me to be looking down on him. Lawyers were trained to seek the upper hand. A seasoned pro, Daddy utilized all the tricks of his trade to his best advantage.

We sized each other up like aging gunfighters on a dusty street.

"Molly."

"Daddy."

"I didn't expect you."

"I wasn't expecting to come."

"You here to apologize?"

My stomach tightened. "No. I still don't want you anywhere near my son."

With that, Daddy sat down and resumed typing, using his index fingers to depress the keys. I'd seen him work a courtroom often enough to know that I should go for the jugular now. He was emotionally vulnerable. But dammit, he was also my father. I couldn't grill him about his infidelity.

I was here as a reporter, following up on a story lead. As long as I remembered that, I could get through this interview. I squeezed the remorse back down my throat. "Were you Barbara Jean's lawyer, Daddy?"

Daddy ignored my question, but I wasn't having that. I walked around so that I stood behind his computer monitor, directly in his line of sight, and repeated my question. "Were you her lawyer?"

He stopped typing, but he didn't look up.

Ah. I had his attention now. "I'm taking that as a yes. I need to know who inherits her property."

"Her will hasn't been made public yet."

No way was he getting off so easily. I tapped my foot on the floor. "Old man Olden owned half the county, and she was his sole heir. Her heirs could have hastened her death. Did that bunch out at the nudist colony benefit from her death?"

Daddy rubbed his curled hands together. "It's unclear who her intended beneficiary is."

Surprised by his admission, I stopped tapping my foot. "You're her lawyer. Didn't you write her will?"

"She had a child. She wanted her kid to inherit her estate."

Whoa. This was news. My spirits lifted. "A kid? Who is it?"

"I don't know."

"How can you not know?"

"Because she didn't want me or anyone else to know. She said if the child wanted her estate, then he or she would have to step forward."

This circuitous logic made my head ache. "How will you know you have the right person?"

"Barbara Jean's name will be on the person's birth certificate. As will the father's name."

"How old is this person?"

He studied the thick blue carpet. "I don't know."

His avoidance behavior tripped my internal alarms. There was something he wasn't telling me. "Did you know her back then? When she grew up here?"

"Yes."

Frissons of alarm clamored down my spine. If they were old acquaintances, chances were good they'd been lovers then as well. I didn't want to ask the next question. I was afraid of the answer, but I was here as a reporter. I clung to that thought and asked anyway. "Are you the father of her child?"

"I don't know."

His whispered answer kicked me hard in the gut. I was Daddy's first born. I was his oldest child. My birth order was a done deal. "Didn't you use birth control measures?"

"We were so young. Barbara Jean and I were barely sixteen that summer."

"Youth is no excuse." So what if my voice trembled. Did I have an older brother or sister out there in the world? As bizarre as the idea was, I needed to know the identity of this secret baby. I took a calming breath and exhaled slowly. "How will you notify this mystery heir?"

"Through an ad I placed in this week's paper. If the child doesn't step forward with proof of his birth within a month, the estate reverts to Barbara Jean's beneficiaries at the nudist colony."

"Is Mama Leon or his aging harem aware of this inheritance loophole?"

"Not yet."

Hmm. If the killer was a nudist, he or she had planned on inheriting Barbara Jean's land. Following that line of reasoning, the secret baby person threw a kink into the killer's scheme. Would the killer strike again? If the person stepped forward to claim his or her inheritance, would he or she be signing their death certificate?

Not if the secret baby had been her killer.

The muscles in my throat reflexively tightened. How could I make any headway in my investigation if every new lead turned up more suspects? At this rate, the entire county would soon be on my suspect list. Worse, with every layer of this woman's life I peeled away, I found Daddy.

As if sensing my silent struggles, Daddy looked at me, really looked at me, for the first time since I'd entered his office. His gaze hardened, and he scowled. "What happened to your face?"

"Clarice."

He nodded. Apparently he was used to her rotten behavior. "She's an unhappy woman."

What an understatement, but before I could reply my cellphone rang. I couldn't tell who was more relieved, me or Daddy. I backpedaled from the room. "I've got to take this. Catch you later."

I clicked open the phone as I exited the office building. "This is Molly Darter. I can't take your call right now. Leave your name and number at the beep, and I'll get back to you. Beep."

"Cut the crap, Molly." Bubba Brown's gravelly voice boomed into the phone. "You really there?"

After the deep chill of Daddy's office, the warm sunshine felt good on my skin. "Yeah. I'm here. What have you got?"

"After your visit on Saturday, I put a rush on the testing. I also expanded the tox screen. The results came back first thing this morning. You were right to suspect foul play. Barbara Jean died of a heart attack, but the amount of stimulant in her blood was off the charts. The excessive stimulant levels triggered heart arrhythmia, which caused her death."

I'd stopped at the crosswalk during his recitation. Now I glanced at the steady traffic on Main Street, waiting for a lull to cross back to the paper. Furtively, I checked to be sure no one would overhear my end of the conversation. "I don't understand. A stimulant? Like caffeine?"

"Coffee was present, but the beverage was a vehicle for the stimulant. The amount of pseudoephedrine in her system would have triggered an irregular heartbeat in a healthy person. In a person with known heart disease, it was lethal."

"Could she have taken the pseudo—whatever herself?"

"It's highly unlikely she would have taken a massive dose at once, or that she would've taken the time to grind the medication up and dissolve it in her coffee. If she was self-medicating, she would've popped a capsule. With her heart history, her pharmacist would have cautioned her not to take this drug."

"Wouldn't she have tasted the stimulant in her coffee?"

"Not likely. The coffee would've masked the taste. Which brings me back to the reason I called. I've officially ruled Barbara Jean's death a homicide. I've requested that Otis go back out in the woods where she was found and look for supporting evidence."

Finally, the traffic cleared. I darted across the street. "Like what? I've been out there. My footprints are on those paths through the woods, and I had nothing to do with her death."

"The stimulant was ground up. It's possible the killer kept the remainder of the medication, or that the grinding apparatus still contains traces of the stimulant. Maybe her coffee cup is still around. In any event, the sheriff is investigating her death as a homicide."

His labeling Barbara Jean's official cause of death as murder chilled me, even though somewhere along the line I'd begun to believe she'd been killed. The proof of foul play verified my reporter instincts were still working. We had a murderer on the loose in Marshview.

"She was poisoned with this stimulant?" I asked. "I thought signs of poisoning were obvious, like blue lips or pink skin."

"Nope. This killer is devious and shrewd. He selected a means of death I wouldn't have picked up on without additional prodding from you. We don't normally do an expanded tox screen on a non-suspicious home death like this. Your interest alerted us that we've got a killer on the loose. You should be proud of yourself."

I didn't feel proud. I felt old and defeated. And it was still Monday morning.

Bubba cleared his throat. "Since you've already been looking into her death, have you got any solid leads I can relay to the sheriff?"

Only photos of Barbara Jean screwing four different men at the produce stand, including the one of Daddy. But Daddy had helped me by giving me a heads-up on Barbara Jean's secret baby. I couldn't turn those photos over to the sheriff yet. Not until I proved they had nothing to do with Barbara Jean's murder. "Nothing solid."

"Otis will interview you anyway. He wants to know who you've been talking to so he won't waste time going over the same ground."

I leaned against the warm bricks of the newspaper building. This county was in big trouble if the sheriff wanted to use my amateurish investigation to solve this case. And Otis wasn't someone I wanted to spend anytime alone with. "He knows where to find me." I glanced at my watch. If I hurried inside and wrote like a maniac, I could get the homicide article on page one of the upcoming newspaper. "Anything else?"

"We take murder very seriously in this county. You can quote me on that. And Molly?"

"Yeah?"

"Watch your step. Your grandmother will murder me if anything happens to you. I called you so that you'd be alerted to the potential for danger."

After the morning I'd had wrestling with my sister and disillusioning my mother, a little homicide didn't scare me. "Don't you read my columns, Bubba? Danger is my middle name."

Chapter Twenty

I was all hot air, of course. If there really was a murderer skulking around in the wilds of Justice County, I didn't want to come across him. Or her. I raced inside the dark newspaper office. "Big news. Barbara Jean McAllister was murdered."

Ted paled. "You sure?"

"Sure as I'm standing here. I'm writing the story for page one."

Ted nodded slowly. "I'll move things around."

I typed up a screaming headline "Murder most foul." Then I started in on the meat of the story, making sure I featured Bubba's quote about zero tolerance for murder. My cellphone rang. I flipped the phone open. "Yeah?"

Mama Leon's voice boomed into my ear. "You found Bea's killer yet?"

The irritation in his voice set me on edge. I didn't have time to deal with a pushy nudist right now. Thanks to my exhausting family dramatics this morning, I was worn out and on deadline. "I've got a paper to put out today."

"Seriously, what progress have you made?"

"Seriously, I don't have time to talk to you today."

"Come on." His deep voice softened. "Your nosing

around has my girls all stirred up. What have you got for me?"

My voice dropped to a whisper. "If you didn't want things stirred up, you shouldn't have asked me to start lifting rocks."

"Those rocks needed to be lifted. You know something. I hear it in your voice. Tell me what you've learned."

Ted shot me a curious glance over the top of his page proofs. He'd approved of my nosing around. I didn't have anything to hide from my boss, so why was I whispering? I cleared my throat and answered in full voice. "I don't have much. I talked to the coroner, who decided to rush the tox screen. Bubba phoned this morning to relay the results. You were right. Barbara Jean was murdered."

The quiver in his voice was unmistakable, which upped my curiosity 100 percent. There was a noisy clatter. Then Mama Leon came back on the line. "Sorry. I dropped the phone. Bubba's sure?"

"Yeah. Somebody laced her coffee with a stimulant. It messed up her already weak heart."

"Coffee? Bea doesn't drink coffee. She gave up caffeine a few years back."

Interesting tidbit. I filed it away. "She drank it on the day she died."

"I don't remember seeing a coffee cup near her body."

"What do you remember about that day?"

"Bea had been working at the produce stand all morning. Norma walked over there to relieve her for lunch. When Bea didn't turn up at the house, Tildy went looking for her." He paused. When he spoke again, his voice was rough with emotion. "And found her dead in the woods."

"That coffee could've come from anywhere."

"I want this guy strung up by the balls."

"We don't know the gender of the killer. It could be a

woman."

As the wife of a former sheriff, I knew poison was normally a woman's tool. Did Mama Leon know that? "Whatever. This is Justice County, and I demand justice for Bea. I want you working on this around the clock. Money is no option."

"Money. You've never mentioned what you're paying me for this."

"Don't you worry. The payment will exceed your wildest dreams."

My wildest dream was to be financially independent. And to find an editor who loved my book. And to raise Jimbo to be a good person. And to make Hadley pay for ruining our marriage. Mama Leon had his work cut out for him if he was going to make all that come true.

My empty stomach rumbled. "Right now, I'd settle for some lunch."

"Done."

Within the half-hour, Mama Leon had a slice of veggie pizza delivered from Calabash's Diner, and I ate it greedily. Ted queued up my story, frowning at my lead. "Is there any other kind of murder?"

He was always trying to ramp down the emotionalism in my writing, but this time, I had good reason to stir up the general populace. "Murder isn't a parlor game. It's a deadly crime, one that's darkening our doorsteps. We have reason to sound the alarm. I can't remember anyone in my lifetime being murdered in Marshview."

He leaned back and tapped his stubby fingers together. I had no doubt he'd come up with an answer since he'd committed all previous versions of the *Marshview Gazette* to memory. Sure enough, he didn't disappoint. "Olden's brother was murdered."

I'd heard Grandma Dee talking about Gator Olden before. Though Barbara Jean was related to Gator, her killer couldn't be the same person. Too much water under the bridge. "That was almost sixty years ago." Long before my time, but folks still talked about it. I strained to remember the details. "It was a medical accident."

"The surgeon shouldn't have been drinking."

Drunkenness was Ted's pet peeve. He didn't believe in drinking, and any sappy group speaking out against alcoholism was given plenty of ink in his paper. I didn't care for public drunkenness myself, but I also saw the medicinal value of a glass of wine with dinner. "Should I have written a different headline? Like 'Naked woman slain by a drunken psychopath'?"

His head popped up, his dark eyes alive with possibilities. "Is that true?"

"Of course not. I made it up."

He sank back in his wheeled chair. "No place for fiction in a newspaper."

Poor Ted. My personal life sucked, but his sucked even worse. "Being a teetotaler has warped your sense of humor. When's the last time you had fun? Huh? When's the last time you went out on a date?"

He brushed off my questions, and we worked in silence until it was almost time for me leave to meet Jimbo's bus. He thrust a photo on my cluttered desk. "Look at this picture of the new condos down in the marsh."

Riverside Estates was the jewel of our development authority, but it was the bane of my existence. My outraged mother had tried repeatedly to get me to write slanted articles against the creeping condominium cancer eating away at our historic town. A batch of nine units went up almost overnight a block from our historic fort. Another condo outbreak had been sighted on the wrong side of the tracks. Concrete footers had already been poured on fill dirt in the marsh.

How they'd gotten permission to build Riverside at the high tide mark was a mystery, but the developers seemed invincible. Local, state, and federal politicians had ignored my mother's letters of protest.

But the photo in my hand looked like the skewed teeth of a Halloween jack-o-lantern. Water dominated the forefront of the picture, so the photo had been taken from a boat. I remembered hearing the road to the new condos was closed for underground repairs. A few repairs wouldn't touch this structural disaster. Concrete pilings, the foundation for the new condos, jutted from the mud at odd angles.

I glanced up at Ted. "Great photo. Where'd the image come from?"

"I shot it yesterday."

"What are they doing to fix this mess?"

"Can't be fixed. Not without more groundwork and permits. I believe the principals are unloading their shares as quietly as possible today."

Riverside Landing had sold out on the day they opened for business. They'd run a bunch of ads prior to their grand opening, and I suspected their reasonable prices for waterfront living had attracted many a speculative investor. "Can they do that? Don't they have an obligation to their buyers?"

"Get real. The developers are in this to make a buck."

"Not all of them. The MarshPlus developers are locals. They said they'd be friendlier than the unimaginative carpetbaggers who built the other two condo boxes. Now they're going to scam everyone? That's not an improvement. At least the other buyers got a solid product for their money."

"My guess is that the developers will claim to lose their shirt, sell the property for a song, and set up shop nearby under another name. Happens all the time."

My stomach clenched. I hated the way Marshview was changing. Progress made people cold and cruel. "Not here it doesn't." Due to the lateness in the day, it was also apparent he'd decided not to run the incriminating photo in the upcoming paper. "Why'd you hold the story?"

"One screaming headline is all Marshview can tolerate

in a week. Besides, things at Riverside will be headed one way or the other by our next edition."

I wasn't so sure. Until things started lining up, every tidbit of news potentially had relevance. "Why don't you pull the organic gardening story? That one isn't breaking news. It won't go flat by next week."

"Nope. The secret garden runs."

Ted acted obtuse from time to time. With him being the boss, there wasn't much I could say or do. I glanced at my watch. "Time to go pick up my son. Are we good? Or do you need me to come back after I get Jimbo?"

There was a flash of red in the parking lot. Ted's eyes narrowed. "I'm good. See you tomorrow."

When I walked outside, Hadley was sitting in the passenger seat of my SUV, his truck parked adjacent to my vehicle. Anger fueled my steps. I flung open the driver's door and leaned in. "Get out."

"You and I need to talk."

"The time for talking is past." I pointed to the scrapes on my cheek. "Look at what talking to Clarice did this morning."

He frowned as his fingers lightly skimmed my face. My pulse raced. I dug deep for resolve. "Get out of my car. I have to be somewhere."

He reached over, caught hold of my arm, and hauled me up in the SUV. "I sent your father to pick up Jimbo."

White-hot anger flashed through me, a dazzling, energizing jolt of fierce emotion. I tried to tug my arm free, but he held fast. "You had no right to do that. I don't want Daddy hanging around Jimbo. He's a bad influence."

Hadley sighed. His clothes were rumpled. Dark circles rimmed his eyes. Whatever else was going on in his life, it wasn't coming up roses for him. He looked awful. The realization should've cheered me. It didn't.

"Joe did seem a mite surprised that I'd asked him." Hadley buckled his seat belt. "Want to tell me why you've turned on your dad?"

I reached over and slammed my door. Marshview had heard enough of my dirty laundry today. "Good old Joe isn't who he seems."

"You're making him sound like an axe murderer," he said dryly. "What happened?"

"Daddy's a liar and a cheater. That's what."

"Those are some mighty big claims you're making. He's your dad, but he can still sue you for slander."

Suddenly I was too weary to fight this battle alone. My world was crumbling around me. Everyone I knew had deep, dark secrets. The only person I trusted implicitly was my eight-year-old son.

I took a long look at my husband. However angry and hurt I was by his actions, Hadley and I had always been a team. A good one at that. Impulsively, I dumped out the packet of incriminating photos in Hadley's lap. "See for yourself."

He cradled the envelope in his large hands and studied each photo in turn. His expression changed from disinterest to incredulous. "Where'd you get these?"

"From the nudists."

Anger darkened his face. "Why didn't you tell me?"

"I'm not telling you anything. You don't exist to me anymore. You or Clarice. I'll interact with you for Jimbo's sake, but we're history."

"The drug case I'm working on involves these people."

I didn't give a flying fig about his drug case with the Georgia Bureau of Investigation. This conversation wasn't about his secretive work. My life was imploding, and I was tired of being a second-rate citizen. "What case would that be, Hadley? The screw Clarice case?"

He thrust his fingers through his hair and leaned back in his seat. "God, I'm beat. Let's go home."

"You don't live with me anymore, remember?"

"I'm guilty of being in the wrong place at the wrong time." His voice roughened. "I didn't cheat on you, anymore than you cheat on me when you 'pass the peace' in the Episcopal church and hug all those dirty old men."

Indignation churned in my gut. "I'm not kissing any of them on the lips, and I'm definitely not fondling their private parts."

"But what if one of them inadvertently turned their head on what was supposed to be a cheek kiss? It would be the same thing. Look, I've been a good sport and honored your right to be angry. I took my medicine like a big boy. Now I want to come home. I want to wake up next to my wife. I want to watch my son sleep at night."

"You're not welcome in my house."

"It's my house, too. Besides, Dee and Bubba have a date tonight, and she kicked me out. I've got nowhere else to go."

I scrunched my eyes shut to block the image of my grandmother and Bubba making love. "You might try Clarice's house on Bonefish Street."

"Forget it. I'd rather sleep in your car."

His dejected tone softened my hard heart. Before this incident with Clarice, I'd never had reason to doubt him. He wasn't making any wild demands. He was acting like my Hadley.

Which made me doubt what I'd seen. Was there a chance I'd misinterpreted that kiss?

Hard to misinterpret a mouth-to-mouth kiss.

Especially when said male had his hand on another woman's breast.

Realistically, I couldn't completely avoid Hadley for the rest of my life. We had a son together. No matter how furious I was with him, he'd always been a good dad.

Plus, I couldn't make it financially without his help. I could afford him the courtesy of a good night's sleep. But not in my bed. He'd lost that privilege. "You can come home, but you're sleeping in the guest bedroom."

Hadley yawned. "Thanks." He was asleep before I reached the edge of town.

Chapter Twenty-One

Hadley's familiar scent swirled around my head, fogging my senses and upsetting my equilibrium. He leaned heavily on me the whole way up the stairs and into the guest room. I wanted to make a big deal about him invading my personal space, but he was dead on his feet.

In the past when he'd come in from one of his extended shifts where he'd been assisting the GBI, he'd slept round the clock. I assumed this instance of crashing would follow the same pattern. While it disturbed me that my body responded physically to his nearness, I limited my actions to what I would've done for any guest. Taking off Hadley's shoes and covering him with a light blanket weren't wifely tasks. They were basic hospitality.

After I finished seeing to Hadley's comfort, I wandered around the silent house, taking stock of my situation. Jimbo was with Daddy and probably wouldn't be home until bedtime. Hadley was home, but he was out cold. That left me footloose.

The click of Goldie's nails upon the wood floor echoed behind me as she followed me into the kitchen where I poured myself a glass of white wine. For the first time in days, my heart didn't feel like it was in the grip of an iron claw. I could take a deep breath without my eyes tearing up. That horrible void of emptiness in my gut wasn't so all-encompassing.

Truth was, with Hadley here, the house felt safer. Granted his stay was temporary, but the normalcy his presence lent was a good sign. Things would eventually come around right.

I sipped my wine. The cool liquid slid down my throat and freed my thoughts. I didn't want to respond to Hadley's nearness. My brain realized that was a terrible idea, but my heart wasn't following orders. My heart didn't care about logic and reason. It cared about the passion this man inspired. It recognized that I both loved and hated Hadley.

I had to get a grip on my turbulent emotions. Hating Hadley exhausted me. Loving him was out of the question. But tonight I'd like to do something normal, something that wasn't so consumed by emotion that I couldn't think straight, something that would keep me too busy to think about that flicker of doubt I now harbored about Hadley and Clarice.

There were two baskets of dirty laundry on the laundry room floor. Goldie needed a bath. My kitchen floor needed to be mopped, and a splotch of mold flowered in the master bathroom. None of those tasks appealed to me. I needed to do something for myself. Something fun.

Like work on my book. That would be more positive than worrying about my impending divorce, and not nearly as emotionally exhausting.

Gauging from past experience, Hadley wouldn't surface from his deep slumber until this time tomorrow, so I didn't have to further exhaust myself by keeping a wall of anger going. I could relax and forget about the nebulous future. Tomorrow would come, whether I wanted it to or not, and there wasn't a danged thing I could do about it tonight. So I wouldn't worry. I would enjoy this brief respite.

Daddy would make the most of this unexpected opportunity with his grandson and drag his visit out to the very last second. I grabbed a quick dinner consisting of cheese, crackers, and an apple and plopped down on the sofa to eat.

My book needed another round of editing before I started sending it out on the contest circuit. But even after I dug out my working draft and flipped through the pages, my story held no appeal for me tonight. I had to face the truth. Fiction couldn't hold a candle to the current events happening in Marshview.

Barbara Jean's murder headed that list. The dead woman was clearly the victim here, but her past didn't endear her to me. She'd sold herself for a living, and judging by the look of pleasure on the men's faces in the pictures I had with her, she'd been good at her trade. Though she was supposed to be retired, she'd reactivated her former career in Marshview.

She'd lived here as a child, and she'd inherited the property the nudists lived on. Those facts must have relevance to her murder. I couldn't picture how the dots connected. The whole secret baby angle threw me. How could she have put her child up for adoption? Didn't she want to watch him or her grow up? To share her life with that child? That baby was part of her heart and soul.

I would never put Jimbo up for adoption. He was my flesh and blood, my legacy for the future. No way would I hand him over to someone else to rear. Barbara Jean had, but at what cost?

Since Barbara Jean was approximately my father's age, odds were her kid was about my age, or maybe even older than me since my parents didn't start our family right away. Or maybe her kid was younger. There was no way of knowing for sure.

I remembered Norma telling me Barbara Jean had suffered from depression, but she'd perked up once she took charge of the produce stand. She thoroughly enjoyed men and sex. Were those qualities inherited? If so, a grown up child of hers might be oversexed, suffer from mental instability, and be physically attractive.

I studied the bottom of my nearly empty wine glass. One name in my generation rocketed to the top of my list of potential Barbara Jean offspring. Clarice. We'd always been so very different. It would explain so much if my sister was adopted. She was undeniably pretty, oversexed, and unstable.

Except I'd never heard any rumor of her being adopted. Wouldn't something like that have come up before? In a small town like this, there would have been stories about how an extra child suddenly appeared in the Campbell household.

I didn't see Mama being altruistic enough to raise another woman's child. But what if it had been Daddy's child? Clarice had my father's eyes, and she didn't look much like Mama's side of the family. I studied Barbara Jean rounded features for some sign of Clarice's face, but nothing matched.

Speculation was getting me nowhere, fast. I rose and stacked my dishes in the dishwasher. As I worked, a familiar dark colored SUV pulled in my driveway. Sheriff Blizzard was here. I didn't want to talk to Otis, especially not when I had an entire evening to myself. Especially not when he was on my list of murder suspects.

I glanced up the stairs to where Hadley lay sleeping. Having him here gave me a sense of security. I didn't want to wake Hadley up when he was so exhausted. I could handle this interview with Otis, but if things got dicey I could always summon Hadley.

When Goldie and I stepped outside, Goldie sniffed Otis, and then peed on his tires. I silently cheered her action. I shaded my eyes with my hand against the late afternoon sunshine. "Sheriff. What can I do for you?"

He tipped his hat at me and stopped about three feet

141

away from me on the driveway. "I heard you've been asking questions about Barbara Jean's death."

The urge to deny his statement clamored in my throat. It would certainly shorten his visit, but I had questions for him. I angled sideways so that I wasn't looking directly into the sun. He adjusted his position as well, this time standing a little closer.

Too close for comfort.

His aftershave swept over me. It was a sickly sweet grocery store blend, and he'd applied buckets of it. My eyes smarted. I blinked away the moisture. "I haven't found out who killed her."

"You knew she was murdered all along?"

The way he said "murdered" made my skin crawl. The naturalists had been suspicious of Otis from the start. They weren't the only ones with suspicions about this man. It still rankled that he'd won Hadley's sheriff job in the vote recount. I didn't trust him.

But I still needed to say something. "Her family out at Natural Woods insisted she was murdered from the start. They asked me to investigate. I asked Bubba Brown to call me about the autopsy results, and he did."

His lips thinned. "The coroner's report is supposed to be confidential."

"Bubba's dating my grandmother. News travels fast in Marshview. What are you going to do, fire Bubba?"

"He should be fired for breaching protocol."

The sheriff's pompous attitude irritated me. As did the overt way his eyes kept sliding down my body, almost like I was naked. "You can't fire Bubba. There isn't anyone else in the county qualified to be the coroner."

"Don't go getting all mad on me. I came out here to invite you to dinner so we could discuss this like adults."

"Otis Blizzard, I am not going out with you. I'm a married woman."

He stepped closer, his beefy palm resting on his gun. "The whole town knows you kicked Hadley out last weekend. I saw Jimbo and your father head out in the creek a few minutes ago with their fishing poles and a bucket of chicken, so there's no reason for you to turn me down."

I could mention Hadley was upstairs right now, but I wanted to handle Otis on my own. I came from a long line of women who were tough as nails. Campbells and Munros kicked butt. I wasn't going anywhere with him, unless it was at gunpoint.

I glared at him, glad Hadley was nearby if I needed backup. "My marriage is my personal business. I don't want you spying on me or my son. I don't care if you are the sheriff. Get off my property and don't come back."

Goldie pushed her way between us. I used the opportunity to retreat toward the door. The dog's hackles rose, and a low growl rumbled in her throat. Retrievers weren't normally attack dogs, but Hadley had trained Goldie to protect us.

Perspiration glistened on the sheriff's brow. His gaze traveled from the wary dog to me and back to the dog. "Call off your guard dog."

I felt the solid bump of the door behind me. I gripped the doorknob and twisted it in my hand. "Can't do that. She thinks you're a threat. And you know what? I believe her. Dogs sense things. Whatever you're thinking, it doesn't bode well for me."

He shook his head. "What's got into you? I'll talk to you tomorrow at work."

Heart pounding in my throat, I stepped inside. Once Goldie cleared the threshold, I dead-bolted the door. I slid down to the floor and hugged her. She was my champion, my protector, my hero.

Otis was bad news. He wasn't a decent guy. He was a lech and maybe more. Maybe even a murderer.

Chapter Twenty-Two

The fireflies were out when Daddy brought Jimbo home at dusk. Goldie barked excitedly at Jimbo's heels as he chased the blinking lights around the yard.

Daddy eyed me warily. He kept his car door between us and nodded in Jimbo's direction. "I fed him."

"Thanks." He'd returned my son healthy and happy. With Jimbo safely home, relief coasted through my veins, softening my attitude toward my father. A good daughter would apologize for threatening to keep him from his grandson, but I didn't have another concession left in my body. After this exhausting day, my emotion bank was bone dry.

"Anytime."

Goldie and Jimbo rolled on the grass. Crickets chirped and marsh hens called as if it was another day in paradise. Except everything had changed. I'd wrestled with my sister and lost. I'd bitterly quarreled with my mother and father. I'd allowed my cheating husband back under my roof. And I'd thwarted the horny sheriff.

Entirely too much drama for paradise. Paradise, now there was a laugh—more like my own private hell.

I wanted to turn back the clock to last week when

everyone was getting along. Then I wouldn't know Daddy had been planning to leave Mama for a hooker. Said hooker wouldn't have been murdered. My heartbreak over Hadley's adultery wouldn't have opened a bottomless black hole in my chest that threatened to suck the life out of me.

"I will pick him up again tomorrow if you like."

"No, thanks. I can manage."

Daddy nodded. I hoped he was going to leave, but he didn't budge. The lines deepened in his face. "I saw Hadley's truck in town. You kids need to patch things up."

A spark of anger flickered. "Hadley dug his own hole."

"You didn't use to be so hard."

"I didn't use to be the victim of adultery."

Daddy sighed, long and mournful. "Don't take your anger at me and my transgressions out on Hadley. He's a better man than I am."

I interrupted him with a wave of my hand. "I won't discuss this subject in Jimbo's hearing."

"I'm not asking you to talk. I want you to listen. Men stumble. I stumbled, and it took me years to come to my senses. Hadley didn't stumble. He was set up. Think about that."

Fresh anger boiled into my blood. "Don't defend him to me. I know what I saw."

Jimbo made another pass by us. Daddy waited until Jimbo was at the other end of the yard before speaking again. "Appearances can be deceiving."

I hated the splinter of doubt wedged in my brain. Even after a week, Hadley's betrayal still took my breath away. But if Daddy wanted to talk about personal business, so be it. "I can't handle deep and symbolic right now. I'm barely getting through each day. But I have a question for you. Was Clarice adopted?"

Daddy recoiled, his body jerking against the side of his car. A copperhead dropping out of an oak tree on his shoulders wouldn't have gotten a stronger reaction. I knew a surge of satisfaction at knocking him off balance.

Daddy gripped the top of the car for support, his face pale. "What made you ask that?"

"I've been thinking about Barbara Jean's secret baby. It would explain so much if Clarice was her child. Clarice never fit in with our family. And she hates me."

"Clarice is your sister." He shook his head sadly. "Christ, I can't believe you asked me that."

"I don't have a sister anymore. I disowned Clarice."

In the waning light, Daddy's sharp look pinned my ears back. "Your family is dwindling by the hour. You've turned your back on your husband, your sister, and you verbally attacked your mother, and now me. Take a good look at your agenda."

Anger sputtered in my veins. Agenda? He was one to talk. "There's plenty of blame to go around." That's what I said, but even as I spoke, my words rang false. I didn't have an agenda or a reason to break with my family. All I had was the enormous hole where my heart used to be. Was I blaming my family for my personal troubles? I hated being at war with my family. I hated that my insides stayed twisted in knots, day after day.

After a hard look at me, Daddy waved goodbye to Jimbo and left. I half-listened to my son's fishing tales as I readied him for bed. Hadley had done us all a favor by allowing Daddy to spend the evening with Jimbo. I certainly wasn't perfect, but Daddy wasn't evil either. What right did I have to judge my father's actions?

I could continue to be outraged, but emotion would eat me up from the inside out. I didn't want to live like that. But how could I condone his behavior? Wasn't adultery a black and white thing?

If Hadley hadn't strayed, if he'd been set up as Daddy suggested, I was letting pride dictate my behavior. I'd been wronged, but what if Hadley had been wronged, too? What if I was stupidly letting my emotions dictate my actions?

I could be throwing away the most valuable thing I'd ever had.

The love of my life.

My head ached with my circling thoughts. I couldn't solve anything tonight. Hadley, Clarice, Daddy, and Barbara Jean would all be there in the morning.

"You all right, Mom?" Jimbo asked at bedtime.

I placed his glasses on his bedside table and kissed him good night. His fresh clean boyish scent reminding me of all the times I'd held him in my arms, of a long ago time when all had been right in my world. "It's been a long day."

"Can I go fishing with Grandpa Joe again tomorrow after school?"

"Going fishing everyday is like eating dessert for dinner. Today was special. You'll have opportinities to fish with grandpa later."

Jimbo frowned. "Sounds like a 'no' to me."

I could be an ogre and solidly put my foot down, or I could bend a bit. The role of ogre had worn thin. I squeezed his hand and reached to turn the light off. "We'll see."

I walked across the hall to my room, glancing toward the closed door of the guest room. I hadn't told Jimbo his dad was here because I didn't want to get his hopes up. Hadley would still be asleep when Jimbo caught the bus in the morning. If Hadley slept around the clock as he had in the past, Jimbo wouldn't even know Hadley had been here. It was better that way.

As I lay in bed trying to fall asleep, Daddy's words replayed in my head. He hadn't answered my question about Clarice being adopted. All he'd said was that she was my sister. He'd used his lawyer-speak to get out of a tight situation without any admission of wrong-doing. Which meant that Clarice could've been adopted. She could be my half-sister.

Wouldn't that be a kick in the pants if Clarice inherited all that property and an organic vegetable farm? She'd never lift a finger again if that was the case. She'd kick the naturalists out, sell the land to the highest bidder, and spend the rest of her days being waited on hand and foot.

There was another possibility. Maybe Clarice was Mama and Daddy's natural child. What if I'd been adopted?

I sat up in bed, my entire body strung tight. Oh God. What if Barbara Jean was my mother? The prospect had me trembling all over.

I hadn't considered that possibility until now. I wanted to be wrong. I prayed it was untrue. But with each passing second, it seemed more and more plausible. If I was Barbara Jean's long-lost child, that explained why she'd taken such a shine to Jimbo. And why she'd invited me to call her by a nickname that only those close to her used.

I didn't look like Barbara Jean. My breasts weren't cantaloupe shaped. They were more like pert plums. No way was I oversexed. I had no intention of having sex with various men. It had been a full-time job keeping up with Hadley in bed. What would I do with multiple partners?

If I was a prostitute's daughter, wouldn't I feel a kinship toward her way of life? I liked being around people, and I definitely liked fresh fruit and vegetables. But I wasn't keen on walking around naked. And I certainly didn't envision me having sex with Mama Leon with all the other naturalists watching.

No.

No way was I her daughter.

It had to be Clarice. Or someone else entirely.

When sleep came, it was fitful and punctuated with terrifying nightmares. After a particularly weird one of me living in a whorehouse dressed up like Miss Kitty on the set of *Gunsmoke*, I awoke in Hadley's arms. Instinctively, I nestled closer to his heat.

One thing led to another, and we made love. Our passion was elemental, a raging inferno of desire, with an edge of desperation unlike any previous lovemaking. A small voice in my head kept chirping this shouldn't be happening, but my body craved this sensual release. Hadley knew what I liked, and vice versa. In this, we were united.

As sleep reclaimed me, I murmured to Hadley's bare chest, "This changes nothing."

His arms tightened around me. "This changes everything."

Chapter Twenty-Three

"Dad! You're home!" Jimbo dove onto the bed and skidded to a stop on top of his father.

Hadley tickled Jimbo. I drowsily smiled at the cozy scene, so familiar and poignant. Sunlight bathed the room in a rosy glow. Awareness dawned with an icy certainty. I was buck naked under the covers. My estranged husband was plastered to my side. From the commingling of our scents, the disarray of the bedcovers, and the apparent moistness between my legs, I had a pretty good idea of what happened last night.

Outrage boiled through my blood. Hadley wasn't supposed to be in my bed. He'd lost the right to be here when he fooled around with my sister. I shouldn't have fallen for his line of having nowhere to go. He was a resourceful man.

Too resourceful.

Fleeting images of our lovemaking steamed through my mind. I had to get him out of here immediately. Two barriers came to mind. My innocent son. And my state of undress. No matter how mad I was at Hadley, I didn't parade around naked in front of my eight-year-old son. Bottom line, I was trapped.

I tugged the turquoise spread up to my chin, held on tight, and waited for an opportunity to clear my bedroom.

Hadley ruffled Jimbo's hair. "How're you doing, sport?"

At Jimbo's happy shrieks, Goldie launched herself up on the bed. Both her front paws landed on my abdomen. I yelped and pushed her away. Goldie bounded back on top of me and licked my face clean. Her tail wagged ninety miles an hour, fanning cold air and fluffy dog hair everywhere.

"Get off me." I pushed the dog off the bed and shook my finger at her. "Stay."

"Aw, Mom," Jimbo said, his glasses askew. "Goldie wants to play, too."

"Goldie can play outside." Cool air brushed against my bare skin. During the tussle with the dog, I'd lost my grip on the spread. It now pooled around my waist. I snatched the spread up to cover myself. Mortification radiated from my face. I'd flashed my son. I glared at him and Hadley. "Out. Everyone out of my bedroom."

Jimbo's face fell. He climbed down off Mount Hadley and dragged his feet toward the door. Goldie slunk after him, her tail dragging the ground.

Hadley's expression turned wary. "Somebody is a little grumpy this morning." He reclined against his pillow, with his near arm draped casually across the headboard. The bold geometric print sheet slid down below his tan line, and he seemed blissfully unaware of his level of exposure.

Not me. That dark hair arrowing down his chest to the very white skin had my attention. I clutched the turquoise spread tightly to my bare breasts. "You didn't play by the rules. You were supposed to sleep in the guest room."

He flashed me a wry grin. "Sorry. I must have been on autopilot after I went to the bathroom in the night."

A likely story. He didn't look one bit sorry. He looked

suspiciously like the cat that'd lapped up all the cream. God. I'd slept with my adulterous husband. How pathetic.

Time to take charge of the situation. "Get your confused self out of my bed."

"That's not what you said a few hours ago."

His sexy voice sent shivers down my spine, adding to my growing distrust of the situation. He'd fooled me, and I hated being a fool, even if I now considered he might have been set up.

I had no business being intimate with him until my mind was clear. "Last night was a mistake. Get out."

He reached for me. "Don't be like that, Molls."

I shrank away from him, but I wasn't fast enough. In one second flat, he had me pinned to the bed. His lips brushed mine possessively. "Hadley," I warned loudly.

"No words."

He kissed me, putting everything he had into that kiss. Thinking became a distant memory as I melted in the onslaught of his passion. I kissed the man I loved with all my heart. My hands cupped his head, his precious head, and his hum of satisfaction resonated in my bones. His fingers threaded through my hair, massaged my scalp. An urgent sigh escaped my lips as he nuzzled my neck.

I was on fire for him. I'd chain him to my bed if he promised to do this every morning for the rest of his life.

"Dad, are you humping Mom?"

Jimbo's curious voice sliced abruptly through my sensual haze. Reality doused my ardor with a figurative bucket of cold water. I buried my heated face in Hadley's broad chest.

"Yes, son, I am." Hadley's deep voice rumbled through his torso. "Close the door."

To my utter amazement, Jimbo complied. I dropped back to the bed and pushed at my naked and soon-to-be ex-husband. "Get off."

He kissed the valley between my breasts. "No can do. I'm busy humping my wife."

I was very aware of the weight of his hands cupping my breasts. In the guise of passion, he'd pinned me to the mattress. "Don't be crude."

His eyes, those dark eyes which had been brimming with passion moments ago, looked guarded. "I'm not the one who taught an eight-year-old to say humping."

I sputtered. "I didn't either. He came up with it on his own. He asked me if you'd been humping someone else the way Goldie humps his leg."

Hadley's gaze narrowed dangerously. "You said no, right?"

A prudent woman would keep her mouth shut. I drilled my gaze into his. "I said yes. I caught you kissing my sister. Your hand was under her shirt."

His features tightened into a hard mask. "I explained all of that."

"You explained nothing. You ripped out my heart and stomped it into the ground. Get off me."

"I love you, Molly."

His body enfolded mine as he kissed me again. I didn't want him to kiss me, but I couldn't keep myself from responding to his advances. His hands skimmed lightly down to my hips, bringing me snug against him.

I shivered. "Don't do this, Hadley."

His warm breath teased my feverish skin. "You want me."

He was right. I did want him. It made me madder than a wet hornet.

I tried to bring my knee up. Hadley disarmed my feeble attack, rolling us over. The turquoise barrier between us fell to the wayside, and my protest died in my throat.

* * * *

After Jimbo got on the school bus, I drove Hadley into Marshview and parked outside the newspaper beside his red truck. Once Hadley left, I would have the mental breakdown I deserved.

"We need to talk," he said.

My face flamed. I was no better than my mother. When it came to the man I loved, I was putty in his hands. Was this why Mama and Daddy were still together? Because she weathered the good and the bad? I wanted more out of my marriage than half a man. "There's nothing to talk about."

"There's everything to talk about. No more games, Molls. I belong in our bed."

"You can make me want you, but I don't trust you. Every time you're out of my sight, I wonder who you're screwing."

"Molls, you're it for me. I haven't slept with another woman since I met you."

He met me in second grade. I was his only female conquest? "How would you feel if you saw Ted's hand on my breast and his tongue in my mouth?"

Hadley glared at the dark windows of the newspaper building. His hands curled into fists. "He did that? I'll kill him with my bare hands."

Though it was wrong of me to gloat inside, Hadley's jealousy felt good. But I didn't want him to attack poor, blameless Ted. "No one is killing anyone else. We've already had one murder this year in Marshview. At the nudist colony. That scenario with Ted was a for instance. I assure you, I have no romantic feelings toward my boss."

"Otis and Ted are putting moves on you?"

Men were such idiots. "No one is putting a move on me. That's beside the point. I'm not your responsibility."

"Yes, you are, and the sooner you realize that, the better off we'll both be."

"Spare me the macho crap. I can take care of myself."

"Don't go out to the nudist colony again."

The jagged edges of the car keys cut into my palm. "You can't boss me around."

"This is for your own good."

His concern for my safety drowned in his macho

attitude. I didn't authorize him to set limits on my personal freedom. I wouldn't allow him to talk down to me like this. "Are you listening to yourself? That's moronic, you telling me how to do my reporter's job. When have I ever tried to tell you how to do your sheriff's job or your lawyer job?"

"We're not talking about me."

"You're not the sheriff anymore, and you're not my boss. I'm deciding what's right for me. Not you."

"You love me."

"Yeah? I hate you, too."

"Then we're even, because right now I'd like to wring your neck for not listening to me."

Enough. I didn't need this lecture. It didn't help that I believed Clarice had tried to lead Hadley astray. He'd kissed her. It hadn't been a peck. There had been more to it than that. I'd seen it myself.

I dropped my car keys in my open purse. "I've got to go to work. Lock the car when you get tired of talking to yourself."

Hadley bolted out of the truck and escorted me into the office. I ignored his overly attentive behavior. "Morning, Ted," I said.

Ted lowered the Florida newspaper he'd been hiding behind. "Morning."

Hadley waited until Ted looked our way, and then he kissed me again, his hand resting firmly on my butt. When he was finished, he murmured in my ear. "See you tonight, beautiful."

I scowled at Hadley's swaggering retreat.

"Got some last night, did ya?" Ted asked.

Heat steamed off my face and neck. "My private life is none of your business."

I couldn't melt down in front of Ted. Not with his journalist friend waiting in the wings for my job. I'd have to self-destruct after work.

I sat down at my desk and reviewed my schedule for the day. I needed to interview a local artist who was having a show in the next town down the road. I called and made an early afternoon appointment with Akysia Mahone.

As I worked, Hadley's sneakiness crept into my thoughts. Had he really gotten disoriented and wound up in our bed? His excuse sounded very plausible, but it also served his purposes of reuniting with me. He expected to sleep with me tonight.

Trouble was, I didn't know what I wanted.

I checked my email and phone messages. No breaking news. The morning passed in a blur of advertisement copy and public notices. I sold newspapers to walk-ins when Ted stepped out for an early lunch. When Ted returned, I headed over to the artist's studio.

On the way, I noticed a foursome dining in the front picture window at Calabash Diner. My blood iced. This particular foursome was an unlikely combination. They were the naked men photographed with Barbara Jean. Their dining together had to be more than coincidence. As a reporter, I didn't believe in coincidence. Every action produced a reaction.

An event must have precipitated their meeting at Calabash's. What was it? Did it have anything to do with the incriminating photos I had of them? Had they received copies of their sexual exploits with Barbara Jean? Was the blackmail ongoing?

Was another murder in the works?

I slowed to take a mental snapshot. The mayor wiped his sweating brow, light glinting on his thick glasses. The preacher's white collar gleamed in the bright sunlight. The hefty deputy shoved a fistful of French fries in his mouth. Thin Judge Humphrey sipped from a water glass.

What were they talking about? I'd never seen this grouping of people socializing before. They were barely nodding acquaintances. The only thing they had in common was they'd all been photographed humping a woman who had recently been murdered.

Something else about them tugged at my thoughts,

but I couldn't retrieve it. Something about the pictures. I needed to review those incriminating pictures again. Good thing I kept them with me. I'd look at them as soon as I parked at Mahone's art digs.

Outside the barn-shaped structure, I rummaged in my purse for the photos.

But they were gone.

Chapter Twenty-Four

Where did the pictures go? I had them last night. Hadley. He must have taken them this morning. But why would he want them?

Akysia Mahone appeared in the doorway of her studio. Her bright magenta batik dress with a matching turban shimmered as she waved me in. I nodded, fully intending to go inside and interview her.

But as I gathered up my gear, my thoughts weren't on Akysia's barn-shaped art studio or her award-winning paintings. They were on my missing pictures and the foursome at the diner. Were the two events connected?

I should phone Hadley right now and demand the return of my photos. I yanked my phone out of my bag, and then thought better of the impulse. Hadley rarely did things he didn't want to do. If he had my photos, I should assume he needed them, and I wouldn't get them back. Most likely, he'd see my name on his phone's caller ID screen and let the call go to his voice mail.

I swore inventively and banged my phone on the steering wheel. Those pictures were lost to me right now. But the foursome at the diner, that was another matter. They were on my murder suspects list, and their public meeting couldn't be accidental.

Something was going on at the diner, and I wanted to know what it was. And if I was going to eavesdrop on their lunch conversation, I'd better hurry.

With that decision made, I poked my head out my window. "Something came up. Can we do this later today or tomorrow?"

"Come back when you can," Akysia said with goofy grin. "I'll be here."

I high-tailed it back to Calabash's. The diner was empty except for the four men. I perused the menu at the front door as if I hadn't read it a million times before. How brazen would it be if I walked up to the adjacent table and sat down?

Probably too obvious.

I edged closer until the murmur of their voices became distinct, and then I chose a booth with a chipped Formica top. I slid onto the red vinyl bench seat.

"Hey there, Miz Molly. What can I get for you?" Erin Henry, manager of Calabash, beamed a smile at me. Erin had been in my class at high school. She'd gotten pregnant in her senior year, dropped out, and done the at-home-mom thing until her common-law husband moved on. After that she'd worked extra hard to keep her four kids fed and clothed.

I'd always felt superior to her before, with my college education and my faithful husband. Now it dawned on me that we weren't so different after all. And she at least knew who her parents were. I swallowed thickly. "I'll have sweet tea and a bowl of your soup of the day."

"You work through lunch again?"

"Something like that."

"Covering something big for the paper?" She leaned close. "Is there more on that woman's murder?"

I shrugged, not wanting to talk about the murder with the foursome nearby. "The police haven't arrested anyone as far as I know."

"They'll get him. That new sheriff is too cute." Erin belatedly realized who she was talking to. Her hand covered her mouth. "Oh. I'm sorry."

I was past embarrassment over Hadley's loss in the polls. "Nothing to be sorry about. Otis is our new sheriff."

Erin nodded. "I'll be right back with that tea."

Once she left, I realized the men had stopped talking to listen to our conversation. All I had to do was wait them out. They'd forget about me in a minute or two. It was so quiet in here. Too quiet. I hoped they weren't getting reading to leave. I rummaged in my purse as if I was searching for something. I picked my phone up and checked my messages. There were none of course, but the men couldn't tell that. I turned the ringer off, flipped open a small notepad, and started writing as if I were taking down messages.

"He's not going to show," Judge Humphrey said finally. His gravelly voice sounded like a death knell.

I heard him loud and clear. Elation shot through me. I might be a natural at this investigative work. Maybe I should consider police work as an alternate career. I doodled on my paper, drawing a chain of daisies, then a row of cubes. I was working on lightning bolts when another of the men spoke.

"Wayne, you said you'd taken care of this." The speaker's voice, pitched low for secrecy, had been spoken so emphatically it reached my ears crystal-clear. I knew what the mayor, the judge, and the deputy sounded like, so the stage whisper must have come from the newest clergy in our fair town, Gil Beasley.

"I did take care of it," Mayor Wayne Frye responded in another loud whisper. "We wouldn't be sitting here if you hadn't lost your nerve."

"That blasted picture could ruin me."

Picture? Adrenaline surged into my veins. Were they talking about my stolen pictures? If so, the preacher had been caught with his pants down, all right, his face radiant with an other-worldly glory. No wonder he sounded edgy. But how did my picture come into his possession?

Who were they waiting for? The blackmailer? Or was it another person, like Daddy, who was a member of this elite group?

"Nobody gives a hoot about where you unzip your pants, Beasley," the mayor said.

"Easy for you to say. If an incriminating picture of you floated around town, you'd sing a different tune."

"I'm smarter than you." Years of Southern refinement rang through in the mayor's cultured words. "I didn't allow myself to be photographed."

My hands clenched my paper napkin in a knot. The mayor didn't know he'd been photographed? Only the preacher's photo surfaced? The surprises seemed endless in this investigation.

"I didn't *allow* it either." Beasley's response vibrated with outrage. "Who sneaks around taking dirty pictures?"

"A blackmailer." This muttered oath came from dour Judge Humphrey.

"No point in leaping to conclusions," Deputy Noah Marvel chimed in. "No one demanded money."

Good old Noah. He'd always had a level head on his shoulders. Hadley had claimed Noah was his best deputy. What did he think of Noah now? When I closed my eyes, Noah's picture with Barbara Jean floated across my eyelids.

"Only a matter of time," Beasley intoned theatrically. "The whole sordid tale will come out. That's the way these things go."

"Keep your voice down," the mayor said. "Some of us would prefer not to be headline news in next week's paper."

I tried to look small and inconspicuous, but it was hard to be invisible when I was the only other patron in the diner.

The front door opened in a flash of sunlight, and Hadley strolled in looking as if he owned the world. Fried food gave him indigestion. I couldn't imagine him choosing to eat here, which meant his appearance wasn't a random occurrence. Was he here for them or me?

From the stern set of his jaw and his direct bead on my booth, I gulped. I wasn't ready to discuss last night. A part of me hoped he would stroll on over to the other table and be the blackmailer. But luck wasn't with me. Hadley kissed me on the lips, and then slid onto the bench across from me. "Hi, hon."

"Don't you 'hon' me, Hadley Darter. Go away."

Erin returned with my steaming soup, beef vegetable by the smell and looks of it. "Look who's here. Ain't seen you in a long time, Hadley. What can I get for you?"

"I'll have the same as my wife."

I winced at his not-so-subtle message, the purpose behind his appearance crystal clear. He came to torment me, and I couldn't ask him about my missing photos with the foursome in earshot range.

Erin nodded and returned to the counter.

"You didn't mention you'd be lunching today at Calabash's," Hadley said.

His accusatory tone rubbed me the wrong way. As did his joining me. If the four men hesitated to talk when I was around, Hadley's presence would turn them into deaf mutes. "There are lots of things I don't mention to you."

"Like what?"

I couldn't think of a single thing I hadn't told him, but that was beside the point. "Like I wanted to have a nice quiet lunch by myself."

The men at the other table got up and filed by. The preacher and the judge walked right out the door, but Mayor Wayne and Deputy Noah stopped to chat with Hadley.

I gritted my teeth. Thanks to Hadley, the men were scattering like roaches. Now I was stuck with a lunch I didn't want and a husband who insisted on having a second chance. Anger churned in my gut. He'd stolen my pictures. Had he passed it on to the holy roller preacher this morning?

Once the men finally left the diner, I lit into Hadley. "What did you do with my pictures? Did you send one to Gil Beasley?"

He picked up a toothpick and rolled it slowly between his fingers. "You sure are wound up tight, hon. I thought we fixed that last night."

I punched him in the shoulder. "I'm not talking about *that*. I'm talking about those pictures. You know the ones I mean."

Erin refilled our tea and brought out his soup. When Hadley smiled at her, I kicked him under the table. Bad enough he kissed my sister in front of me, he didn't have to flirt with the waitress too. Had he always been this way? Surely I would've noticed flirty behavior. Wouldn't I? Why was he acting like this?

When we were alone again, I rephrased my question. "Where are my pictures?"

"I have no idea."

"Did you take them?"

"I did."

"And you lost them?"

He put the toothpick down. "Didn't say that."

"What are you doing here? Don't you have drug cases to work on?"

"I was working. Then I saw you barge in here."

His statement got the wheels turning in my head. Those four men were blackmail victims, and the blackmailer might be connected to Barbara Jean's death. Now it appeared that Hadley's investigation had run head-on into my own. "Those four are involved in a drug deal?"

He downed a couple of spoonfuls of his soup. "Not bad."

"Forget the soup. Are those men drug dealers?"

"Yeah."

"But they're our town's leaders. The people in this

community look up to them."

He shrugged, his spoon working double time. I couldn't eat a bite of my soup, and he was inhaling his. Where was the justice in that? He'd messed up my investigation. Had that single act made him ravenous?

Not fair. But if I lost my temper, Hadley would know how far under my skin he'd crawled. I sipped my syrupy tea and gathered my thoughts. "It doesn't make sense."

His spoon scraped the bottom of his bowl. "Crime rarely makes sense."

My mind churned. "You think the mayor, the judge, the deputy, and the preacher conspired to move drugs through Justice County?"

Hadley tossed a twenty down on the tabletop and took my arm. "Let's take this conversation outside."

I had no choice but to follow. He stopped between our two vehicles, which were slotted side by side in the deserted parking lot. I shoved my dark glasses on to keep the strong sun out of my eyes. "Wait a minute," I said. "Those men are my murder suspects."

"They're also drug runners."

"What proof do you have?"

"We know who they are and where they operate. We don't know the why and the how. That's why we haven't moved on them yet."

I tried to add this up in my head, but nothing computed. "Did Barbara Jean's death have to do with drugs?"

He nodded slightly. "Looks that way."

"Was she running drugs out of the produce stand?"

"We're not sure how she ties in. That's why we set Beasley up with the photo. Figured he'd be the easiest nut to crack."

"I want my pictures back."

"I don't have them anymore."

"You had no right to take them."

"I'm doing what I think is right."

"You can't steal from me and sleep with me, too. You breached my trust."

His hand rested on my arm. "I sincerely wish I didn't have to take those pictures this morning. But I did it, and I'd do it again. I don't want you mixed up in this. These people are dangerous. Barbara Jean was murdered."

I backpedaled into the side of my SUV, torn between swatting Hadley with my purse and screaming my frustration. "I don't have any choice. Daddy's up to his eyeballs in this mess. He's going to jail if I don't figure this out."

Hadley matched me step for step, his gaze focused on the way my hands tightened on my bag. "Joe can look out for himself."

"Daddy isn't as tough as he lets on. He loved this woman. I don't want him dragged into either investigation."

"You can want all you like, but that won't change how things are."

"You're the most infuriating man I've ever met."

He lifted my chin, his laser sharp gaze penetrating my sunglasses. "I'm your husband, and I mean to keep you safe. Stay away from the Naturalists. They're going down."

"The naked people are part of the drug ring?"

"Weren't you paying attention? We established that first."

"We established nothing."

He closed the last inch of space between us, his breath warm on my face. "Wrong. We established you still want me." He kissed me on the lips again, taking his time about it. "I'll see you tonight."

"Not if I can help it."

Chapter Twenty-Five

The sense of déjà vu hit me as I drove onto the studio's crushed shell drive ten minutes later. I was running around in circles—with Hadley, with Barbara Jean's murder investigation, and with my life—and getting nowhere fast. I needed to make forward progress; otherwise, I'd keep plowing myself deeper into the shifting sands of coastal Georgia.

Interviewing this award-winning artist was a step in a different direction, one that wasn't tainted by my family or naked dead people. Still looking tropical in her magenta batik dress, matching turban, and bare feet, Akysia Mahone waved from the open doorway. Her friendly come-to-the-islands smile radiated good cheer and irritated the crap out of me.

I probably should have waited until tomorrow to do this interview, but Ted's journalist friend waiting in the wings for my job weighed heavily on my mind. Until he had a job elsewhere, I had to watch my step.

Besides, this should be a fluff piece. All I had to do was photograph her work and her award, and then listen to her until she gave me a decent quote. I could do that in my sleep.

How would Ted feel if he heard I'd eavesdropped on the fab four? He'd voted for the mayor, and he played poker with the judge. If his cronies were involved in the drug ring, what did that make my boss? An accomplice?

The potential ramifications took my breath away. If I solved this case and Ted was involved, he'd go to jail. Which would put the newspaper out of business and leave me jobless. Not good at all. I could only pray Ted wasn't part of this.

"Welcome. I'm so very happy you returned today." Akysia latched onto my arm and powered me into a dimly lit interior. The ceiling fans whirled lazily, moving thick currents of patchouli-scented air around the small space. The centrally located divans were strewn with reclining naked people, naked people I recognized in spite of the green grape clusters resting on Kim's perky breasts, the pile of oversized M&M's resting on Tildy's pubic area, the leafy halo above Mama Leon's glittering ears, and the ugly blue violin in Alma's hand. Norma wasn't here. I filed that fact away.

"About time you returned," Mama Leon said.

"What's all this?" I asked. The sight of the naturalists caught me off balance, voiding my logic about this being an easy assignment. First, I didn't expect them to be here, so I hadn't mentally prepared myself for so much bare skin. Second, their nakedness and brazen sensuality made me uncomfortable. Steam rose from under my shirt collar.

Not five minutes ago, Hadley said the naturalists were most likely involved in a drug scheme, so they weren't innocent of wrongdoing. How much wrongdoing could be laid at their dirty feet? They'd claimed their beloved Barbara Jean had been murdered, but if they inherited her land, they had motive to kill her. Were they using me to see if their guilt was detectable? Would I be the next person they killed?

"I've wanted to do a nude study for some time," Akysia stood by her easel, a colorful palette of watercolor paints in her hand. "My friends volunteered to sit for me. They prompted me to arrange this interview."

I glanced at the abstract paintings lining the walls. Akysia was an award-winning artist, but her works gave me the shivers. The canvases were filled with blobs of paint, squiggly lines, and shadows. Lots of shadows. I snapped a few pictures of her work.

"Let's cut to the chase," Mama Leon said, his hand fingering the mounds of grapes on Kim's bosom. "What do you have for us?"

"Nothing new," I hedged. "You were right. She was murdered."

Alma leaned forward, one of her long gray braids slithering over her shoulder like an arthritic snake. "How'd she die?"

Not only was I uncomfortable with so much nudity, I felt vulnerable in this hedonistic lair. Ambushed, even. Akysia stood between me and the doorway. Was she in cahoots with the nudists? "Heart failure. She ingested an agent that caused her heart to malfunction. The tox screen proved it wasn't natural causes."

Mama Leon smacked his palm against his bare leg. "Yesterday evening the sheriff and two deputies showed up with a warrant and went through our house and our woods. What were they looking for?"

His question put me in the hot seat. I didn't trust the naturalists. One of them had slipped me those pictures of the men having sex with Barbara Jean. Someone wasn't what he or she appeared.

If one of them had murdered Bea, my telling them about my conversation with the coroner might prompt the killer to destroy evidence. I didn't want to do that. But I couldn't pretend I knew nothing.

I'd take a page from Daddy's legal playbook. I'd tell enough to make them think I was on their side. "A coffee cup. Barbara Jean drank coffee right before she was killed."

Tildy shook her head emphatically. "She never drank coffee. The caffeine made her too jittery."

Caffeine was a stimulant and caused heart palpitations in certain people. Barbara Jean would've avoided caffeine because of her heart condition. So why drink the darn stuff? "All I can tell you is she drank coffee before she died."

"Imagine that," Alma said. "Her last meal was coffee. I want mine to be steak and lobster. And Norma's strawberry pie."

Tildy munched a handful of M&Ms. "At least they're looking for her killer now. They wouldn't have done anything unless Molly made a fuss. This whole town wants us gone. Mayor Frye wouldn't care if we were murdered in our sleep."

Good point.

"I need a cigarette," Mama Leon said. "I can't bear to think of my precious Bea dying all alone like that in the woods."

From between her sprawled legs, Kim withdrew a cellophane wrapped pack, tapped out a cig, lighted it, and handed it over.

Thank God for cellophane. Otherwise, no telling what would be on those cigarettes.

"Where's Norma?" I asked.

Alma plucked at her blue violin. Discordant notes echoed in the heavily scented room. "Running the produce stand. She's taken over Barbara Jean's duties."

Was Norma screwing the men from the photos? Was she the new blackmailer? She'd been in the back room with Daddy on Saturday morning. Even though Daddy said he wasn't doing her, maybe she was doing his checkbook. And Otis had been hanging around her stand. Was he a target or an accomplice?

"There's no justice in Justice County. I demand justice for my Barbara Jean. Sheriff Otis doesn't know his head from a hole in the ground." Mama Leon paused to blow out a perfect smoke ring. "What else did you find out?"

Did I tell them about Daddy's prior relationship with Barbara Jean? That odd notice he'd paid for was printed in the paper, the one asking the secret baby to step forth and claim his or her inheritance. Why weren't the naturalists asking me about her missing kid? Were there already bulls-eyes drawn on my father and Barbara Jean's long-lost child? I studied the carpet next to the divan. "Not much."

Mama Leon's leafy halo slipped a bit as he sat upright. Eyeliner ringed his bloodshot eyes. "Come on, gal. I can see in your face you're holding something back."

Where was my poker face when I needed it? All I could think was "don't look down." I didn't want to know if he was aroused. "I have some ideas," I began slowly. "But I don't have any proof. A murder conviction requires proof."

"Yeah. You want proof, we'll get it. What are we looking for?"

"People don't kill without a reason. Or I should say, they rarely do. I don't think we're looking at a serial killer because we've only had the one death. Whoever killed Barbara Jean wanted her dead."

Alma put down her violin. "Well, duh. Every writer knows the basics of murder. Revenge, greed, and passion." She quickly ticked them off on her fingers. "All we have to do is figure out who had the most reason to kill her."

Murderous Alma vaulted to the top of my suspect list. If she knew half the things she claimed, she was a very viable killer.

"She was so sweet," Tildy said. "Everyone loved our Barbara Jean."

"Not everyone," Alma offered. "She used to be Mama's favorite. Now Kim is."

Ah. A bit of insider knowledge. Kim had taken Barbara Jean's place as Mama Leon's chief consort. She seemed to be the youngest and most attractive of the bunch. The other women weren't competition for her in the looks department. And Kim had abandoned me in the garden. She liked being in control.

The grapes slid straight down Kim's taut stomach as she rose. "Wait a minute. I had nothing to do with this. I loved Barbara Jean like my own sister. I would never hurt her."

Mama Leon's face tightened. "You playing me, Kim?"

Kim's eyes teared up. "I swear. I didn't kill anyone. You've got to believe me, Mama Leon."

Mama Leon patted Kim on the head, and then pulled her astride him. Green grapes rolled off the divan and bounced on the floor. "It's all right, sugar. You don't have a mean bone in your delightful body."

I gagged. I didn't believe Kim's "I'm-being-wrongly-accused" performance for a second. Mama's brand of comfort turned carnal. I didn't need to see that again.

I turned to Akysia who hummed happily at her easel. Her paintbrush edged across the canvas. "I'm sorry, there isn't enough time left for me to do your interview before I meet my son's school bus. Can we reschedule?"

Her eyes were dilated, and she didn't respond.

Hmm.

My brain whirled with possibilities. Was Akysia on drugs? The naturalists were somehow related to Hadley's drug case. I had a dead nudist who'd been photographed screwing five city leaders, including my father.

"You say something?" Akysia asked. She looked over at me, but I swear her eyes focused on the raunchy tableau behind me.

She could have them. Kim's heated stream of sensual encouragement to Mama Leon nauseated me. "Yeah. Gotta run. Can we finish tomorrow?"

Akysia nodded and went back to her humming, zoned-out mode. I glanced down at her canvas. In the center, like a giant beacon, stood a monumental, fire engine red penile-shaped tower. It was surrounded by lesser, shadowy rounded shapes. Whether they were grapes, M&Ms, breasts, or body parts, I couldn't tell.

All I knew was that I had to get out of there before I barfed.

Chapter Twenty-Six

Though the odor of patchouli clung to my clothes, my head cleared when I stepped out of the art studio into the fresh air. Once in my car, I automatically checked my voice mail for messages. Sure enough I'd missed a call. I queued up the message. Hadley's voice came across loud and clear. "Don't rush home for the school bus. I'm picking up Jimbo so we can straighten out the humping misinformation. We'll both be home about six tonight."

I erased the message and pulled out of the studio driveway. After our lovemaking last night, Hadley believed everything was fine. I didn't believe that, not by a long shot. And I didn't want to argue tonight in front of Jimbo. But I wasn't up for any arguments right now. I needed peace and quiet. If I went back to the office, I could start the artist story and see what was on tap for tomorrow. Anything was better than worrying about where Hadley would sleep tonight.

Clarice lit into me like a vengeful harpy as soon as I stepped out of my Suburban. "You went too far, Molly."

Town gossip Mrs. Rolanda Murphy stopped in her tracks outside Liquor Land, the store to the immediate right of the paper. Murph always had her ear to the ground, and today was no exception. I could easily imagine all of her well-trained ear hairs leaning in our direction.

She was destined for disappointment. I had already disowned Clarice. Ignoring her, I stalked toward the front door.

"Molly. Stop." Clarice shrilled, her girly shoes clicking on the sidewalk behind me.

She could run all she wanted, but I wasn't stopping for her. I marched into the office, wishing I could lock the front door.

Ted sensed conflict and immediately went into lurking mode. I swear he kept the Savannah paper near his desk for juicy situations like this. Few people noticed he was hiding back there in the dark corner because of his talent for reptilian stillness.

Clarice caught me, her bright pink claws latching onto my arm. "Stop. You can have your stinky old Hadley. But you can't have Mama. She's mine."

I didn't own Mama, but my arm was another matter. The hackles on my neck rose at the touch of my enemy. "Get your hand off me."

"Not until you call Mama and take back those awful things you said about me."

I didn't want Clarice touching me, and I certainly didn't take orders from her. "I'm taking nothing back. Everything I said was the truth. Unlike you, I don't take what isn't mine."

Clarice blinked rapidly. "You've got everything. Why'd you have to go and take Mama, too?"

I should've known better than to try to reason with an ego-maniac. "I didn't take Mama. She's an adult, and she makes her own decisions. Let go of me, Clarice."

"No. You've got to make this right."

Fury simmered in my bones. "Let go of my arm."

"Quit bossing me around and listen. For once in your life, hear what I'm saying."

She had selective hearing, not me. A highlight reel of

Clarice's past dramatics ran through my head. "Why not throw in tears for good measure? What about the quivering chin or the trembling shoulders? Or maybe you'll faint like the time at the state fair?"

Clarice stomped her foot. "That wasn't my fault. Those state fair animals reeked. I wasn't about to go into the barns and be surrounded by stinking manure. If you hadn't insisted we go see the baby pigs, I wouldn't have had to take such drastic measures."

"You can't blame me for your histrionics."

"I surely can. If you'd have voiced even one complaint as a kid, I wouldn't have had to do all the complaining. I've always had to play the weak one. That's who I became. And now you've taken that away from me. Mama looked right through me today and told me to grow up."

Good for Mama. "About time."

"I'm being persecuted unjustly. I didn't sleep with Hadley, but I wanted you to think that. I heard you pull up, and I knew he would go bounding over to meet you when he'd been yawning at my side for the past six hours. I wanted to have some fun."

Fun? Her idea of fun was to make me think my husband cheated? Her fun was breaking up my marriage and depriving my son of his father's company. An invisible steel band constricted around my chest. My mouth went dry. "I wasn't laughing then, and I'm not laughing now."

"Okay, so I need to work on my sense of humor. Hadley's been making me flirt with the judge and that new preacher guy out at the Twin Willows Truck Stop, and I thought it would be fun to tease him a little."

My fury flashed from a slow simmer to a rolling boil. "You baited him to hurt me."

"Everything came to you so easily. Your steady boyfriend, your college degree, your husband, your career, your child. You've got everything I ever wanted."

Outrage gave me the strength of three women. I

yanked my arm out of her hand. "Nothing came easy to me. I worked hard for everything. If you'd paid more attention in school and to making friends, you'd have a different life."

"I don't want to slave away at the grindstone. I want my goals handed to me on a silver platter. Until that happens, I want Mama fussing over me again. She won't speak to me, and that's your fault."

I looked at her with disgust. "Mama is right. Grow up. You're way overdue."

"I didn't sleep with Hadley. You're persecuting me for no reason."

Adrenaline roared through my veins. Clarice's ill-conceived actions had consequences. She had to face them. "Because of what you did, my life is in a shambles. I've always had a plan for the future, and you snatched it out of my hands."

"From where I'm standing, you've still got everything. Adorable Jimbo. Mama and Daddy's respect. Hadley's going nuts because he thinks you're divorcing him. You have a real job. You didn't settle for working for your father. All I had was Mama's sympathy, and now I don't even have that. Fix it."

"Let me get this straight. Your crowning achievement, your reason for living, is that you can manipulate Mama?"

Clarice winced. "It sounds bad when you put it that way, but I'm not a deep person. Please, you have to help me. I'm begging you. Forgive me. Help me. If I don't have Mama in my corner, I've got nothing. You've got more than that. You've got you're a career, a child, a husband—"

"Stop." I interrupted her litany of my achievements with a wave of my hand. I rubbed my aching temples. I couldn't take much more of Clarice's self-serving dramatics.

"You'll do it? You'll tell Mama I didn't sleep with

176

Hadley."

The hopeful note in her voice soured my stomach. "You came between me and my husband, and you did it to be mean. Your revised claim won't change the reality of the rift in my heart and in my marriage. I don't forgive you."

Clarice's face fell. Her shoulders slumped. "Then you're banishing me from Thanksgiving. Mama said you wouldn't come if I was there, and she won't have Thanksgiving without her precious grandson. If you don't make things right, I'll be stuck at home on turkey day eating cold grits by my lonesome."

I banged my fist on the news counter, causing the glass bowl of paper clips to clang. "You make it sound like one word from me will miraculously fix everything. I don't have that kind of power, plus I do blame you. You are the most rotten, self-centered, egotistical sister in the world."

"All I want is to have Mama back. What's so hard about putting in a good word for me?"

My skin crawled. I couldn't take one more second of Clarice. She'd shut up if I agreed, and frankly I wanted to be rid of her. "All right. I'll talk to Mama. Leave me alone."

Relief washed over her face. "You'll come to Thanksgiving, too?"

"Don't push your luck."

"Why punish the entire family because you hate me? Couldn't you pretend to like me for one meal a year?"

Her comments momentarily stilled my racing heart. God. Was that what I was doing? Punishing everyone else for Clarice's shortcomings? I wanted things to be easy and clear-cut, planned out. Why couldn't she see that? Why was she so blind to my needs?

No answers came to mind. I couldn't think straight with Clarice in the room. "I'll think about Thanksgiving. I'm not making any promises."

Clarice engulfed me in a big hug, which I stoically

endured, and then she trotted out the door humming to herself.

I still hated her, but I understood she couldn't be any other way.

Crap.

Nothing in life was fair.

Her revelation about purposefully baiting Hadley slammed through me. She'd punched my buttons, all right, and I'd reacted like a wronged woman. What was I now? An overreacting woman? I didn't quite know.

I hated uncertainty. I wanted to trust in what I'd seen, but both Hadley and Clarice claimed Clarice had instigated the kiss. Hadley could've pushed her away, so he wasn't Mr. Innocent either. How was I supposed to sort this out? I'd been wronged. That was clear. But had I wronged everyone else with my wrath?

The newspaper rustled behind me. "Quite a show you two put on," Ted said.

I slumped down in my wheeled chair behind my desk. "Don't remind me. I caved like a spineless wimp. I hate myself for giving into my sister."

"She's a powerful persuader, that's for sure."

That dreamy glint in his normally shrewd eyes concerned me. "God, Ted. Tell me it isn't true. Tell me you don't have the hots for my neurotic sister."

"Wouldn't want to lie to you, seeing as I know how you feel about liars." He rose and stretched. "Hold down the fort for me, would you? I need to pop over to the bank before they close for the day."

Ted and Clarice as a future couple? No way. The man had no idea what he was getting into. "If you know what's good for you, stay away from Clarice. She annihilates men."

He nodded his agreement. "Passion. A guy would be lucky to have that passion directed at him."

"A truck stop cutie would be safer than tangling with a shrew like Clarice."

"I'll take my chance when the time comes."

I stared after him, too dumbfounded to speak. Ted and Clarice together. The first time he gave her his patented death glare, she'd fall to pieces. Then she'd rip out his heart and stomp it into the ground.

But Ted and Clarice's potential romance was the least of my problems. I was suddenly ravenous. I should've eaten that soup at lunch. I dug my emergency candy bar out of my purse and inhaled it. The gooey caramel and the rich milk chocolate made short work of my headache and empty stomach.

How did I sort out everything that had happened today? I'd allowed my straying husband back in my bed, I'd halfway reconciled with my trashy, manipulative sister, and I'd agreed to think about attending a family Thanksgiving.

I'd learned the nudists were involved in Hadley's drug running investigation, and so were four of the men photographed with Barbara Jean. Daddy couldn't be involved with drug running. I quickly qualified that. I didn't know what my father was capable of doing. Joe Campbell was a stranger to me.

Hadley had used Clarice to get closer to the four men who ran our town, and his investigation had wreaked havoc in our lives. If he hadn't slept with Clarice, only kissed her, could I forgive him in the cold light of day? Or would I only welcome him in my bed in the dark of night?

My head throbbed again. Life was rushing at me like a speeding locomotive. Could the train be controlled or would it career off the tracks and crush everyone? I couldn't deal with the entire train at once. But Mama. I could speak to her for Clarice.

God. I hated caring so much about what my family thought of me. I couldn't stand the thought I was punishing all of them. I only had one family. Nothing good could come of me ripping it asunder to soothe my wounded pride.

Maggie Toussaint

I hated this being so hard. Why couldn't I turn back the clock to when my family was united?

I glanced at my watch again. Mama would be home now, starting dinner. The longer I waited to call Mama, the more I would dread it. I gulped down a shot of invisible courage and dialed her number.

Chapter Twenty-Seven

My mother answered the phone on the first ring.

I wasted no time on polite chitchat. My goal was to have this unpleasant task completed before Ted returned from the bank. He didn't need to hear me groveling. "I'm speaking to Clarice again."

"I'm so glad you girls made up. I've been praying for the two of you. Now, what about Hadley?"

Her chipper voice aggravated me. Did she turn on Clarice to force me to deal with my husband? "What about him?"

"Did you reconcile with him, too?"

That imaginary steel band tightened on my chest again. I stared up at the water stains on the ceiling. "That's between me and Hadley."

"And Thanksgiving?"

"Thanksgiving is months away. Who knows if we'll even be alive?"

"You won't come to Thanksgiving dinner?"

"Mama, this isn't about Thanksgiving. This is about Clarice ruining my life." A clicking noise sounded in my ear right in the middle of my protest.

Mama interrupted me. "Hang on a minute, dear. I

have another call."

I fumed in phone limbo. I doubted Mama had heard a single word I said. All she could think about was her Thanksgiving meal.

Her other caller was probably Clarice. Were they comparing notes on how to best manipulate me so I didn't ruin Mama's perennial family gathering? I had half a mind to start my own Thanksgiving tradition. Who said I had to spend the holiday in the company of relatives? It would be much nicer to cook a simple meal at home.

Mama came back on the line. "Get Hadley and meet me at the jail."

The quiver in her high-pitched voice alerted me to the seriousness of the matter. "What's wrong, Mama?"

"It's Joe. He's been arrested for that woman's murder, and he wants Hadley to be his lawyer."

Time froze. I couldn't think. I couldn't move. My lungs doggedly pushed air in and out of my chest. Was my heart beating? I couldn't hear anything for the ruckus inside my head.

Daddy's arrest implied that law enforcement had reasonable cause to think he killed Barbara Jean. Had Hadley given the new sheriff the photo of Daddy with Barbara Jean? If so, he would be the worst person to represent Daddy. Should I hire a big-gun lawyer from Savannah?

Mama screeched in my ear, snapping me back to the present. "Molly? You there?"

"Yes. I'm here."

"Why aren't you on your way to the jail? You can't let your father's floozy cause trouble from the grave."

My chocolate-coated stomach clenched. I was going to be sick. "You knew about Barbara Jean?"

"Of course I knew about the Olden girl or whatever she calls herself these days. A woman knows when her man is catting around."

Strangely, her terse words encouraged me. I'd never

felt an emotional distance from Hadley prior to finding him kissing my sister. Maybe the whole scene with Hadley and Clarice was merely a product of Clarice's diabolical scheming. Maybe I could salvage my marriage. I dug out my purse and started a note to Ted so he'd know why the office was locked when he returned from the bank.

I tucked the phone to my ear with my shoulder as I wrote. "You're handling this much better than I would have."

"We Munro women have our own styles. Clarice pouts, you stomp around and make people miserable, and I, well, I keep putting one foot in front of the other."

She'd already launched into martyr role, her true style, not that I would point that out for all the tea in the world. I wasn't stupid. "Ignoring a problem won't make it go away," I countered.

Mama's hoarse laugh echoed through the phone. "Wrong. I've still got my husband. All she's got is a marble slab for a pillow."

"Mama, I've got to hang up to call Hadley."

"I'm coming to town. I'll meet you at the jail."

I grabbed up my keys and darted out the door of the paper. After locking the building, I punched Hadley up on speed dial.

"Darter."

I quickly filled him in as I ran down the street to the jail, narrowly avoiding a collision with Mrs. Murphy in front of Liquor Land.

"I'll be right there. Should I drop Jimbo at his friend's house?"

I tugged on my hair. I couldn't remember if Eric and his family were home tonight or if this was his night for drum lessons, and this was no time to be guessing. The most important thing was to get Hadley to the jail as soon as possible. "Bring him with you. I'll be responsible for him."

Hadley hung up. Good thing because I was already at

the jail. I stepped right up to the thick Plexiglas separating me from the dispatcher. "Buzz me in, Betty Sue."

I must have looked fearsome because she didn't give me any of her normal lip. Since these used to be Hadley's digs, I knew the layout. They'd be holding Daddy in the back office.

Sheriff Otis and Daddy rose when I entered the barren room. Of the four institutional desks in this room, the sheriff occupied the only one with a computer. The other desks were markedly empty. Nothing had been left behind that could be used by a criminal to gain a toehold back in the real world. This room represented the end of the line.

Deep furrows lined Daddy's pale brow. My heart immediately went out to him. Whatever else Joe Campbell was, in that moment he was my Daddy, the man I loved and knew. And he was in trouble.

"Molly, you shouldn't be back here," Otis said.

He couldn't run me off that easily. "You shouldn't have arrested Daddy. He didn't kill Barbara Jean."

Otis' pinched face suggested he smelled sewer gas. "Our investigation says otherwise."

Daddy sat back down beside the desk. His hands hadn't been cuffed, which meant he was getting VIP treatment. So far, so good.

I perched on the edge of an adjacent desk, refusing to back down. "Daddy wouldn't hurt a flea, and you know it."

The sheriff's face darkened. "I've seen Joe in action in the courtroom. He's not as innocent as all that. Besides, he admits sleeping with Barbara Jean right before she died. That's opportunity in my book."

I glanced over at Daddy for verification.

Daddy shrugged. "No point in denying the truth. DNA doesn't lie."

A chill ran through me. DNA? Daddy had screwed Barbara Jean right before she died? He hadn't mentioned that tidbit before. Though his innocence now seemed less certain, I knew deep in my heart that he wasn't a killer. "Doesn't mean he killed her. He cared for her."

"Which is why we believe he murdered her. We recently came into the possession of several photographs of the victim having sex with Joe as well as four other men. No man in love with a woman would stand for that. He's got opportunity and motive. Two strikes."

I gulped. He had to be talking about the same photographs I'd seen. Had Hadley fingered Daddy for the murder by handing the photos to the sheriff? "Photographs can be faked."

"We didn't arrest Joe solely because of the pictures. He takes the same decongestant found in her system. He bought a month's supply at the Marshview Pharmacy two days before she was killed. That ties everything up neatly. Three strikes. He had the means, the motive, and the opportunity. He's our man."

That sounded circumstantial, for sure, but I knew better. "That decongestant is an over-the-counter product. Tell him about your allergies, Daddy."

Daddy nodded slowly, as if in a daze. "I take the decongestant because of my allergies. Ask the pharmacist. Heather knows I buy that stuff like clockwork. Same as I buy antihistamines from her. That doesn't make me a killer."

Otis sat back down and typed out every word we said. I glanced at my watch again, sure that hours had passed since I'd arrived. Where was Hadley?

Ted sauntered into the office area. "What's going on here?"

I was so surprised to see Ted that I stood up. He had a folder under his arm and a strange expression on his usually inscrutable face. "Otis has mistakenly arrested Daddy for Barbara Jean's murder," I said.

"No mistake about this." Otis chortled with glee. "Joe had means, motive, and opportunity for the murder.

DNA evidence puts him at the scene. I've got him dead to rights."

"Tell him about the will, Joe," Ted urged.

Otis stopped typing and looked up. "What will?"

"Barbara Jean's Last Will and Testament." Daddy sighed and sagged back into his chair. "She left her estate to her child, as long as the child stepped forward to claim it in a timely manner. The notice is in this week's paper."

"What child?" Otis glared at my father, and then toward Ted. "I don't know anything about a child. I thought the naturalists were her family."

Didn't he read the paper? I thought everyone knew about the secret baby by now.

"Barbara Jean grew up an Olden," Daddy said in a weary voice. "All that land is Olden property, and it is her wish for her estate to go to a child she put up for adoption thirty-eight years ago."

Otis picked up a pencil and tapped it on the desk. "Her will doesn't change the facts about your arrest. You're still the guy who killed her."

Ted opened the folder and slid an official-looking piece of paper across the desk to Otis. The sheriff picked it up and read it, his eyebrows shooting up to his hairline. Suspicion further marred his perfect features. "Is this for real?"

Daddy pulled out his reading glasses and reached for the paper. He read it, too, and then handed it back to the sheriff. He carefully folded his glasses back into his pocket and stared at Ted.

Ted stared back.

"What?" I reached for the sheet of paper.

It was an official document.

A Georgia birth certificate.

I scanned the official text to find his parents names. Ted's mother's name was listed as Barbara Jean Olden. Ted's father was Joseph Theodore Page.

I didn't know any other Pages, but Joseph and

Theodore, those names were very familiar. Those were Daddy's first and middle names.

My gaze swiveled between my boss and my father.

How had I missed this before? The two men were of a similar height. Both had brown eyes. Both had the same shrewd, intelligent gaze. The same grim sadness. The same hard line against injustice.

Ted Page was Barbara Jean's secret baby.

My jaw dropped.

He was also my half-brother.

Chapter Twenty-Eight

I staggered back into an empty metal desk, the drawers creaking at my sudden impact. My hand covered my gaping mouth. My gaze remained locked on Barbara Jean's secret child. My brother.

Blood roared through my head. Dear God. All those years I'd wished I for someone to play with, someone who wanted to climb trees and build forts. All Clarice ever wanted to do was play dress up and have tea parties.

My beleaguered brain stumbled over my sister's name. I had a sister and a brother. A brother who was romantically interested in his half-sister. Protective instincts welled up from deep within my core. "Stay away from Clarice."

Ted's lips thinned. Had it finally dawned on him that he had a thing for his half-sister? Or had he figured out that Joseph Theodore was Joe Campbell? Was Ted trying to help Daddy or drag him deeper into the pit of lies?

Daddy glanced up sharply. "What's Clarice got to do with this?"

"Nothing!" Ted and I spoke in unison.

Speculation flashed across Otis' face. His gaze drilled into Ted. "Where were you last Wednesday morning between nine and noon?"

Ted went into his reptilian-still mode. "Right where I am every Wednesday morning. At the newspaper office, selling papers."

"Can anyone confirm that?"

"Molly can."

Suddenly all eyes were on me. I couldn't remember if Ted had stayed in the office all morning on Wednesday. Sometimes one or the other of us slipped out to run errands. Had he done that this past Wednesday? I couldn't remember. Wednesday seemed a lifetime ago.

If I confirmed Ted's alibi, would that tighten the screws in Daddy's coffin? Did I have to make a choice between my father and my alleged brother?

Wait. No point in getting too spun up over this. Whether he was my brother or not, Ted was my boss. And he'd been a good boss. I trusted him. "Sure. He was there. With me."

Ted reached over and squeezed my shoulder as Hadley walked in.

Hadley brushed Ted's hand away and angled in for a possessive kiss. "Hands off, Page. She's taken."

Ignoring the jolt of electricity his kiss elicited, I scowled at him. His macho gamesmanship was unnecessary. "Where's Jimbo?"

"He's out front finishing up Betty Sue's crossword puzzle." Hadley glanced over at Otis. "What are the charges against my client?"

The sheriff met and held his gaze. "He's being charged with the murder of Barbara Jean McAllister."

Hadley nodded tersely. "I'd like a moment to confer with my client."

Otis, Ted, and I filed out of the small room into the wide hall. Hadley closed the door, shutting us out. If only it were so easy to shut out my racing thoughts.

I had a brother.

I glanced sideways at Ted and discovered him

checking me out. Heat suffused my face. "How long have you known who your parents were? Is that why you hired me? Because we're related?"

Ted's gaze appeared to be fixed on the distant series of locking doors. "My parents didn't tell me I was adopted until I was sixteen. I needed my birth certificate to apply for a driver's license. That's the first I heard about it. The names on the document didn't mean anything to me. I didn't know either of the people listed as my birth parents. They didn't matter because they hadn't wanted me. A few years back, my adopted parents died, and I wondered about my birth parents. I tracked Barbara Jean to Marshview."

"Daddy didn't know about you. I swear he didn't even know he had a son. He never would've let you be adopted. He would've raised you himself."

Ted smirked. "Lila Campbell would've loved that. Doesn't matter. I had a great childhood with my adopted family."

Another ramification of Ted's secret identity emerged from the chaos in my head. "Dang, Ted. You own a nudist colony. What are you gonna do with it?"

"I'm not doing anything until I find out who killed my mother."

His deep voice broke on the word mother.

The door buzzer sounded, and Mama sailed down the hall, an avenging angel in ice blue. Her heels rapped imperiously on the tiled floor. As she neared, I saw that her skin tone was very pale.

"Where's Joe?" Mama stood toe-to-toe with Otis in the institutional green hall. "What have you done with my husband? Have you stuffed him in one of those nasty cells?"

My heart ached for her. Daddy's arrest meant she had to deal with the reality of his relationship with Barbara Jean. I reached over and patted her arm. "Daddy's fine, Mama. Hadley's with him in the interrogation room."

"Well, get him out of there. Post bail or whatever has to be done. Joe needs to come home with me tonight. He can't be arrested. That's not right."

Otis looked at Mama speculatively. With the evidence of Daddy's extracurricular sex life standing next to him in the person of Ted Page, Mama was a person of interest in the murder investigation. "Where were you last Wednesday morning, ma'am?"

Mama glared at him. "Why do you want to know?"

"I'm asking everyone involved in the murder case."

"Well, I never." Mama huffed. "I can't believe you'd have to gall to ask me about my whereabouts. My ancestors settled this town. I'm a card-carrying member of the Daughters of the American Revolution, and the founder of the bridge club. I'm not a common criminal. Let me assure you there's nothing common about Lila Munro Campbell."

Otis remained unfazed by the recitation of her lineage. "Where were you?"

"I was at home. Alone. There, are you satisfied?" Mama's voice broke. "I have no alibi. But I didn't kill Barbara Jean McAllister, much as I would've liked to wring that hussy's neck for leading my husband astray."

Ted stiffened.

I grabbed Mama by the arm and guided her down the hall. "Look, Mama, it doesn't do Daddy or you any good to go around slinging blue-blooded mud in here. You hate airing dirty laundry in public, so let Hadley handle this. He'll get Daddy released. Then we'll regroup at home."

Mama sniffed copiously. "I can't bear to think of my Joe wasting away in a tiny jail cell for the rest of his life."

"Daddy didn't kill Barbara Jean. Hadley will get the charges dropped." I studied her for a second. Even when she was in a state, Mama looked perfectly pulled together. How much of her composure was an act?

I prayed she was as composed as she appeared. "There's been a new development in this murder case."

Mama stopped in mid-sniff. "What kind of development?"

Guilt gnawed at my stomach. I shouldn't tell her. No, I should. She shouldn't hear the story from one of her bridge cronies. Telling her now was the best thing.

I cleared my throat. "Barbara Jean willed her estate to a child she put up for adoption thirty-eight years ago. That grown-up person, her son, is Ted Page. His birth certificate lists a Joseph Theodore Page as his father."

"Oh!" The remaining color drained from Mama's face. She crumpled in slow motion. Diving like a soccer goalie, I caught her head before it smacked on the hard tile floor.

If I could manipulate time so that there was only one problem at a time to deal with, I could manage. As it was, shock strangled me, too.

I had a brother.

An older brother. One I hadn't even known existed until now. My trashy sister expected me to forgive her. My cheating husband wanted me to take him back. My father had been arrested for murder. And Barbara Jean's killer was still at large. Her killer somehow tied into the drug case Hadley was investigating.

Clearly, Hadley and I needed to pool resources to straighten this out.

Jimbo's sneakers squeaked as he stopped next to me. "Mom, what's wrong with Grammy?"

Cold from the floor seeped into my butt. Telling Mama the truth hadn't done her any favors. My eight-year-old son didn't need to be burdened with truth. He'd had enough to deal with these last few days. "She got a little light-headed. Ask Betty Sue for a glass of water for her."

Jimbo dashed down the hall and returned immediately with a cup half full of water. A trail of spilled water dotted the hallway. Mama stirred in my arms. "Here, Mama, drink this." I pressed the paper cup to her lips.

Otis and Ted hovered nearby, ready to help. When

Mama reached to steady the cup, her hand trembled. Water sloshed onto her ice blue blouse. Mama pushed the cup away, closing her eyes as if tuning us all out.

"You can and will let me in." Clarice's irate voice echoed down the empty hall.

Great. A second drama queen. If Betty Sue had a lick of sense, she'd leave Clarice out in the unsecured area.

With Daddy and Mama in trouble, I didn't need Clarice back here causing a ruckus. I heard the low murmur of Betty Sue's voice. I silently cheered that the door buzzer hadn't sounded. Betty Sue was holding her own against Clarice.

"Buzz me in, Betty Sue, or I'm going to tell everyone about your secret tattoo," Clarice threatened in her cheerleading voice, the one that carried clear across Marshview Stadium.

At the sound of the buzzer, I shrunk inside. Clarice would stir things up, and we'd be lucky to get out of here without the entire family being arrested. Otis would have a Campbell in every cell. I braced for Clarice's arrival.

Clarice rounded the corner in a flash of hot pink and lime green, and spotted Mama on the floor. Her eyes locked with mine.

Fury churned in her gaze. "What have you done to my Mama?"

"She's my Mama, too." From my vantage point on the floor, the flashy rhinestones on Clarice's girly sandals sparkled as she raced down the over-bright corridor. My muscles tensed.

Clarice hit Jimbo's trail of spilled water and skidded into the wall at full speed. Like an animated cartoon character, she slid face down to the floor, each frame of her descent searing itself into my permanent memory.

"Clarice!"

I wasn't sure if Otis or Ted yelled her name, but both men sprinted to her aid.

Ted checked for a pulse and started CPR. After the

third puff, he glanced up at Otis. "Call an ambulance." Otis raced into the dispatch room and ordered Betty Sue to make the call.

Beside me, Jimbo squirmed. "Am I in trouble?"

Lord. Poor Jimbo. He blamed himself for Clarice's fall. "No, sweetheart. It was an accident. Aunt Clarice should've looked where she was going."

The door buzzed again.

This time, Bubba Brown and Grandma Dee walked in. As the coroner, Bubba had more medical knowledge than the rest of us. He took over Clarice's CPR. Ted picked up Clarice's hand and held it. The concern on his face wasn't brotherly.

I shivered at the thought of the two-headed babies they would have if Ted pursued his romantic interest in his sister.

Grandma Dee headed toward where I sat cradling Mama's head in my lap. Jimbo knelt at my side, tears welling in his eyes.

"Be careful, Grandma Dee," I said. "There's water on the floor."

"I see it. I'm not blind." Grandma Dee leaned down and lightly cupped Mama's face with her hands. "Lila. Pull yourself together. Your family needs you."

Mama moaned. Jimbo sobbed openly. Silent tears rolled down my cheeks. Unlike Jimbo, my guilt had a basis. I should've kept my mouth shut.

Hadley and Daddy exited the office. "Lila!" Daddy shouted. He knelt beside Mama, cradling her in his arms, keening softly. Sirens wailed in the distance.

Hadley scooped Jimbo up in his arms and looked like he would murder anyone who touched his precious child. He glared at me. "My God, Molly. Did you declare war on your entire family?"

Tears rained soundlessly down my cheeks as I hugged my knees to my chest. Grandma Dee offered Bubba her support. Ted had a death grip on Clarice's hand. Daddy had Mama. Hadley had Jimbo. Even Betty Sue had Otis to hold onto.

I was the only one without someone.

And Hadley believed this disaster was my fault.

Trouble was, he was right.

Chapter Twenty-Nine

With lights flashing and siren wailing, the ambulance carrying Mama, Clarice, and Daddy sped away from the jail. Thank God Clarice had started breathing again on her own after Bubba took over her CPR. With any luck, her worst consequence would be a concussion.

Ted bolted down Main Street to get his Jeep. Grandma Dee and Bubba Brown left with Jimbo, who would now spend the night with Grandma Dee. Otis disappeared back in the jailhouse. I guess he'd had enough of the crazy Campbell clan for one day. I'd certainly had enough of him.

That left Hadley and me alone in the parking lot. Well, as alone as we could get with thirty townspeople milling around, watching our every move.

Given his earlier crack about me declaring war on my family, he probably didn't want my company. But it was senseless for us to drive separate vehicles twenty miles to the hospital. When Hadley unlocked his pickup, I climbed in the passenger side.

I clicked my seatbelt in place. "Is Daddy still under arrest?"

"Yes."

His clipped tone aggravated me. As did his comment about declaring war. I had made remarkable strides in mending fences today. Besides, I had enough guilt over Mama's heart palpitations for the two of us.

Maybe Hadley would lighten up if he knew how upset I was for opening my big fat mouth. "I'm sorry about what happened in there. I shouldn't have told Mama about Joseph Theodore Page being on Ted's birth certificate, but she seemed so calm I thought she could handle the news. And I'm truly sorry about causing her medical distress. That's my Mama in the ambulance, and I helped put her there. But I swear to God, I didn't make Clarice run into the wall. She did that on her own."

Hadley didn't answer. His lips pressed tightly together, and he drove as if his life depended on it. His brooding silence filled the truck, swirling in thick eddies around me. My shoulders bowed under the weight of his disapproval.

All during the previous week when I was furious with him, I'd felt bereft, but I knew I wasn't alone because I had my parents' love and support. Right now my parents were speeding toward a hospital and neither one of them was in a position to help anyone. My injured sister was in that same ambulance.

My family was dropping like flies. Their needs came first. I had to be strong for them. I had to make Hadley understand that I wasn't vindictive. He'd known all week that Clarice led him on, and that the big kiss was staged to get my attention, but I'd just found out. No, that wasn't right. I'd believed the image of their embrace more than the subsequent explanations.

Hadley had been a victim same as me. He should get that, right? He was smart. But he'd been taken in by Clarice. Could it be that he didn't trust his intuition where Campbell females were concerned?

Mile marker posts flew by as we merged onto the interstate. I pulled my visor down and turned it to the side window to block the late afternoon sun. The speedometer hovered near ninety. My grip on the armrest tightened. I couldn't remember if this truck had passenger side air bags. If we wrecked going ninety miles an hour, an air bag might not save us.

It seemed my earlier premonition about my life being analogous to a speeding train wreck was unfolding on the interstate highway. My physical safety depended on the man I loved, but at this moment I believed he'd rather crash into a guardrail and be done with me.

I hugged my tummy. The tension in the truck was thick enough to slice. "Daddy didn't kill Barbara Jean," I put forth into the fractured silence.

Hadley navigated around the RVs, mini vans, and rental trucks as if they were standing still. His single-minded preoccupation with driving fast worried me. If I could open a dialogue between us, I could fix what was wrong. I tried again to draw him into conversation. "Getting us killed on the way to the hospital won't help matters."

A muscle in his cheek spasmed. If I hadn't been staring at him, I wouldn't have known he'd had any reaction at all. It dawned on me that Hadley's behavior was different. He wasn't responding to me.

And he was racing at top speed after the ambulance with my sister in it.

A fresh tide of jealousy crested and spilled over my churning thoughts. I couldn't make the nasty insinuations in my head go away. Was he driving so fast because of Clarice? He'd said he didn't love her. He'd said he loved me. Did he think he could have the both of us?

I wouldn't suffer in silence as Mama had done. "Is this about Clarice? Are you upset because she's hurt? I won't share you with another woman, and especially not my sister."

His eyes never left the road. "You don't get it, do you?"

I most certainly wasn't getting it. I didn't have any idea what "it" was. "Look, I don't know what's going on inside your head, but this isn't a life or death situation. My mother and my sister will recover, but I'm going crazy with worry. Why won't you talk to me?"

"Did you ever stop to wonder why you and Clarice butt heads so often? Clarice isn't the only one that thinks the world revolves around her. You do, too."

Outrage joined the dangerous cocktail of emotions poisoning my thoughts. "I do not."

"Why do you think your entire family has been walking on eggshells around you this week? You're unhappy, and you made sure everyone else was unhappy, too."

Hot tears flooded my eyes. I was not going to cry again. Crying was a sign of weakness. "That isn't true."

He cast me a cool glance. "Isn't it?"

"You broke my heart."

"We're even. You broke mine, too."

"Don't make this into a competition." I wanted to shut my eyes and have this situation go away, but I was too afraid of dying to close my eyes. If Hadley hit something, I didn't want my death to be a surprise. I didn't want to be one of those lost souls that perpetually wandered the earth. If I was dead, I wanted to be the first to know.

"I'd win hands down," Hadley said. "You've single-handedly turned my personal life upside down. And six months of investigative work has been trashed."

How dare he put that burden at my feet? "If you weren't so secretive about your work, I might have a clue of what you're talking about."

He shrugged. "It doesn't matter now. With Clarice out of commission, my drug investigation is dead in the water."

Disappointment rocked me. "Clarice. It always comes back to my sister. I can't believe she's indispensable to you."

"She's spent the last six months infiltrating the drug ring. Tonight was supposed to be the big finale."

"Your entire investigation hinges on my whack-job sister? That's incredibly poor planning."

"Clarice gained the confidence of the drug ring members. Without her, we don't have an in."

This entire conversation was so absurd. We were zooming down the highway like a hot needle with a burning thread. The fate of the entire free world depended on my screw-up sister. A bizarre suggestion popped into my head and out of my mouth. "So use me. I'll do whatever she was supposed to do."

His Adam's apple jumped. "My wife doesn't dance with other men."

My heart warmed in spite of his brusque tone. He called me his wife. For a moment I thought I'd morphed into the Anti-Christ. "Clarice's undercover job is to dance with men? I know how to dance."

"She meets with the four men from the photos. She's become their mascot out at the truck stop."

"Wait a minute. Everyone in town knows Clarice works for Daddy. How come she's accepted into the bad guy gang?"

"She wears a red wig and calls herself Candy Apple."

When we were little girls playing dress up in Grandma Dee's old clothes, I'd been Delta Dawn and Clarice had been Candy Apple. I was well aware of how Candy Apple moved and thought. I dug an ink pen out of my purse and held it like it was a cigarette. In my best Mae West throaty voice, I drawled, "What's a gal gotta do to get a drink round these parts? Sell her soul?"

"You've got her voice down, but the answer is no. These people have already killed once."

His protest made no sense. He was willing to risk Clarice's neck, but not mine? How dedicated was he to getting bad guys off the street? "You'd rather sulk about six months worth of field work going down the tube, than let me step in and help? Talk about stubborn. You take the cake."

"There's always a chance Clarice could come around and be available for work tonight."

"You know good and well Clarice is going to milk this for all it's worth. She'll have the entire hospital staff hopping to her every whim. Let me help. Tell me how the set-up works."

He held his silence for a long moment. "Clarice goes into the truck stop, flirts outrageously with every man out there, but especially with our four drug kingpins. They keep buying her drinks and then they forget she's not one of them. We're listening in."

"You are? How?"

"Clarice wears a concealed wire under her blouse."

"You never had any high tech spyware when you were sheriff."

"The GBI has the works, but I have to turn the electronics in every time I sign them out."

I nodded as he pulled in the Emergency Room parking lot. "Those systems must be very valuable."

"They are. I was removing Clarice's wire when she decided to kiss me."

His words settled on me like nuclear fallout, burning my skin, filling me with panic. I quickly connected the dots.

Clarice's wire was under her blouse. He had to turn the wire in every day. With a few drinks in her, Clarice would have enjoyed tormenting Hadley by being uncooperative about removing the wire.

I hung my head. The man I'd vowed to trust, I'd given him nothing but doubts and accusations. I hadn't witnessed him fondling Clarice. "You never groped my sister?"

"Nope."

"Why didn't you tell me?"

"I tried all week, but you wouldn't listen."

"The investigation—"

"I couldn't jeopardize blowing it this close."

The world outside my window came into focus. Thin blades of parking lot grass rippled in the breeze. He was right. I hadn't listened to him. But I was changing all that. I laid my hand on his shoulder. "I'm listening now."

Chapter Thirty

As the afternoon shadows lengthened, Hadley switched off the ignition. "You're gonna make me say mushy stuff, aren't you?"

I made no move to unbuckle my seatbelt. I needed and dreaded hearing whatever he had to say. Though we sat motionless in the hospital parking lot, I had the sensation of tumbling head over heels through outer space. "A woman likes to hear mushy stuff every once in a while."

Hadley stared through the steering wheel at the instrument panel like it was the most fascinating thing he'd ever seen. There'd been moments this past week when I'd wanted to tear him limb from limb for betraying me. Now that we'd both calmed down, we needed to talk past the hurt.

Seconds ticked away. Out of the corner of my eye I saw Ted hurrying into the Emergency Room. Ted's deep concern for Clarice was a problem. But I couldn't worry about Ted now. Not with my future with Hadley on the line.

My hand ached. I realized I had a death grip on the armrest and forcibly relaxed my fingers. Emotions played across Hadley's face like a fast moving summer squall, and my tough gal stance wavered. I loved him. He loved me. He loved Jimbo. I should let him off the hook. I cleared my throat. "Hadley—"

He waved his hand in the air. "Don't make it easy for me."

When he turned to face me, I saw him clearly for the first time in days. Dark circles rimmed his doleful eyes. Deep lines bracketed his mouth. His broad shoulders looked as if they'd been bowed by a heavy load.

Sadness filled his gaze. "I hurt you, and I'm sorry for that," he stated quietly. "If I could erase that moment from history, I would. But I can't change what's done. All I can do is reassure you that it wasn't what it seemed. I made a mistake and kissed your sister, but I have no romantic feelings for Clarice. It was a mistake. I've been miserable this past week, knowing you were considering divorce. You wouldn't talk to me. All I could do was throw myself into my work, and now that's messed up, too. I need to know where we stand." He drew in a ragged breath. "I need to know you forgive me."

Nothing could erase the memory of him kissing my sister. That horrific scene was permanently engraved in my brain. But I realized, no, I now *accepted* the truth. My sister's twisted logic and jealousy had spawned the kiss. All that remained was for me to reconcile my heart and my head. "I want to forgive you."

At the hesitation in my voice, he cocked an eyebrow at me.

Hadley had to be thinking of how he'd laid his heart on the line for me. He'd only done that twice before. The first time was when he asked me to marry him. The second was when Jimbo was born. Now he wanted my forgiveness.

"This isn't easy for me either," I said. "My affections don't swing like a pendulum. I believed what I saw. I was there. You kissed Clarice. Your hand was under her shirt."

"She kissed me. And I explained—I was removing her wire."

"You didn't try very hard to convince me of that at the time."

"You were throwing everything that wasn't nailed down at me. Plus, I was guilty, so I let you."

"But now you don't feel so guilty?"

"Now I know I can't live without you."

My hand clutched my heart. I tried to speak, but no words came out.

"Do you love me, Molls?"

The despair in his ragged voice was real. I believed he loved me. I believed it with my whole heart. I wanted this rift to be healed. I wanted our old life back. I could certainly try forgiveness.

Still unable to speak, I nodded.

The light returned to his eyes, and the grim lines eased around his mouth. He leaned across the center console, his breath warm on my skin. "Kiss and make up?"

I gave him a peck on the cheek, the kind of kiss he should've given Clarice. "I should make you suffer, after all you've put me through."

"We're more than even, Molls. I went through hell, too." A slow fire warmed his eyes. He reached for me.

When his lips closed on mine, I didn't think of anything else for a while. Hadley could be very persuasive when he put his mind to it.

The hurt receded from my heart. Though I didn't trust him implicitly, I wanted to trust my feelings for him. Weren't feelings more important than logic? Logic didn't keep me warm at night. Logic didn't make my blood hum. Hadley Darter did those things and more. I'd have to figure out the rest later.

Hadley's hands framed my face. "We're good?"

"Yeah." I gave a shaky laugh. "We're good."

After we locked the truck, Hadley clasped my hand, and it felt like old times. My step lightened, and my heart rallied. Warmth radiated up my arm.

I should feel guilty for feeling so good when Mama and Clarice were in the hospital, but I couldn't help it. I wanted to turn cartwheels.

I glimpsed Ted at the reception desk and stopped short on the sidewalk. I leaned into Hadley. "Did Daddy tell you about Ted?"

"He did. Because of the amount of money involved in Barbara Jean's estate, I've recommended Ted have a blood test to confirm his parentage."

"Ted won't like that."

Hadley's eyes chilled me with their cop intensity. "Ted is a person of interest in Barbara Jean's murder. He's known for some time that Barbara Jean was his birth mother, but he sat on the information until he benefited financially. That's highly suspicious behavior if you ask me."

Loyalty compelled me to defend my boss. "I've spent a lot of time working with Ted at the paper. He isn't a murderer."

"If Ted isn't the killer, we need to come up with another viable suspect fast. Otherwise, Otis won't look any further than Joe. Or Lila."

The thought of my parents being imprisoned was abhorrent. They didn't belong in jail, but who did? I should be able to figure this puzzle out, but I couldn't piece the extraneous facts together by myself. I needed help from someone with real investigative experience. "How do the drugs fit into the murder?"

With his hand on the small of my back, Hadley propelled me forward into the bright lights. "When we know the answer to that, we'll have our killer."

Chapter Thirty-One

"Miz Campbell is right in here," the plump nurse said as she pulled aside the curtain to Clarice's cubicle.

Hadley and I joined Ted at the foot of Clarice's hospital bed. Monitors beeped. A plastic sleeve was clipped on Clarice's fingertip. In spite of knocking herself out cold, Clarice had the appearance of a fashion model. Her picture perfect makeup and softly curling hair were probably the envy of every woman in this hospital. She looked so serene, so composed. I knew better. This was Clarice, after all.

"How is she?" I asked.

Ted rubbed the back of his neck. "No change. She's still out cold."

Clarice had to be faking. She hadn't fallen that hard. I nudged her sheet-covered foot. "Clarice, can you hear me? You won the lottery, only you have to claim the prize tonight."

Clarice's long, thick lashes stirred, renewing my faith in her acting ability. "I won the lottery?"

"You won the get-out-of-hospital-free card," I said. I was glad she was okay, really I was, but Clarice wouldn't lift a finger to help Hadley tonight, not when she had an entire medical team waiting on her hand and foot.

Clarice struggled to sit up and failed, collapsing with a theatrical moan. I eyed her closely. I'd heard that exact moan when she played Juliet one summer for the Campbell version of the Shakespearean tragedy for our parents. Actually I'd heard that moan day and night for most of the summer as she worked to get it right. Nice to know she hadn't wasted all that effort.

Taking my acting cue from her, I leaned in close, patting her shoulder in sympathy, pitching my voice low. "Stay put, sis. These hospital folks want to run a few tests on you, to see if you have a concussion. Your key still in the same place?"

Her heavily mascaraed eyelashes fluttered to almost closed. She answered in a strong whisper. "Why do you need my key?"

"I'm helping Hadley tonight."

Clarice's eyes rounded. "Oh?"

I didn't appreciate the questioning look she sent Hadley. This undercover job had definitely put ideas in Clarice's head where he was concerned. He'd be wise to leave her out of his future investigations. In fact, I would insist on that very thing.

"Hello. I'm still in the room," Ted said. "You don't need to keep secrets from me, now that I'm family and all."

I opened my mouth to answer him, but Hadley stopped me by wrapping his arm around my shoulder and tucking me close to his side. I got his message loud and clear. Ted wasn't to know what we were doing.

"Clarice has some things I need on my current case over at her place," Hadley said. "With all of the excitement today, I didn't get finished up with today's work. Molly has agreed to pitch in tonight, since her sister is detained."

"I don't know about Molly working two jobs." Ted frowned. "Doesn't your contract say you can only work for me?"

Was his concern for my ability to meet his editorial deadlines or was there an ulterior motive behind his question? I hated the suspicion that colored my thoughts where he was concerned. "I don't have a contract with you, Ted. You said contracts were for wimps."

"Yeah, but I knew you were family. Besides, you're the most truthful person I know."

He'd known we were related for years. Interesting. And sneaky. I didn't like being deceived one bit. I felt like I needed a few hours to mentally review all of our past conversations and interpret them in this new light.

I stared at my boss. "Got a news flash for you, Ted. Relatives are the last people you should trust."

Ted seemed to consider the double meaning of that nugget of wisdom, and then nodded in our direction. "Good to see you two worked things out."

My cheeks heated. "We are a work in progress, and I don't want to jinx anything by talking about it." I glanced down. Clarice was drinking in every word under her lowered lashes. "Clarice appears to be in good hands. We'll head over to check on Mama. Give us a call when you get discharged, and we'll pick you up."

"I'll take her home," Ted offered.

Hadley reached around me and shook Ted's hand. "Good deal."

We walked down the tiled corridor to cubicle seven where Mama was billeted. She was wired to the gills, with twice as many monitors flashing and beeping. Daddy huddled at her bedside. He looked up at our approach. "How's Clarice?"

Poor Daddy. Technically he had to return to the jail as soon as he left the hospital. He must feel like his world was coming apart. I leaned close, hugged him, and whispered my reply. "Clarice has regained consciousness. They suspect she has a concussion, and they're going to run a few tests. What about Mama? What did the doctors say?"

Mama opened her eyes and fixed me with a frigid glare. "They say I'm doing great for a coot my age. It was my silly heart acting up."

Mama's heart trouble had kept her out of serious manual labor for most of her life. We'd tried to get her to have it fixed, but she was having nothing of that. The only person better at getting out of work than Mama was Clarice. That apple didn't fall far from the tree.

Daddy patted Mama's hand as the heart monitor blipped in the background. "She's going to be fine."

The concern in his eyes tore at my heart and added to my confusion. If he cared so deeply for Mama, what was he doing with Barbara Jean? I didn't understand men at all.

Some of my frustration must have reached my eyes. Hadley squeezed my fingers in warning.

Or was he urging me to say something? I glanced over at him, and he nodded toward my mother. Okay, he expected me to speak. He didn't want me to talk about Ted being Daddy's son, but that was all I could think about. That and Daddy sleeping with another woman before and during his marriage to Mama.

"Molly's sorry for upsetting you, Lila," Hadley said.

Oh. Yeah, I should play nice and make up. I bowed my head in contrition. "I am sorry, Mama."

"You should be. I wouldn't be stuck here in the hospital if it weren't for you."

My spine stiffened at her barb. Same as it had when she told me that I had to allow for Clarice's teenage laziness. We wouldn't be in this mess today if Clarice had been held to the same standards I'd had to abide by every day of my life. My back teeth ground together.

Hadley leaned down and kissed Mama's cheek. "Since your condition seems stable, Lila, we have some work to finish. Joe, call us if there's any change."

I also kissed Mama's cheek, but it was all I could do not to stomp out of there. Conscious of the don't-air-dirty-laundry-in-public rule of the Campbell clan, I held my tongue until we sat in Hadley's truck. "She couldn't wait to light into me," I said.

"She's honest. That's what you value above everything, right?"

I groaned in frustration. "For the next fifty years, Mama will lord this over me as the time I put her in the hospital. And you know what? She's known for ages that Daddy cheated on her. She told me as much a few days ago, when she told me to overlook you and Clarice, so don't go telling me what to do. She's playing us, same as Clarice."

"You didn't think much of her advice, did you?"

I shook my head. "She's wrong. Fidelity matters. Look what happened when Daddy cheated on Mama with Barbara Jean. Ted appears to be Daddy's love child."

"Joe and Barbara Jean were lovers. Barbara Jean is dead."

"She was murdered. Big difference."

"And if Otis reasons out Lila's motive, she will be arrested, too. Jealousy is a powerful motive for homicide."

"But Mama wouldn't have used a drug to kill anyone. She'd have ruined them socially and run them out of town." As I spoke, it occurred to me that had already happened years ago. Barbara Jean had left town under a cloud as a teen, and to some extent, the powers-that-be had been mounting a campaign to have the nudists expelled from the county by raising their taxes. Had Mama been behind the scene pulling strings all this time?

She cared deeply about her prized begonias, about her antique furniture, and about her family's reputation. She'd fight like a cornered grizzly bear if someone threatened her personal empire.

But murder? Had she taken Daddy's sinus medicine and slipped it into Barbara Jean's coffee? That seemed unlikely when Barbara Jean had given up coffee. And my mother and Barbara Jean weren't friendly enough to share a cup of coffee.

A couple hurried out of the ER. The man's limping gait and his cadaver-thin physique brought his name to mind. He was Judge Humphrey, one of the drug kingpins and one of Barbara Jean's recent lovers. The rounded woman in earth-toned flowing garb also looked familiar, but I couldn't place her. I tapped Hadley's arm. "Who's that with the judge?"

Hadley studied them for a moment. "The better question is, who are they visiting in the hospital? The judge should be home right now, getting ready for his fun evening with his pals and Candy Apple at the Truck Stop."

"You know his schedule that well?"

"The man is like clockwork. He doesn't deviate from his routine one iota."

"Maybe he had a sick relative."

"His kids and grandkids live in Atlanta. His wife is dead. His drug buddies are his life."

Humphrey and the woman got into a low-slung charcoal gray convertible. The judge buckled himself in, but the woman tipped her head back, laughing ebulliently at some private joke. When they roared off in the deepening twilight, the woman raised her arms in a victory salute, her white blonde hair whipping around her cherubic face.

I'd seen that face before. Only, where? I'd been so many places lately everything was running together. She hadn't been at the jail. Or at the produce stand. Or the newspaper office. But her face haunted me.

Her face. That was it. I did know her face, but not the rest of her body because last time I'd seen her she'd been naked. Judge Humphrey was hanging out with one of the nudists. Tildy Smith to be exact. The woman who had "discovered" Barbara Jean's dead body in the woods.

She'd been thrilled about her hospital visit. What was her role in all of this? Had she taken over Barbara Jean's male clients? It didn't look like she was blackmailing the judge. Their behavior indicated that they were friends, which led to more questions about their relationship.

Hadley had been right. His drug ring connected to the nudist colony murder. But we still needed proof. That's why I was dressing up as Candy Apple tonight. I'd get that proof and put the killer in jail. Doing so would keep my parents out of jail.

The bad guys were on the move, and we were in the dark.

But not for long.

The tide had turned.

Chapter Thirty-Two

Behind my locked bathroom door, I dressed in the skimpy clothing I'd borrowed from Clarice. Her ultra-padded push-up bra had done wonders for my breasts. I shimmied into a fluorescent green outfit that clung to me like a second skin. The short-short skirt skimmed my bare butt cheeks, the plunging neckline revealed everything but my nipples. Thanks to the miracle of spandex, my narrow waist was evident, showcasing my hour-glass figure.

With the red wig, heavy makeup, and stiletto heels, I was Candy Apple, plus I felt sexy as all-get-out. With a final wink at the mirror, I opened the door and sashayed into the bedroom where Hadley waited. I gave him my best come-and-get-it look, lacing my husky voice with a breezy flirtiness. "Whatcha packing, sailor?"

Hadley's gaze heated with desire. He tackled me, tumbling us both down on the bed. My thong went flying, as did the miniature spandex outfit. I caught his excitement and tugged at his clothes. Urgency fueled our actions. Yes, my body sighed. This was what I needed. I gave myself up to delicious sensations and let him have his way with me.

Later, after he caught his breath, he supported himself on one elbow and scowled down at me. "Seriously,

Mrs. Darter, you aren't going anywhere dressed like that."

My inner vixen had been released. "Think again. This is the big night, remember? You said you needed Candy Apple to charm the truck stop four tonight."

"Every man who sees you in this rig will have the same reaction I had. I can't protect you from the parking lot."

"Clarice dresses like this for her play-acting role. Don't I look the part?"

"You look hot. And available. I don't want my wife looking like every man's fantasy."

My grin stretched from ear to ear. All week long I'd felt asexual. For him to jump me like that confirmed I still had sex appeal.

I lifted up from my pillow to kiss him. "Hadley, that's the sweetest thing you've ever said to me." I dressed slowly, with exaggerated undulations for my rapt audience of one. I felt saucy, and encouraged that my life was finally back on track. Helping Hadley tonight would further mend the breach between us, and it would aid both investigations. Definitely a win-win situation for both of us.

From the bed, Hadley groaned. "You're killing me, Molls." He stomped off to hop in a cold shower.

I hummed inside and out. Life was good.

*　　*　　*　　*

The whine of tires on asphalt carried through the open truck window near the interstate interchange. Travelers on the busy north-south route wouldn't exit at our tiny town this time of night unless they were desperate. Who could blame them? Marshview rolled up its sidewalks at five p.m.

Except for Twin Willows Truck Stop. Judging by the overflowing parking lot of big rigs, pickups, and dark sedans, it was a happening place. A single male parked nearby and hurried inside. The door to the bar opened and closed, a sharp blast of foot-tapping music blaring into the parking lot.

The time was a little after ten. Despite my earlier bravado, I had definite reservations about my upcoming performance as Candy Apple. It was one thing to seduce my husband in the privacy of our bedroom, but he already lusted for my body. Could I really enthrall a room full of men? Wouldn't I do or say something to mark me as a boring married woman?

My stomach twisted and turned like a berserk roller coaster ride, the knot in my throat made it hard to breathe. I concentrated on filling my lungs with air.

With the aid of a flashlight, Hadley made one last adjustment to his electronic control panel on the center console. "Say something."

I dropped my chin and spoke to my chest. "Test one, two, three."

"Don't look down. Folks will think you're wearing a wire."

"You mean women aren't supposed to go around looking at their own breasts?" I cupped my plumped up breasts. "I can't believe Clarice walks around like this on a daily basis. I feel like a meat counter."

Hadley scowled. "You better not be touching anyone else's meat. Anyone lays a hand on you, I'll be all over them like shrimp on grits."

I waggled a finger at him. "You better rein in those macho thoughts. I'm here to catch you a drug kingpin, and hopefully flush out a murderer. I can't do my job if you go caveman on me."

He looked contrite, and guilt assailed me. It was easier to fuss at him than to acknowledge my own fears. He couldn't help that he was hard-wired to protect me. Aside from me exposing a great deal of my skin, I wasn't in imminent danger tonight. After all, Clarice had played the role of Candy Apple night after night, and nothing had happened. There was no reason to believe that this round would be any different.

Even so, a part of me was fearful, no matter how I rationalized my actions. And that fear made me mad. Because in this instance, I wasn't meeting the standard Clarice had set.

My sister had always been afraid of things. As kids, I'd been the one to taunt the ghosts in Grandma Dee's house. I'd been the one to slide down the steep bluff on a plastic tray. I'd been the one to poke the dead frog to see if his legs still worked.

Clarice had been bold in other ways. She'd emerged from the womb thinking the world revolved around her, so maybe she approached this acting job the same way. She wouldn't be overwhelmed by a roomful of ogling males. She would expect their attention. No, she'd demand their attention.

Hmm. That felt right. If I was pretending to be Clarice, I darn well better pretend that I expected masculine attention.

Hadley massaged my clenched fists open. "You all right?"

I lowered my eyelashes the way Clarice did and roughened up my voice. "I'm fine, sugah. The finest kind."

Hadley blinked in astonishment at the way my tongue flickered along my lower lip.

His bafflement bolstered my flagging courage. Clarice was onto something with this masculine teasing. It sure added zest to my sex life. I'd do well to remember this lesson in the privacy of our bedroom. But for now, God willing, I'd see about enthralling drug dealers and a murderer.

I opened the door and slid out of Hadley's red pickup. "Don't you worry your little head about a thing. Candy Apple is on the case."

With that, I sauntered off toward the blinking neon lights.

Chapter Thirty-Three

Honky-tonk music rolled over me like an eighteen wheeler when I entered Twin Willows Truck Stop Lounge. My gut reaction was to cover my ears and grimace, but Clarice, no Candy Apple, wouldn't do that. She'd dance to the beat.

So that's what I did. I leaned into the vaguely familiar looking muscle-bound, shaved head guy guarding the door. "How you doing tonight, sugah?" I purred in his ear.

He leered at my chest. "Doing all right now that you're here, Miz Candy."

I chuckled deep in my throat, wishing I could remember his name. I was certain he'd been a few years behind me in school. "Don't you let any bad boys in this door. I'm counting on you to keep this place safe."

His eyes reluctantly left my chest, fixating on my glossy red lips. "You can count on me, ma'am."

I waggled my tail like an excited puppy, and then I sashayed toward the bar, keeping my chin high. "Hey there, big fella," I said to one hulking guy who blocked my way. "Where you from?"

"Tennessee. My name's Joe Dog Brownley, ma'am, and you're 'bout the purtiest thing I ever did see."

He laid a beefy palm on my arm about an inch from my plumped up breast, and my body tensed like a piano wire. I wanted to knee him something fierce.

The big guy from the door rushed to my rescue, knocking the guy's hand away. "Nobody touches Miz Candy."

Joe Dog's face fell.

I felt sorry for him. "Tell you what. You can buy me a drink, Joe Dog. I'm mighty parched." I glanced up at the bouncer, and wonder of wonders, his name popped into my head. "Thanks, Bud. You're the best."

Bud nodded to the wiry female bartender. "Sally, a glass of champagne for the lady."

His request took care of my not knowing the bartender's name or what Candy preferred to drink. I should've known Clarice would go for something over the top like champagne. It was the one beverage I had absolutely no tolerance for. I could knock back shots of Jack Daniels in a pinch, but I'd always been a cheap champagne drunk. I didn't have to drink it, though, I could pretend to sip it. After all, pretending was the reason I was here.

I sidled up to the bar, Joe Dog on my heels, and accepted my drink. "Thank you, Sally. You're a doll."

Sally's startled expression told me I'd messed up. Too late, I realized Clarice wouldn't have thanked a woman for service. She would have taken and taken from everyone.

Joe Dog plunked down a twenty for my drink. "Keep the change," I told Sally.

Mesmerized by acres of my white breast meat, Joe Dog nodded his agreement. Sally whisked the money away and kept her mouth shut. I took stock of the bar patrons. Clusters of people dotted the tables in the center of the room. Singles lined the bar. A few couples danced on the postage stamp dance floor off to the side, and my party was ensconced in the rear booth.

I ran the gauntlet at the bar first, introducing myself

and Joe Dog. "How y'all doing?" I asked each man. Most flirted back, increasing my confidence. One guy told me to go away.

I leaned into Joe Dog as we moved away from the grump. "He's not the friendly type, is he?"

His cheeks flamed at my closeness. He shot a glance over at Bud and lifted his hands in surrender, as if to say he didn't invade my personal space. "No, ma'am."

"You're too cute, Joe Dog."

I worked the tables, managing to unobtrusively spill most of my champagne. By the time I started on the row of booths, I sent Joe Dog off to refill my empty glass. I quieted my nerves and poured on the charm. And the breasts. Finally, I reached the rear booth.

"How you fellas doing tonight?" I leaned over their tabletop using my plunging neckline as crab bait. Sure enough, this natural lure caught their eyes.

Gil Beasley, the charismatic preacher, sputtered beer in mid-swallow, spraying Deputy Marvel at his side.

Noah Marvel wiped at his wet polo shirt, and then punched Beasley's shoulder. "Cut that out."

Mayor Wayne Frye had two empty shot glasses in front of him. How shocking. He hadn't taken a drink in years. Not since his three-year-old son wandered off and drowned in four inches of creek water. He patted his lap, light glinting off his thick eyeglasses. "Come sit with me, Candy girl."

His wife would bust him good if she knew what he was doing. Both for drinking and for cutting up on her. Mrs. Mayor took her civic duty personally and held herself above reproach. Wayne had always seemed to be faking his goodwill and civic-mindedness. Tonight's discovery proved he was a fraud. He didn't deserve the public's trust.

Cadaverous Judge Humphrey sat in the back corner. Muted light glistened off his bald head. Four empty shot glasses sat in front of him, but his sharp eyes missed nothing. I had the distinct feeling he was the brains of this operation.

"Wasn't expecting you tonight, toots," the judge said.

His comment rattled my nerves. He'd been at the hospital with Tildy. Had he put it together that Clarice was Candy? If he thought Clarice/Candy was out of commission, would that alter his plans to move the drugs tonight? I tamped down my fears. Plenty of time to worry later. Right now I had a job to do, and that included finding out the inner workings of the drug operation.

I wedged myself into the booth next to the mayor and leaned across him, fluttering my eyelashes like I had sand stuck in my eye. "Why ever not? Don't you pine for me when I'm not here?"

Gil Beasley nodded like a bobble-head doll, sweat glistening on his shiny brow. "We sure do, gal. You sure light up a room."

Joe Dog returned with my glass of champagne. I gestured broadly toward the tabletop. "Set it down right here. You boys know my new best friend, Joe Dog?"

The men grumbled, and shook hands with hulking Joe Dog.

"Wanna dance?" Beasley asked over the thumping music.

I liked the perkiness of this number, and the little bit of champagne I'd sipped seemed to have loosened my tight hold on my inhibitions. No question in my mind that Clarice would have strutted out on the dance floor without reservation. "Thought you'd never ask."

Beasley beamed as he slid out of the booth. He went to touch the small of my back and Joe Dog stepped up. "No one touches Candy."

"Call off your hound, sweet thing," Beasley said, through clenched teeth.

"It's okay, Joe Dog," I said with a flutter of eyelashes. "Gil here is an old friend."

I pranced through the tables to the tiny dance floor, praying I didn't ad-lib my way into trouble. I knew how to dance and I knew how Clarice danced. What I didn't know was how Candy danced. I figured she'd maximize all her assets, something I'd never quite done before.

The cheating lyrics washed over me, and I started stepping to the beat. I shimmied my curves like a woman possessed, letting it all hang out, and prayed to the gods of spandex that nothing essential would break or snap. If Hadley had any idea of how suggestively I was gyrating, he'd rush in here and pull the plug on the whole investigation. I was on a steep learning curve.

That forbidden element lent a dash of excitement and quieted my nerves. I gave myself up to the music and let go. My smile became genuine. I shouldn't worry so much. Having fun was so much better than worrying.

I snaked my way around the floor, conscious of Beasley trailing along behind me, and of the questions in his eyes. Something I was doing wasn't quite right, but what?

The song ended and I flashed him a thousand watt smile. "You cut quite a rug, big fella."

He reeled me into his arms as the fiddle music swelled around us. Great. I didn't want to slow dance with him, but I didn't have much choice. We fit together like hand and glove, his parts hard and lean, mine thickly padded. I tried not to gag at his nearness. He smelled wrong, and he felt wrong.

I wished it was Hadley holding me.

Gil's heated lips brushed my ear. "You're on quite a tear tonight, Candy. Trying to make me jealous by flirting with every man here?"

I hated him holding me this closely. I pushed against his broad chest and spun some lies. "Now Gil, you know a fun-loving woman like me is death to your holy reputation. Twin Willows is the only place you can be seen with me. You think I wait in the closet for these brief glimpses of heaven?"

"Baby, things aren't looking good for the church gig.

I've been thinking we should hop in my van and drive on down the coast, see where the road leads us."

I stopped dancing and poked him in the chest with my pointer finger. "Ain't no way I'm running off with a man unless he's got a cool million or more."

"Cut it out. You want them to see us fighting?" He guided me back into his arms and shuffled us slowly around the dance floor. "I'll have the money. Don't you worry your pretty little head about that."

"Give me a time table. I can't pick up and leave without any notice."

"Two days. My ship comes in two days from now."

"You're not toying with me, are ya? That would break my little ole heart if you turned out to be a liar like the rest of these clowns in here."

"I swear on my mother's grave. Me and the fellas is putting together a deal." He nodded over to his companions in the booth. They were all leaning in close, deep in conversation.

I hoped I wasn't missing something big. Hadley would kill me if I danced away this golden opportunity. I needed to get back over to the booth and find out what was happening in the next two days. This was just the info Hadley needed.

Joe Dog hovered at the edge of the dance floor, holding my thin champagne flute in his beefy palm. From their earlier reaction to Joe Dog's presence, the fab four didn't like Joe Dog hanging around their booth. No way would they talk freely in his presence. I had to get rid of him. I needed a plan, fast.

My gaze caught on the sassy, pony-tailed brunette dancing with the bald man in a Harley T-shirt. Erin something. Erin Henry, the waitress from the Calabash diner. If I set Joe Dog up with Erin, he wouldn't be so focused on me. As the song wound down, I stepped out of Gil Beasley's clutches and fanned my face. "I declare, I'm parched from all this exercise."

I made a beeline for Erin, tapping her on her shoulder as I drew near. "See that guy over there?" I pointed to Joe Dog. "He's got a thing for you, but he's too shy to do anything about it. Come on and I'll introduce you two. Why don't you ask him to dance?"

Erin seemed surprised that I'd spoken to her. "Sure, Candy."

So she was a regular here, or at least she knew who I was supposed to be. I snagged my champagne out of Joe Dog's hand and made introductions. Sure enough, Erin linked her arm through his and dragged Joe Dog out of the dance floor. Joe Dog sent me a look of pure masculine frustration that had me laughing hysterically.

"What's the joke?" Gil asked.

"I'm feeling on top of the world tonight. You and me are gonna take your cool million and get out of this one-horse town."

Alarm flared across his face. "You tell anyone our plan, and the deal is off. If the fellas knew I was planning to skip town, no telling what they'd do to me."

I sidled up to him. "It'll be our little secret."

We threaded our way back to the booth. I took Gil's seat in the booth. He straddled a spare chair.

"Don't you two look pleased with yourselves," the mayor said.

"Dancing always does a girl's heart good," I answered, sipping at my champagne. The bubbles tickled my nose.

The conversation lulled. I couldn't learn any secrets if they weren't talking. I squared my shoulders, thrusting my main assets in deputy Marvel's direction. Everyone in town knew of his sweet tooth. "You been dreaming about Candy's Apples?"

Noah Marvel turned beet red. I almost felt sorry for him. Then I remembered he was a nasty drug pusher and possibly a murderer.

"I got me a fierce longing for some of them apples,"

he answered fervently. His gaze zeroed in on my chest.

"How about you, judge? You in the mood for some candied apples tonight?"

"Gal, you the biggest flirt I've ever seen. Every man in this room wants to ride that ass of yours."

"You play your cards right, and this may be your lucky night."

"We're playing cards?" Marvel blinked rapidly at the other men. "Deal me in."

"No cards tonight, braino," the judge answered. "We're out enjoying the mighty fine scenery."

"You said I could choose the game next time," Noah whined. "You said I could run the boat this time. You ain't changing the plan, are ya?"

I didn't know whether I should jump back in the conversation, or let it take its natural course. What would Clarice have done? She wouldn't be a wallflower. "I hate riding in boats. My hair gets all tangled up."

"I'll untangle it for you," Gil said from my elbow.

"I bet you would." I sipped my champagne. "But the mayor is such a take-charge kind of guy, maybe I'd let him help me with my hair. Would you do that, Mr. Mayor? Would you take care of me on our boat ride?"

Wayne Frye seemed stunned by the sweep of my fake eyelashes and the dazzling white skin plumped up on my chest. I was certain his wife, one of Mama's good friends, would gut him from head to toe if she had any idea he was looking at another woman's breasts.

"I get to drive the boat," Marvel said.

"No one is driving the boat just yet," the judge said. "Our plans have to remain fluid."

As the music faded away, I noticed my glass was empty. Oops, I hadn't meant to actually drink the champagne. I turned the glass upside down. "All done. I win the prize."

Gil rose. "I'll get you a refill."

"Get her a good one," the judge said. "Get us all

refills."

"Yeah," I added. "No more of this cheap crap. Break out the expensive stuff."

"Would you really go on a boat ride with me, Miss Candy?" the mayor asked.

The wistful note in his voice worried me. Maybe the reason he was cutting up so bad was because his wife was mean to him. If he had a woman who understood him, maybe she'd set him on the straight and narrow path.

Not that I was attracted to the mayor, or any of these guys. My interest laid elsewhere, a long lanky man with soul-piercing eyes. I sank back into my seat, glowing with love for my guy. Then I realized the men were waiting for my response. For Candy's response about the boat ride.

This whole situation felt so contrived. To think that these men, three of whom I'd known all my life, didn't know who I really was. It made me want to laugh and laugh. All they saw was my breasts. None of them had even looked closely at my made-up face. "I could wear a scarf around my hair, like the movie stars do."

"I'd rather you didn't," Mayor Wayne said. "I'd like to see you sitting on the bow of my boat, your hair blowing wild and free."

I had a sudden vision of the gal silhouetted on big rig tire flaps. Lots of tits and ass on that girl. I twisted to the side and imitated her pose, arching my back until it was shaped like a backward 'C.'

Marvel hooted and clapped his hands. "Yeah girl. That's what we like."

So did the other men in the bar who'd caught a glimpse of my privates. Hadley wouldn't like that. But he wasn't here. I straightened up and smiled at the men I was deceiving. I was putting my ass on the line, and I was doing things my way.

Gil returned with a tray full of booze. Beer for him and Marvel, shots for the mayor and the judge. I took a healthy swig of my bubbling champagne.

The judge lifted his glass, and everyone followed suit. "To the plan," he said.

Glasses clinked. "The plan," everyone echoed.

The mayor and the judge downed their shots in one gulp. Gil sipped his beer slowly while Marvel sucked the foam off the top of his. I slurped more champagne.

I tried to get the conversation back on track. "So when is this boat ride? Are we going tonight? Will it be a moonlit boat ride?"

The judge's face thinned even more. "Don't you worry about the boat ride. You'll have the ride of your life."

His voice sounded too slow, like an audio recording at the wrong speed. The lights of the bar blurred and sharpened. I shook my head to clear it. I shouldn't have drunk any champagne. Why couldn't Candy Apple drink beer or shots?

My limbs weighed a ton, my eyes felt gritty. I needed to splash water on my face or I was going to blow this investigation. "Pardon me fellas, I gotta hit the head."

The room spun when I stood. Gil steadied my arm to keep me from busting my ass. "Let me help you, Candy."

"Appreciate it," I managed, my syllables slurring together. "The room's a little tippy."

Gil cinched me close to his side. Somehow, I walked across the dance floor, but I'd never been so tired in my life. Not even after sixteen hours of labor when I gave birth to Jimbo. Numbness crept down my legs, my arms, and my throat. All I could think of was going to sleep.

My eyes drifted closed.

I tried to make sense of my altered reactions, but my thoughts weren't connecting. One word bullets fired through my mental fog. Frazzled. Exhausted. Numb. Sleep. Need. Sleep.

Fresh air hit my face, momentarily rousing me from my stupor. The world twirled and I realized Gil had picked me up. I tried to lift my arms, to say a word of protest, but

I was powerless.

Warning bells clamored inside my head.

I'd been drugged.

Gil had drugged my champagne.

Gil, the man I'd made fake plans to run away with. Had he been laughing at my play-acting ability all night? Had he known from the start that I wasn't Candy Apple? Was he going to kill me?

My eyelids drifted shut again.

It was too late to even whisper a warning to Hadley.

It was too late for anything.

Chapter Thirty-Four

"She knows too much. I say we kill her," an angry voice insisted.

"Killing's too good for her," a rougher voice said. "I say we shoot her full of junk for a week and drop her off in a red light district of Miami. That'll teach her to mess with us."

Fragments of conversation penetrated my slumber, shocking me out of my warm cocoon of sleep. My unease grew with each beat of my heart. Why was my mind so groggy?

"I wanna screw her first."

"Nobody's screwing her. We gotta figure out what Darter knows."

The voices drifted away, and I became aware of my surroundings. Was it night? I squinted into the darkness.

The gentle slap of water against fiberglass added to my disorientation. The aromas of fish, tar, and diesel fuel permeated my sinuses, providing a clue to my location. I was on a boat.

A boat? Terror paralyzed my limbs. I blinked myself awake, but I couldn't find an object to focus on in the unrelenting blackness surrounding me. I craned my neck around, but I couldn't even see the nose on my face. The sky was wrong. Where were the stars?

My mouth wouldn't open. I tried to reach up and discover what was wrong, but my hand wouldn't lift. My limbs weighed a ton. I renewed my effort to raise my hand, only to learn that moving my hands moved my feet as well.

My pulse skittered. I was tied up.

I struggled against my bonds, but it was no use. What had happened to me? Why couldn't I gather my thoughts?

I was tied up. Hog-tied, with hands and ankles bound together. Not good. My breath came in short pants.

I fought back the scream in my throat and remained still. No telling what would happen if my captors knew I was awake. I needed to gather my wits. If I could get my bearings, I could figure out what was going on. Then I would get off this boat.

The taste of stale champagne lingered in my mouth. I didn't drink champagne. Where was I? Why couldn't I remember how I got here?

Memories paraded through my head. Daddy in jail. Mama and Clarice in the hospital. Hadley making love to me. I couldn't get a timeline going. Had those things happened today?

What day was it?

I didn't know. My head ached, my scalp itched, and my empty stomach rumbled. I was so sleepy I could barely keep my eyes open. It would be easy to close my eyes and forget this nightmare.

But I couldn't. I was a prisoner. On a boat. And in danger. That much I knew.

Was my kidnapping related to Hadley's work?

Or had I stumbled onto something while working on a newspaper story?

My mind was blank. All I could do was lay here and worry. Only my groggy brain wouldn't cooperate. I couldn't get a good worry going. My eyelids drifted shut again.

*   *   *   *

When I next awakened, the rumble of the diesel engines indicated we were underway. My mind seemed clearer. Wherever I had been, I was fixing to be somewhere else.

Would I become shark bait?

I wasn't ready to die. I had a boy to raise and a husband who needed me. My family needed me. I couldn't lay here and accept what had happened. I had to fight back.

My fingers curled into the irregular bedding underneath me. I felt knots. Bunches and bunches of fibrous knots. They were connected, like a mesh or webbing. Or a large net.

Awareness dawned. I was on a shrimp boat, most likely below deck. These powerful fishing trawlers ranged the entire Atlantic seaboard. I could be anywhere in the vast ocean.

How long had I been out? My watch. It glowed in the dark. I stared down in the vicinity of my hands, but I didn't seem to have my watch on. Strange. I always wore my watch.

And what the heck clothes did I have on? They didn't cover much of me. Where were my customary jeans and T-shirt?

God, why couldn't I remember?

Following a scraping sound, someone with a flashlight descended to my level. My fear mounted. Would this person be my executioner? I needed to hide.

I inched backward on the net.

"Good. You're awake," the person said.

I couldn't make out the person's features, but the higher register of the person's voice indicated a woman had spoken.

The light shone directly in my eyes. "I want answers," she said. "If you lie to me or aggravate me, I'll kill you where you lay. Got that?"

My heart pounded in my dry throat. I nodded. Survival was my goal. If I didn't screw up, I'd see my son again. I clung to that hope.

The woman leaned down and ripped the tape from my mouth. An anguished cry tore from my lips. She slapped me hard across the face. "Cut that out. You're annoying me."

My face throbbed. Tears massed in my eyes. I blinked against the bright light. Who was she? Why was I here?

"What does Hadley Darter know?" the woman asked.

That was a trick question. We'd been married for long enough that I knew I hadn't a clue what Hadley was thinking about anything.

When I didn't answer right away, her booted foot knocked the wind out of me. Instinctively, I hunched into a ball to protect my abdomen. I also caught sight of my skimpy lime green spandex outfit. These weren't my clothes. Why couldn't I remember anything?

"I don't know," I slurred out.

The light moved closer to my aching head. Would she use the flashlight to bash in my brains? She'd mentioned that she'd shoot me. Did she have a gun, too?

"What do you know?" the woman persisted.

"Where am I?" I asked.

She moved as if to wallop me with the flashlight. "I'll ask the questions here."

I cringed. "I can't remember anything. I swear that's the truth."

The woman swore inventively. "I told him to only use one roofie in your drink. He must've screwed up. Gil, drag your sorry ass down here."

Roofie? The date rape drug? Had I been raped? I couldn't tell.

Horror clawed at my gut. I wanted to go home right now. Where was Hadley when I needed him?

Another person descended the stairs with a dimmer light. It was dark above the stairs, so I assumed it was nighttime. But what day was it?

The woman cuffed Gil on the head. "How much did you put in her drink?"

"Only what you said, sis. I swear."

Sis? This pair was related?

I wracked my brain for Gils. The only Gil I could come up with was Gil Beasley, the new preacher in town. What would a minister be doing mixed up with a kidnapper?

If only my head would work.

Gil. I knew something about Gil Beasley. I'd seen a photo of him recently.

"She claims she can't remember nothing," the woman sneered.

Both lights beamed on my face. Gil knelt beside me, his hand lingered on my arm. "Come on, Candy girl. Tell us what we need to know."

Candy? I frowned. My name was Molly. Why did these people think my name was Candy? Did it have something to do with my odd get-up? I needed to satisfactorily answer their questions. But the only thing in my answer bank was more questions.

Gil seemed to like me. I tried to use that. "Turn me loose, Gil."

He gazed expectantly up at his sister. "She don't know nuttin', Til. Let me have her. Me and her's got big plans."

"She's playing you. She ain't who you think she is. God save me from stupid men. Flash a bit of tit in your face, and you're worthless." She yanked hard on my head, and then lifted something up to show him. "See? She's been playing you."

Gil's voice trembled. "Candy?"

I dug deep through the murk in my thoughts. I vaguely remembered dressing up in my sister's clothes and her wig. Clarice never would've let someone take her wig off. "Give me my hair back."

Tildy dropped the wig on the fishing net. "Take a good look at her, Gil. Her name isn't Candy."

Gil leaned close enough that I could see his nose hairs and the sheen of sweat on his brow. He recoiled. "It's Darter's wife. That newspaper reporter." Anger darkened his face. "Where's my Candy?"

His sister bopped him in the head again. She wore one of the shapeless shifts from the produce stand wardrobe. "You moron. There never was a Candy. Her sister has been playing you fools for weeks. Then when her sister got hurt today, this one took her place. Now you see why I don't leave any of the decisions up to you men? I have to constantly be on my guard."

Gil cowered. "I didn't know. I swear, I didn't know."

"You didn't know about Barbara Jean's curiosity either. That bitch almost ruined everything."

"Don't you talk about her like that. Barbara Jean was a saint."

"She was a whore. That's all she was. And she gave it away for free. I swear I can't trust nobody to keep their pants zipped."

I soaked in this heated exchange. I recognized the woman now. She was Tildy Smith from the nudist colony. She was Gil Beasley's sister, and she hated Barbara Jean.

Errant facts slid into my mind. Tildy was the one who'd found Barbara Jean's body. Barbara Jean had been murdered. Odds were I was looking at Barbara Jean's killer.

I stilled, trying not to draw attention to myself.

"A man needs his zipper," Gil said.

"You hound dawgs are all the same. You can't be trusted."

"You're mad 'cause that other gal with the perky tits moved in on Mama Leon. When Barbara Jean died, you thought you'd get to be Mama's lap dog again. It don't work that way, Til. Life marches on, and it don't take no notice of invisible folks like you and me."

If Tildy had killed to remove her rival, she wouldn't hesitate to kill me, too. It might buy me some time if I could pit brother against sister. "Barbara Jean was murdered. Her killer knew about her heart condition and knew about drugs. Her killer spiked her coffee. That was you, wasn't it, Tildy?"

"So what if I killed her? You'll never find where I buried that coffee cup." She kicked me again. This time in the shoulder.

I groaned in pain. My mouth hurt. My head pounded. And my shoulder ached.

Gil howled. "Say it isn't true, sis. Look me in the eye and tell me you didn't kill Barbara Jean."

"She took what I had, and she wouldn't give it back. I had to kill her. It was the only way."

Gil bellowed and charged his sister. A gunshot rang out, deafening me. Both flashlights clattered to the floor. I scooted further back on the net until I fetched up against the hull, all the while chanting "oh God" in a helpless litany.

Gil fell to his knees, his hand clutched to his bloody chest, his face pale and scarred with disbelief. "You shot me. I'm your own flesh and blood, and you shot me."

"You would've told the others about Barbara Jean. With you out of the picture, I can still make this sweet drug-running scheme work."

"I should've listened to Pop. He always said you were no good."

"Pop was a fool. He couldn't keep his pants zipped either." Tildy held the gun to Gil's head. "Pop couldn't forgive himself for screwing me. But he's a has-been, and I've got my eyes on the future. Mama Leon and me, we're gonna have it all."

"Pop and you?" Gil's voice broke. "Pop had relations with you?"

"I slipped in his bed when he was three-sheets to the wind. I seduced him, and I was the best piece of tail he ever had. He told me so, right before I killed him.'"

"That ain't right," Gil said.

I shivered uncontrollably. I was bound hand and foot and at the mercy of a crazy woman who had a gun in her hand. Suddenly, all of my aches didn't matter so much. One squeak from me, and I'd be sporting a bullet hole, too.

Tildy jabbed the gun at her brother's head. "You think I'm trash, too, don't ya? I can see it in your eyes, big brother. You don't know what it was like growing up in that house, with him watching me night and day. He was always walking in on me in the bathroom, always hanging out of his drawers. He didn't touch me, but his eyes ate up my body, and he made damned sure I saw his equipment. He drove me to it."

Her chilling words renewed my determination to survive and keep my child safe. With her attention on Gil, I silently tugged and pulled against my bonds. I couldn't imagine growing up in those circumstances.

"You shoulda told someone," Gil rasped between labored breaths.

"Nobody in that town cared about us," Tildy said. "We were dirt under their fingernails. They're all going to pay. I'm going to take the drug money and buy that whole town and turn it into a pig farm. Nobody ignores me and gets away with it."

The thick tape binding my hands and feet didn't budge. I was truly incapacitated. My brain was my only hope, but it wasn't much help.

What would Tildy do with me? My family wasn't rich enough to pay a ransom. I had to think of something. Prayer. I could pray. So that's what I did. *God, I'll be the best mom ever, the best wife ever, the best whatever you ask me to be, if you could see fit to save me.*

Tildy picked up my wig and threw it at Gil. "You're a loser. Like Daddy. Like Barbara Jean. And Molly Darter. I'm on a mission of mercy, ridding the world of stupid people."

I heard a horn blast, followed by a booming voice. "Prepare to be boarded."

My hope soared like a fourth of July fireworks display. I was being rescued!

Tildy swore a blue streak. "I come down here for five minutes and everything screws up on deck. Otis was supposed to keep the heat off my back."

With that, Tildy abandoned Gil. She yanked me up to a sitting position by grabbing the back of my stretchy top and dug the gun barrel into my temple. "Molly Darter, you're my ticket out of this floating nightmare."

Chapter Thirty-Five

My hopes plummeted. Just when I thought things couldn't get any worse, I wound up with a gun jammed in my head. The person crouched behind me holding the weapon wouldn't hesitate to pull the trigger. My chances of seeing dawn vaporized.

And that made me mad. The best way to get me moving was to tell me something was impossible. Right now, my survival seemed impossible. Even if a rescue party boarded this boat, Tildy was mean enough to shoot me because she could. "You don't want to do this."

"Shut up." Tildy shook me viciously. "Nobody tells me what to do."

Adrenaline spurted lighting-strike fast through my blood stream. I wasn't going down without a fight. "You kill me and my husband will hunt you down like a dog."

"I am not going to jail."

"You should've thought of that before you started killing people."

More blasts of a boat's horn sounded. Feet thundered overhead. My ears were still ringing from the gunshot, but the advent of rescue fueled my hope.

Gil Beasley's life was ebbing away. His whacked-out

sister had shot him at point blank range in the chest. I didn't know much about gunshot wounds, but getting shot this close up surely decreased his odds of survival.

"Molly!"

My heart leaped for joy at the sound of Hadley's bellow above deck. I'd never heard quite that note of desperation in his voice before. He'd come to rescue me. Had he also come to his death? If both of us died, who would raise our son? Why hadn't we made out our wills? Hadley was a lawyer. We should've made out wills.

Hadley raced down the wooden ladder, a light attached to his helmeted head. His steps slowed as the grisly scene illuminated before him.

"Stop right there," Tildy ordered.

Hadley stopped three steps from Gil. "Let her go. You don't need Molly."

"I need a helicopter and a pilot. You go back up there and arrange that, and then we'll talk."

"I'm not leaving my wife." Hadley whipped out a two-way radio and relayed her request. He ended with, "Send a medic. One white male sustained a gunshot wound to the chest."

"He's as good as dead," Tildy said. "You will be, too, if you stay down here. Get off my boat."

"Can't do that. I'm not going anywhere without my wife."

"Hadley, do what she says," I interjected. "Save yourself."

He shot me a dark look. "We're sticking together."

"Suit yourself," Tildy said. "It doesn't matter if I put a bullet in one or both of you."

"You okay, Molly?" Hadley asked.

Tears welled in my eyes. I didn't trust my voice to speak. I nodded.

Tildy grabbed a hank of my hair and pulled hard. "None of that husband and wife encoded language."

I gasped aloud at the pain. Hadley's lips pressed

tightly together. He stared intently into my eyes, and then his gaze focused on the killer.

"Let's talk, Tildy Smith," Hadley said matter-of-factly, as if a man wasn't bleeding to death at his feet. "We need to get a medic down here to save the good reverend. You hand over the gun, and I'll see about getting your sentence reduced for cooperation."

"Will Judge Humphrey hear my case?"

"Humphrey? Not likely. He's going to be tied up with his own legal problems for quite some time."

Gil moaned. I couldn't believe he was still alive.

"Beasley isn't dead," Hadley continued. "His life could be saved, and you wouldn't be facing his murder charge."

"I don't care if the bastard dies."

"Gil's her brother," I whispered.

"Shut up," Tildy said. "What does it matter if he dies today or tomorrow? We're all terminal. I'm doing him a favor by saving him from a rotten life. He'll never waste away with cancer. He'll go out at the top of his game."

Hadley had edged around to the right where Tildy held the gun to my head. With his very long legs, he could kick the gun away. It was a good strategy, as far as strategies went, if you forgot about the crazy person controlling the trigger.

"Judge Humphrey's up there singing for the feds," Hadley said. "The thought of doing time with the crooks he's put away motivated the judge to better his chances for freedom. He claims he's the head honcho in this outfit."

Tildy and her gun trembled. "Ha. Humphrey wouldn't know his ass from a hole in the ground. I'm in charge of sales and marketing. Me. I make the decisions."

"Like you were in charge of Barbara Jean?"

"She had a death wish. She waltzed in and thought she was queen of the world. Well, she wasn't, and I didn't let her hog all the glory."

"So you killed her?"

"Just call me Dr. Kevorkian."

I'd heard of Kevorkian. He'd made a name for himself by performing humane euthanasia on very sick people. Tildy wasn't in his league. From all accounts, Barbara Jean had been thriving and had shown no sign of wanting to end her life. Which made Tildy a cold-blooded murderer.

A murderer holding a gun to my head.

"Your plan backfired when Mama Leon asked Molly to investigate her death," Hadley said.

Tildy snorted. "Mama Leon thought Barbara Jean walked on water. He couldn't see she was using him. We're much better off without her."

"You screwed up big time. Barbara Jean willed the property to her son."

Her voice cracked. "What son? She didn't have a son."

"Yes, she did, and the land is his."

"You're lying. I saw her will. The land comes to us, her naturalist family."

"She changed her will. I've seen the new document, and it's perfectly legal."

"I don't believe you. Where's my chopper? It ought to be here by now."

My impatience mounted during this rapid-fire exchange. When Hadley was sheriff, he received all kinds of specialized training. He knew how to officially charm the legs off a grasshopper. Why was he being confrontational? Shouldn't Hadley be using his fancy-schmancy hostage negotiating techniques?

And why was his foot tapping? He never tapped his foot.

Unless he was trying to send me a message. Hope flared wildly.

Hadley had a plan.

I might live to see the sunrise after all.

Chapter Thirty-Six

The engine quieted. Tildy stiffened. "What's going on?"

Hadley nodded toward the hold opening. "Chopper's here. You got what you wanted. Let Molly go."

I glanced up at Hadley. He cut his eyes toward Gil repeatedly. I wasn't sure what his message was, but I sensed Tildy's attention was divided now that the chopper was here.

My best guess was Hadley was signaling me to roll away from Tildy and her gun. Did I dare do anything that might incite Tildy to violence? Heck, she didn't need any extra prodding. She was crazy. But I wanted to live. If Hadley was right, this was my one opportunity to save myself.

I inhaled a shaky breath. This would either be the bravest thing I'd ever done, or the stupidest. I sent up a quick prayer, and then lunged toward Gil. Tildy's grip on my spandex top slackened, and I crumpled on my side outside of the pool of light. Momentum rolled me over one hundred and eighty degrees so that I ended up facing Hadley and Tildy, with my back to Gil.

My breath stalled in my throat. Tildy leveled her gun

at me.

Hadley kicked the gun out of Tildy's hand. He launched himself on top of her, one hundred and ninety pounds of angry male, intent on one single purpose: to neutralize the threat. In all his years as sheriff, I'd never seen him do a takedown. What I saw was a violent side of my husband I'd never witnessed before. His movements were meant to inflict pain, his anger palatable.

Tildy thrashed like a ferocious shark out of water. "No. No. It can't end this way. I'm in charge. I give the orders here."

Hadley jammed his knee in her back and cuffed her. "You're jail bait, that's what you are." He read Tildy her rights.

He secured the scene and cut me loose with his pocketknife. "All clear," Hadley yelled over his shoulder. He wrapped me in his arms and held me close. Though my limbs were now free, they ached with pins-and-needles sensations. I choked in a breath of Hadley's precious scent. Sobs ripped from my throat. Tears rained down my face.

"It's over now," Hadley whispered in my hair. "I've got you."

I couldn't stop the horrific images from replaying in my head. The blood stains on the floor reminded me of how near death I'd come. Hadley's body heat surrounded me, but I couldn't stop shivering. My teeth chattered through my sobs.

A team of medics tromped down the ladder. They lashed Gil to a stretcher and lifted him out of the hold. Moments later, the rescue chopper departed. Next, a squad of DEA agents descended to remove Tildy from the hold.

"I can buy and sell everyone on this boat," Tildy screamed. "I'll give a million dollars to anyone who takes these cuffs off and sets me free. You'll never have to work again in your life."

One of the hulking agents turned and winked at me. I dashed the tears from my eyes, because I recognized Joe

Dog from the bar. "You trying to bribe a federal agent, ma'am? Shame on you. We'll tack that on your list of offenses." He lifted her to her feet and propelled her up the ladder.

I couldn't believe Joe Dog was a fed. No wonder he'd been keeping an eye on me. If I hadn't tried so hard to get rid of him at the bar, I might not have been kidnapped. Or they might have drugged us both.

It was over. I had to keep remembering that. I'd identified Barbara Jean's killer, and Hadley had concluded his drug investigation. We'd accomplished our goals. Now I wanted out of here. Never would be too soon for me to be in a shrimp boat hold again.

I tried to stand up, but my rubbery legs wouldn't support my weight. I couldn't stop bawling. I'd nearly died. This could've been it for me. If not for Hadley, I would have had the same fate as Gil Beasley or worse.

I leaned into Hadley's warmth, needing everything he had to give. The welcome thumping of his heart resounded in my ear. His hands shook as they stroked my back.

After a while, he cupped my chin in his hands, his headlight beaming down in my face. "Don't ever do anything like this again."

His scolding brought a wave of normalcy to my thoughts. "You think I planned this? I was minding my own business when they drugged me at Twin Willows."

His fingers caressed my cheek. His expression tightened. "I mean it, Molls. I lost it when you weren't where you were supposed to be."

I snugged my arms around his waist. "I was never so happy to hear your voice as I was a few moments ago. I kept thinking that if I could stay alive until you found me, I'd be all right. Then I worried we would both die, and Jimbo would be raised by Clarice or my mother. Why don't we have wills?"

"I'll get them written up as soon as I can bring myself

to let you out of my sight. I thought I'd die when you disappeared from that bar."

"Yeah. How'd I get here? How'd Joe Dog miss seeing them haul me out of there?"

"Joe Dog got tangled up with a woman, thanks to you, and missed your exit. Near as we can figure out, they walked you out the back door and hauled you over to the shrimp docks. We had their boat staked out, but the surveillance team missed the vehicle's approach. They saw activity on the boat, and a man carrying a sleeping woman on board. We gathered forces to rescue you."

The sequence of events made sense to me, but I couldn't stop thinking about poor Gil Beasley. "Is Gil going to make it?"

"You got a thing for Beasley?" His voice sharpened.

I patted his arm. "No, of course not. He drugged me and kidnapped me. Tildy shot him from close range. What are his chances?"

He shrugged. "His survival is out of our hands now."

Truer words were never spoken. "I'm glad it's over."

"You and me both."

Undercover work wasn't for me. Clarice could have the excitement, as long as she didn't try to take my husband, too. The glamour of pretending to be someone else paled beside having a gun rammed into my brain.

I needed the routine of newspapering. The slow and steady grind of obituaries and town meetings. This rapid freefall of consorting with criminals was too nerve-wracking.

"Will Tildy stand trial for killing Barbara Jean?" I asked.

"We've got her in custody on drug charges, but we can't prove the murder charge, not without the coffee cup. We've ordered another search warrant for Naturalist Woods. Maybe we'll catch a break."

"She told me she did it."

"Her confession helps, but proof would be better."

Hadley guided me over to the ladder. "Can you climb the steps? If not, I can have the boys drop a sling down here and hoist you up."

"Heck no. That'd be too embarrassing. I can do this. And I want to go on record as saying I never want to put my big toe on another shrimp boat as long as I live."

Helping hands reached for me as I cleared the hold. Overhead, stars filled the sky, twinkling like lights on a Christmas tree. Fresh air brushed against my cheeks, and I began to shiver uncontrollably. A blanket was draped over my shoulder. I clutched it close. Hadley talked to his associates for a few minutes before he joined me on the stern of the boat.

I leaned into his embrace. "Are we going home?"

"Yeah. The fab four have all been taken into custody. The drug ring is busted, and we took a killer out of circulation. Not bad for a night's work."

At the eastern horizon, pink streaks appeared, warming the dark sky. Over the next few minutes, the bands of pink increased in size and intensity. Dawn. I'd thought to never see another day. This was the most glorious sunrise I'd ever seen. And the most precious.

I'd survived a brush with death.

Grandma Dee had been right about the mettle of Munro women. We came from sound stock. We didn't bend, and we didn't give up.

I wouldn't give up on justice for Barbara Jean either. Tildy had pushed me to my limit. Now I was gonna push back. I glanced up at Hadley. "Make sure the search warrant covers the garden. My money says she buried the coffee cup under those marigolds she replanted in the garden."

Chapter Thirty-Seven

The ring of a phone jolted me awake. I listened to the ring tone. Not the house line. Not my cell. Hadley's phone. I could relax.

My eyelids drifted shut. Beside me, Hadley tensed and answered his phone. "Darter."

I snugged the covers close, intending to go right back to sleep. But the tension radiating from Hadley set my nerves on edge. Something had happened.

I opened my eyes and studied him, marveling how he'd fought for our love. I'd been wrong not to trust Hadley before. Wrong to believe his feelings for me had changed.

My hurt pride had ruled my actions. Pride and stubbornness. I'd learned a valuable lesson this past week. Love and hate were opposite sides of the same coin. When love soured, hate flourished. But hate poisoned from within.

Tildy hated Barbara Jean. That hate shaded her every thought, word, and deed. That hate drove her to kill her rival. Maybe she'd been turned wrong from the start, maybe she became hateful later in life. Whatever. Hate wasn't good.

But love. Love was something else altogether. I smoothed my hand down Hadley's bare back, tracing the familiar muscled contours. Love was a precious gift, and I'd almost squandered mine.

Hadley ended his call, deposited his cell on the bedside table, and reached for me. His eyes warmed as I came into his arms. This was the way my life was supposed to be. His lips closed over mine, and I gave him everything and more.

A long while later, I lay content in Hadley's arms. "Who was that on the phone?"

His hands stroked through my hair. "You think you can ply me with sex and I'll tell you anything you want to know?"

I leaned up on one elbow, not bothering to hide my nakedness. "Will that work?"

Appreciation darkened his gaze. "Every time."

"So, tell me."

He skimmed his finger along the line of my neck. "I'll tell you something. You, dear wife, are a genius."

I swatted his hand away. "I already knew that. Who was that on the phone?"

His hand came right back, skimming across my shoulder. "Your buddy, Joe Dog from the DEA. They used metal detectors to search the garden out at the naturalists' property. They located a digital camera, the stainless steel coffee thermos, a package of pseudoephedrine, and a log book. The log entries were made by a woman, and they match a sample of Tildy's handwriting."

I sat up and scooted out of his reach. "What kind of log book?"

"The kind that says what Barbara Jean did every minute of the day. Tildy fixated on the woman. She'd been obsessing about her for years."

"What about fingerprints? Were her fingerprints on the coffee cup?"

"Prints were lifted from the coffee thermos. They appear to be Tildy's and Barbara Jean's but DEA is running them as we speak. She's going down. We nailed her for the drug charge, the attempted murder of her brother who, incidentally, survived, and for the murder of Barbara Jean."

I nodded slowly. "That's the best news I've heard all day."

"And it's all because of you. How'd you know to look in the vegetable garden?"

"I had a hunch."

Hadley came across the bed after me. "Well, it was a good one. Tildy Smith will be behind bars for the rest of her life."

I let him catch me. "Good deal."

*   *   *   *

Later that afternoon, Clarice held court in my mother's sewing room. In an earlier life, the room had been Clarice's, but now, the day bed was surrounded by mounds of fabric scraps and a basket of clothes to be mended. After being released from the hospital, both Mama and Clarice had been instructed to take it easy. Mama ignored the orders. Clarice had yet to get out of bed.

Hadley propped a hip against the sewing table. I sat on a corner of Clarice's bed.

Clarice frowned at my encroachment. With a tragic sigh, she shifted her feet. "You don't look dead."

"I'm not dead," I said. "But I could have been."

"Did you go to the hospital?"

"No."

She nodded. Did she think her hospital stay trumped my being held at gunpoint? Only my sister would think a concussion rated more attention than being drugged and kidnapped. I exchanged a glance with Hadley. His eyebrows waggled.

"Where's my wig?" Clarice asked in a petulant tone.

I had no idea where her wig was. Once Tildy had yanked it off my head, I hadn't given it another thought. "The last time I saw it was on the shrimp boat."

"The wig is evidence," Hadley said.

Clarice scowled. "I paid good money for that wig. I expect to have it back, or else get paid in full."

Her comment floored me. "I almost died, and you're worried about your wig?"

Clarice smoothed her fingers along the satin border of the comforter. "You survived, didn't you? That's more than I can say for my wig. What about my clothes? Did you ruin those, too?"

Hadley cleared his throat. "You will be reimbursed after I submit my expense report."

With a performance that rivaled an Oscar nominee, Clarice sniffed. "Better be. That's only fair."

Daddy entered the room. "What I don't understand is how the drug ring tied into the murder investigation."

"The mayor, the judge, the preacher, and the deputy smuggled drugs," Hadley explained.

"Yeah," Clarice echoed. "They were trouble with a capital T. I went undercover at Twin Willows to find out details of their operation. We knew another drop would be made in the next few days. What we didn't know was the time or place."

"After Clarice was injured, Molly took her place at the truck stop," Hadley said, pacing the room. "That's when it got weird."

Clarice snickered. "Trust Molly to screw it up."

Hadley shot her a dark look. "From our interviews with them, it appears they already suspected Candy was an undercover operative. They planned to eliminate her last night."

"So I didn't blow the operation," I said.

"Yeah, it didn't matter who played the part of Candy last night. The operation was already compromised," Hadley said. "We suspected the drug smugglers were acting in concert with someone else, but we didn't know the identity of their associate. That's why we didn't move on them earlier, because we wanted to take out the whole supply chain."

I cleared my throat. "I thought the whole undercover thing was going well until they drugged me. Gil even asked me to run off with him and his million dollars."

Clarice's eyes rounded with wonder. "He did?"

"You couldn't have seriously liked the guy," I said.

Clarice's bottom lip shot out. "Maybe I did."

"He drugged me, Clarice. He delivered me to a crazy woman who planned to kill me. And his good buddy Noah Marvel wanted to rape me."

Clarice's nose went up in the air. "Gil has a cute butt."

"He was under the thumb of his sister." I shivered. "They all were."

Hadley stopped behind me. He squeezed my shoulder. "Because of Tildy Smith's intense jealousy for Barbara Jean, she learned those men were sleeping with her rival. She set up the camera at the produce stand and planned to use the photos for blackmail purposes, only she gave the photos to Molly instead to cast suspicion on Barbara Jean's character. She didn't want Barbara Jean's death investigated. She planned to take over Barbara Jean's premiere place in the nudist colony but that plan backfired when Kim stepped into the leading lady role."

"I'm missing something." I looked up at Hadley. "If Tildy was an outsider, how did she gain control of a local smuggling ring?"

"Tildy's revenge against Barbara Jean started years ago. Tildy knew drug lords in Atlanta. When the nudists relocated down here, Tildy met her contact offshore on the mayor's shrimp boat. She arranged the bi-monthly drug drop at sea, opening a new drug pipeline from South America. You were on an intercept course with a drug boat last night."

I shuddered, remembering the dark and airless boat hold. "I wasn't sure I'd see the sun rise today."

"We caught the local kingpins, the Atlanta connection, the Colombian drugs, the trucker bound for the D.C. area, and a murderer to boot. Quite a haul for the GBI and the DEA."

"I heard the DEA offered you a full-time job," Daddy interjected. "Am I losing my law partner again?"

Hadley shook his head in denial. "Not taking the job. The stakes are too high. I don't want Molly to ever be in that situation again. But there is another job I'm interested in pursuing. We found out during our investigation that Tildy used her drug contacts to pay Justice County residents to vote for Otis. I wasn't voted out by the people. Tildy bought my job for Otis, a man she thought she could control."

"Why didn't they want you to be the sheriff?"

"She thought she could use Otis's weakness to make things go her way."

"Weakness? What weakness?"

I remembered seeing Otis repeatedly at the nudist farm, and the puzzle pieces fell into place. "Oh my God. Otis is a closet naturalist?"

"Yep. Anytime he's not on the job, he's letting it all hang out at the farm."

Clarice's eyes rounded. "Otis the tight ass is a nudist?"

"That would make him more likely to lend a friendly ear to their cause," Daddy said.

I squelched my unease. "I don't even want to think about what else he's lending to their cause. With the notable exception of Kim, those women are all in their sixties."

My mother walked through the door bearing a tray of freshly baked chocolate chip cookies. "Nothing wrong with the sexual appetite of sixty-year-old women."

Grandma Dee followed her, accompanied by Jimbo

and Bubba Brown. "Nothing wrong with eighty-year-olds, either. We still like to have our fun."

"Mom!" Jimbo made a flying dash and tackled me.

"I'm fine," I protested.

Hadley grabbed Jimbo and tossed him in the air, to Jimbo's delight. "How would you feel if your dad ran for sheriff again?"

Jimbo frowned. "I thought you gave it up."

"I changed my mind. I want to run again. But I'd need a good campaign manager. What do you think, son?"

Jimbo nodded solemnly. "You gotta do it. To keep the bad guys away from mom."

Chapter Thirty-Eight

Hadley parked his truck in front of the *Marshview Gazette* at high noon the next day. I'd tried to escape my husband's eagle eye by saying I needed to hand-deliver my story to my boss, but he was wise to my evasive maneuver. I sure hoped his need to keep me safe from the big bad world eased up real soon. I didn't like having my wings clipped.

As I reached for the door, my cellphone rang. Mama Leon's voice blasted through the phone. "I expected you to come by here and give me a full report. And there is the matter of paying your fee."

My fee. Once Ted said I could look into Barbara Jean's death on the paper's nickel, the thought of charging Mama Leon for my investigative services hadn't crossed my mind. However, I understood him needing to tie up loose ends. I felt that way, too. Seeing Mama Leon again would give this investigation closure. And maybe, just maybe, the whole idea of visiting the nudist colony would disgust Hadley so much he'd let me go alone. "I could swing by there in the next half hour. How's that work for you?"

"See you in thirty." The connection ended.

"I thought you were taking the day off," Hadley said,

the corners of his lips turning down.

"I am." I pocketed my phone. "Dropping this story off is the only newspaper-related thing I'm doing today. That call was from Mama Leon. He wants to pay me for my investigative services."

"What kind of money are we talking about?"

"I never set a rate. I have no idea what he's come up with. I can drop you at home as soon as we're done here and scoot over there."

"Not on your life. I wouldn't miss this for anything."

"I'll be right back." I climbed out of the truck and headed into the office.

Ted scowled over the top of his computer. "You could have emailed your story. You didn't have to file it in person."

I nodded over my shoulder at Hadley. To the casual observer he was leaning against the bumper of his truck as if he didn't have a care in the world. I knew different. His cop eyes had already cleared the street for signs of danger. It appeared he didn't consider Ted a threat to my personal safety. "I tried to escape, but I couldn't shake my devoted husband."

Ted nodded sagely. "Cut him some slack. He nearly lost you."

I frowned. "Did Hadley tell you to say that?"

"He didn't have to. I know too well what it's like when something bad happens to the one you love."

Poor Ted. The results of the DNA test hadn't come back yet. If Daddy was a match for his parent, Ted would have found his dad, but lost his chance to date Clarice. I honestly didn't know what he wanted at this stage. "You sure you can handle this alone today?"

"I'm pulling canned news stories off the wire. That, plus your front-page feature, should do the trick for this week's edition."

"I could come back later today and help. All you have to do is say the word."

"Allow Hadley to coddle you. You deserve another day off after what you two went through."

"I'm not the only one with changed circumstances. What will you do with your nudist colony?"

Alarm flared in his brown eyes. "It isn't mine."

"The property is yours. That's prime real estate out there. I bet the Lyle brothers would give you ten million for it, since their condo project in the marsh went belly up. You could sell the paper and drink piña coladas on a tropical island for the rest of your life."

A dark look flickered across his face. "I'm not selling anything. Not the property. Not the paper. Get out of here so I can put this issue to bed before midnight."

"Don't try to pull that martyr junk on me. I've been manipulated by the best, and frankly your technique needs work."

As I spoke, Daddy's Buick pulled up alongside Hadley's truck. Daddy and Bubba Smith conferred with Hadley.

"I wonder what that's all about," I said. "Do you think your test results are back?"

Ted's silence spoke volumes.

All three men marched toward the office. I swallowed thickly. "Whatever it is, it can't be good."

Ted stood. "But maybe it won't be bad, either."

The door opened, and they filed in. Funny how having four men in here filled the space. I'd had the entire second grade in here last fall, and the office hadn't felt this full.

Bubba handed Ted a sealed envelope. "This is for you."

The color drained from Ted's face. I couldn't imagine reading an important document with people watching me. Ted needed privacy. "We should be going," I said.

Ted examined the official looking envelope. "Stay. This concerns everyone in this room."

Hadley took my hand as Ted pulled the pages out and

scanned them.

Ted looked over at Daddy. "I'm not your son."

I let out the breath I'd been holding. Ted wasn't my brother. I didn't know whether to feel relieved or sad.

Daddy nodded. I guess he didn't know what to say either. I mean, what did one say to the illegitimate son of your former lover?

Daddy cleared his throat. "You're a fine man, Ted. I would've been proud to call you my son."

"Thanks." Ted studied the paper again. "I came here to find my biological parents. What I learned is that opening doors to the past is painful."

"In that we agree," Daddy said. "I'm sorry about your mother. She meant the world to me."

"Are you still going to look for your father, Ted?" I asked.

Ted shook his head. "I'm taking time off from the search. I've recently discovered an interest in something else, something that will require a good bit of my time."

My hand covered my mouth. "Good Lord. You're going to court Clarice, aren't you? She'll run you ragged."

Ted grinned. "Yeah, but it sure beats the alternative."

Chapter Thirty-Nine

"There's naked people in here," I warned as we passed through the gate leading to Naturalist Woods. I reached for the bug lotion and slathered some on.

"I've seen naked people before." Hadley scanned the tree line. "What about the dog?"

"The dog is imaginary. However, the naked people are very real. And there's naked good and naked ugly." I headed down the shaded path to the left. "Trust me; this isn't the good kind of naked."

Hadley caught my hand and stopped in the one spot of sunlight on the wooded path. "I do trust you. But do you trust me?"

I bit my lip. I'd trusted him with my life, but was I ready to let him fill my heart again? A part of me felt too raw still, too vulnerable. "This isn't a kid's boo-boo we can kiss and make better. I want you and I need you but I don't have complete confidence in us. I believe you about the wire, and I believe Clarice instigated the kiss. However, you kissed her back. I saw you and that image isn't something I can file away as a mistake. I want us to be like before, but I feel on edge."

"You've been through a lot. That edgy feeling will pass."

"I thought so, too, but it hasn't lessened. Even though you're driving me crazy by hovering over me, there will come a point where we take each other for granted again. That's when I'll wonder what you're up to. That's when I'll wonder if you're kissing someone else."

"Don't say that, Molls."

"You asked for the truth, so I'm giving it to you."

His eyes bored into mine. "What happens next? Will I wake up tomorrow and have you kick me out of the house again? How long will I have to pay for my mistake?"

"I don't have an answer for you. Why don't we content ourselves with taking one day at a time?"

"I want this settled."

"You shouldn't have married a Munro. We're all a bit crazy."

"As long as you're only crazy with me." He kissed my forehead. "You okay with Ted muscling his way into your family?"

I smiled. "Clarice is going to eat him alive. He has no idea what he's in for."

"Ted's a big boy. He'll figure something out." Hadley nodded ahead. "Let's get this over with so we can go home."

Alma bounded down the path toward us, her waist-long gray braids flopping alongside her long skinny breasts. "Hey, Miz Molly, sorry I'm a few minutes late. I see you brung your man."

My man. In spite of my reservations, the thought warmed me. I made introductions.

Alma's face fell. "He don't need killing no more?"

I laughed aloud at the scathing look Hadley sent me. "Not this week. I'm keeping him after all."

She nodded stoically. "If you change your mind, I'm eaten up with ideas, hypothetically speaking, of course. Did I tell you about the woman who found out her man cheated on her, and so she shoved him in the tree chipper? Her blue-ribbon garden was the envy of the neighborhood."

"I'll keep that in mind." I winked at Hadley. He scowled back.

The two-story Victorian house came into sight. "Nice house," Hadley said.

Alma gestured toward the door. "Go on in. They're out by the pool. I'm headed to the garden to pick fresh vegetables for our snack."

"I know the way," I volunteered, dragging Hadley up the porch steps and inside the house.

Hadley caught sight of the vibrant wall color. "Whorehouse red."

His narrow-minded comment irritated me. "It is not. This room is very tastefully decorated. The walls happen to be red. You wouldn't find matching prints by local artists or hand-embroidered throw pillows in a whorehouse. This place is a home."

Hadley's gaze narrowed. "Would you sit on that sofa?"

I shuddered. "Heck, no. No telling how many bare butts and God knows what else were on those cushions."

He smirked. "Just checking."

Strangely, I didn't feel out of sorts here. I knew this place now. I still wasn't entirely comfortable with nudity, but I could manage the concept for short-term.

Norma bustled into the house to greet us, her apple-shaped breasts bobbing. A blast of sandalwood scent accompanied her. My gaze shifted upward to the slow-moving ceiling fan.

"Miz Molly, we've been waiting for you." Norma saw Hadley and brightened. "Oh, you brought a guest! We have a clothing-optional rule here. If you'd like to remove your clothes that would be fine with us."

Hadley's lips barred enough to show teeth. "My clothing isn't optional."

Another wisp of graying hair slipped out of her loose topknot. "Pity."

"Molly's clothing isn't optional, either," he added.

"Both of you need to loosen up. Clothing does more than shield your body. It constricts the brain and interrupts the flow of creative thought. As a writer, Molly, you should be aware of the limitations you are placing on yourself."

I could imagine what Ted would say if I showed up for work at the newspaper naked. I'd be arrested for indecent exposure in a heartbeat. And Hadley would have plenty to say about my public nakedness. "Maybe I'll look into it. I could try naked writing at home."

"That's the spirit." She grabbed up some papers from the kitchen counter and motioned for us to precede her out to the pool.

I caught Hadley ogling her very round breasts, so I latched onto his hand and set him in motion. Heat and the odor of chlorine hit us as we strolled out of the air conditioning into the pool area.

Mama Leon and his aging courtesans lounged around the pool like a family of sun-drenched lizards. Full-figured Kim hand-fed Mama red grapes, one at a time.

"Hey, everyone," I said. "Don't get up."

Mama Leon scrambled to his feet and extended his hand in greeting. "My pleasure, Miz Molly."

Hadley's fingers tightened around mine. A low rumbling sound emitted from his throat. Mama Leon dropped his hand and backed up immediately.

"Like that is it?" Mama Leon sat back down and signaled Kim for another grape. "My, what a difference a week makes. Good fortune smiled upon you and crapped on me. I still can't believe our Tildy was a cold-blooded killer. She seemed so sweet."

I tugged Hadley over to a nearby lounger and sat. His eyebrows shot up at my precipitous action, but I'd already thought this through on a previous visit. Between the sun and the chlorine from the pool, these chairs were sanitized.

Alma came in bearing a tray of cherry tomatoes, baby

carrots, broccoli clusters, a stack of small plastic cups, and a bottle of Jim Beam. She passed the vegetables around and started filling cups with straight booze. "That Tildy was nothing but a dirt-mouth cracker, and she got what's coming to her," Alma said.

My jaw dropped. "You suspected her?"

"Heck no, but she always tried to one-up the rest of us. Weren't no call for that. This isn't a competition."

Norma hand-delivered the booze to everyone. "Good riddance to her. She didn't want to be here with us or she wouldn't have been so hateful."

Kim's eyes glistened. "She murdered Barbara Jean. That's beyond hateful."

I eyed the three fingers of booze in my cup. If I drank all that, I wouldn't be good for much the rest of the day. But with Hadley keeping an eye on me, I wasn't likely to get into too much trouble.

When everyone had a drink in hand, Mama Leon lifted his cup high. "Here's to our special investigator. She got justice for Barbara Jean and earned our everlasting gratitude."

The others echoed his sentiment and drained their cups. Though Hadley didn't sip his at all, I tried mine. The alcohol burned a fiery trail down my throat, clanking in the bottom of my empty stomach. Heat radiated from my core and a goofy smile on my face seemed impossible to erase. When I'd been in this same position before, I hadn't trusted the nudists. Now here I was drinking their booze, eating their organic produce, like I belonged.

"Do you have the folder, Norma?" Mama asked.

Norma handed Mama Leon the papers from the kitchen.

Last time they'd handed me a sheaf of papers, I'd been the recipient of pornographic photos. Now that we knew who had killed Barbara Jean, there wasn't any reason for my heart to beat so fast, was there?

Mama Leon opened the folder and removed a thick

piece of paper. "Molly, in honor of your outstanding achievement, we're making you an official member of the Naturalist Society. You have a lifetime free pass to the facilities on-site."

With relief, I took the certificate from him. It was written out in a frilly computer script on marbled paper as if it were a graduate degree or other worthy endeavor. Laughter bubbled out of me. Of all the payments possible, this was one I hadn't seen coming. "Thank you. I hardly know what to say."

"We have the pool and the garden. You can come over for a swim or pick produce from the garden whenever you like. Bring your son."

I popped another bright red cherry tomato in my mouth. The taste was delicious, but not so delicious I'd risk seeing naked people to get it. And I wouldn't dream of exposing Jimbo to a pool full of naked old people. I'd rather swim in the creek with the alligators. "Thanks."

"And," Mama continued, "if we're not evicted, we're thinking of building a meditation temple on the property. You will also have lifetime usage rights to the temple."

Oh goody. I could sit on the floor with a bunch of chanting naked people. Glory, hallelujah. Beside me, Hadley shifted his weight from foot to foot, tensing his legs as if he were getting ready to vault into a basketball slam dunk.

I got the message. He'd had all the fun he could stand. I put my cup down. "Thanks again. We've got to go."

A man with a lot of pristine white skin where there should've been clothes approached the pool area. Looked like the nudists had snagged a new member. I definitely didn't want to hang around and make his acquaintance.

"Hadley! Hold up."

Uh-oh. I recognized that deep voice. Otis the fashion plate. Otis the sheriff. He was out of uniform and totally naked. Guess he bought into the theory of clothing restricting the brainwave process. And now I would see him naked. I shuddered. Some things were best left to the imagination.

"Otis. I wasn't expecting to see you." Hadley's voice was grim and terse.

"I've been coming out here for a while. I tried to hide my association, but that felt gol-darned wrong. So I'm going with my gut now. I've moved out here, lock, stock, and barrel."

On the plus side, he wouldn't have to worry about doing his laundry now. But on the minus side, he was still our high sheriff. I didn't see how he could be very effective as the naked sheriff.

Hadley's face remained devoid of emotion. "I see."

I could tell that Hadley, like me, was trying to keep his gaze at eye level. I definitely didn't need to know what Otis's penis looked like.

Otis reached over behind the tiki bar counter and collected a small object. "No, you don't. Here." He handed Hadley a shiny metal object. "This is yours."

Hadley stared at the sheriff's badge in his palm. "I can't take this. You won the election."

"There were election irregularities. I resign, and you were the next highest vote getter, so it's yours. Besides, I wasn't very good at the job anyway. Marvel and his buddies had a drug smuggling operation going on right under my nose, and I didn't suspect a thing. I'm done with working for the county. I'm looking into a different line of work now."

"What would that be?" I asked.

"I come from a long line of farmers, so I have a keen interest in the operation here. And, I have an interest in meditation. I'm going to attend training seminars down in Jacksonville. When I return, I'll lead the meditations at our new pavilion."

Hadley's fingers closed around the shiny badge. His chin quivered. He'd loved that sheriff job so much. Now to have his post back, without having to wait until the next election, must seem a dream come true.

"We're calling the site the McAllister Pavilion in honor of Barbara Jean," Norma said.

"She didn't die in vain," Alma said. "She'll be remembered for years to come."

"And naming a structure for her has nothing to do with currying the new owner's favor," I observed.

"That's the way the real world works, sweet cheeks," Mama Leon said. "You scratch my naked back, and I'll scratch yours."

Hadley tensed beside me. He'd go for Mama Leon's throat if we stayed here much longer. "We should be going," I murmured.

As we moved toward the door, Mama Leon's words stopped me. "Don't forget our date next week to start on my memoirs."

His memoirs. Now that should be a real trip.

*   *   *   *

I'd survived the nudists, my scheming sister, a shaky marriage, the drug ring, a clueless sheriff, and an armed killer. Not bad for a gal from a one-horse town. After this, I wouldn't take anything for granted. Each day was a precious gift, each breath a treasure beyond words.

Hadley's pickup roared to life, banishing my musings. "I thought we'd never get out of there," he said. "Quite some company you keep."

"You thinking to ban me from visiting my new friends?"

He grinned. "Heck no, we should go home and let you practice."

"Practice?" I tilted my head to gaze up at him. The cracks in the foundation of our marriage remained, but I needed to cling to the illusion of togetherness for a bit longer. "What kind of practice?"

"Nudity." Hadley executed a three-point turn and sped down the highway. "I've discovered I have a passion for naked women. Make that one naked woman. You."

Throwing caution to the wind, I fanned the heat from under my T-shirt. "I don't mind playing your naked harem girl, so long as it's a harem of one."

His gaze warmed. "Done."

ABOUT THE AUTHOR

Formerly a contract scientist for the U.S. Army and currently a freelance reporter, author Maggie Toussaint writes mystery and romantic suspense. From journaling to short stories to full-length books, the lure of the printed word holds her spellbound. A native Georgian, Toussaint's worldview is shaped by her childhood experiences as a shrimper's daughter, her college years, and her family-rearing years in the Washington, D.C. area.

Her mysteries include In For A Penny, On the Nickel, Death, Island Style, and Murder in the Buff. She was nominated for the Silver Falchion Award with On the Nickel. Her latest mystery, Dime if I Know, will release in September 2013.

Her romantic suspense titles include House of Lies, No Second Chance, Muddy Waters, and Seeing Red. Her debut release, House of Lies, won Best Romantic Suspense in the 2007 National Readers Choice Awards. She finaled in the Beacon writing contest with Muddy Waters. Her upcoming romantic suspense, Hot Water, will release in July 2013.

Maggie lives in coastal Georgia, where secrets, heritage, and ancient oaks cast long shadows. Yoga, beachcombing, and music are a few of her favorite things.

Visit her at http://www.maggietoussaint.com
http://mudpiesandmagnolias.blogspot.com
http://www.facebook.com/MaggieToussaintAuthor
http://www.twitter.com/MaggieToussaint